BITTERSWEET OBLIVION
MOLLY SUTTON MYSTERIES 11

NELL GODDIN

Goddin
Books

ISBN: 978-1-949841-21-3

If you prick us, do we not bleed? If you tickle us, do we not laugh? If you poison us, do we not die? And if you wrong us, shall we not revenge?

— WILLIAM SHAKESPEARE

CONTENTS

❧ I ❧

JUNE 2008

Florian Nagrand, coroner of the village of Castillac, drummed his fingers on his desk and looked out the window.

"Must you?" said Matthias, glaring at the drumming fingers as he swept the floor for the second time that morning.

"Must *you*?" said Florian. "We're not going to eat off these floors, you know." He heaved a sigh. "Nobody ever tells you that the worst part of a job is when there is nothing to do. It is torture. We sit and we sit, and no one dies. I feel entirely useless. Are we to do nothing but sit here and pick our noses, day after excruciating day?"

Matthias jammed the broom into a corner, trying to dislodge a bit of dirt wedged up in there. He was lanky and tall for a Frenchman, in his late thirties, with longish hair that looked well taken care of. "'No one dies' is generally thought of as a positive," he said. "So sorry no one has expired for your entertainment."

"That is not what I meant," said Florian, springing up from his chair as well as he could, given how his weight had ballooned from giving up cigarettes. "Let's go have lunch."

"It is 10:00," said Matthias.

Florian dropped back into his chair with another dramatic sigh, combing his fingers through what was left of his hair, which though sparse, could have used a trim.

"Bonjour fellas!" said Molly Sutton, poking her head around the door. Her curly red hair was untamed as it usually was; she was short and sturdy, built a bit like a fire plug. A cute fire plug.

"Never thought I'd hear myself say I'm glad to see you, but here we are," rasped Florian, getting back up and going to kiss Molly on both cheeks.

"I will do my utmost to take that as a compliment," she said. She looked at Matthias. "I don't believe we've met? I'm Molly Sutton, I run the *gîtes* at La Baraque just outside the village, on rue de Chêne."

Matthias shook her hand and made a rather courtly bow. "My pleasure," he said. "I am Matthias de Clare, minion of Monsieur Nagrand."

Molly considered him. "Have you been here long?"

"In Castillac? Since birth, Madame."

"Funny that I haven't met you before, the village being so small."

"What she means to say is, Madame Sutton has raised the bar on our local custom of knowing all we can about everyone else's business. First as a civilian, and now...well, still technically a civilian, but a professional one. You might have heard of Dufort/Sutton Investigations?"

Matthias nodded. "You've done some good work," he said, bowing again. "Excuse me," he added, and took his broom into the next room and continued to sweep.

Molly smiled to herself, amused that she had met another serious sweeper, having a few months earlier made a friend in Aix-en-Provence who also swept with a great deal of dedication.

"I tell you, Molly, as perhaps you are the one person of my

4

acquaintance who would truly understand—there's nothing for me to do, absolutely zilch, zero, *nada*—and it is really too much to bear. I figure our local Angel of Death knows what I'm talking about," he added. He might have winked but Florian was not a winker.

"Angel of Death, that's going a little far. And a bit rich, coming from a coroner."

"Eh, you can call me...uh...Minister of Death? No, that's no good. Death Wizard?"

"Nice try," said Molly. "Maybe we should play Dungeons and Dragons sometime."

Nagrand snorted.

"I'll have you know that one of the many reasons I moved to France was to escape crime. All I wanted was peace and safety."

"It's been my observation that what we think we want is rarely the whole story," said Florian.

"Life takes unexpected turns," she said with a shrug.

Florian rubbed his thumb and forefinger together, missing cigarettes with a sudden obliterating passion.

"So what's the deal with Matthias de Clare? How long's he been working for you?"

"Oh, forever. He lives...well, I don't know the exact house, but somewhere toward the south end of the village. Good worker. Keeps to himself."

"I'll say. I thought by this point I'd met most everyone in the village."

Molly had moved to Castillac on something of a whim, looking to get over a divorce. That had been just three years ago, but there had been a great deal of water under the bridge since then. (If by water, you think dead bodies and their murderers, plus marriage, and an entirely new career.)

"Well, I just dropped by in case...not that I had any hopes, really...it does seem as though this calm and peaceful period in the village shows no signs of abating. As bad as that is for business, it's obviously the best news and I'm glad about it. I was out for a walk and figured I'd come say *bonjour*."

"*Rebonjour*," said Nagrand, mocking her for saying it twice and after they had already been in conversation for some time.

"Oh for heaven's sake," said Molly, grinning. "All right, I'm going before you find something else to make fun of. See you on the flip side."

The door banged behind her. Florian closed his eyes and listened to the sound of Matthias sweeping in the next room.

Maybe I should take up cigarettes again, he thought, just for a week or so. The idea seemed a very good one.

§&

MOLLY STOOD ON THE STREET, at something of a loss for what to do next. It was Friday, a day of the week when the gîte business was not especially demanding: current guests left and new ones arrived on Saturdays, with a few hours in between to accomplish the cleaning and tidying. Friday was as close as she came to having a day off.

She gave her pal Frances a call. "How about a walk? I'm only a few blocks from your place."

"I would love a walk. Or a swim. Or really anything at all. But I am absolutely tied to the piano this afternoon. Jingle deadline."

"You're still working? Shouldn't you be lazing around doing nothing but being pregnant and eating a lot of liver and oysters?"

"I found out that babies apparently require quite a bit of money to raise. So I took a few contracts. She's not coming until September."

"*She*? Have you been holding back news?"

"Well, I wouldn't call it confirmed news. Not from a third party. But you know I have certain witchy powers and I'm saying this baby is a girl."

"Mm," said Molly. "What does Nico think?"

"He doesn't get a vote," says Frances. "Enjoy your walk, I've got to get back to work."

Molly drifted up one street and down another, looking into people's gardens as she'd been doing ever since coming to Castillac, and mourning her scooter which was in the shop again. It was *magnifique* to be back in the village, her beloved home. She walked a little faster toward home, wanting to see Ben even though they had finished breakfast together only a few hours ago.

$\mathcal{H}$ 2 $\mathcal{H}$

B enoît's face was pale, his eyes dull. His wife stood in the doorway of their bedroom—or former bedroom, now sick-room—and gazed upon her husband with an expression of concern and anxiety.

"*Chérie,*" she said softly, stepping into the room and placing a tray on the bedside table, careful not to bump the lamp. "Did you have a restorative sleep? Do I see a bit of bloom in your cheeks this morning?" She scrutinized his face and he turned away.

"Ben-oît," she singsonged.

"No, I did not have a restorative sleep," he said, shrugging. "I lay awake for hours staring at the ceiling, my heart thumping too fast, wondering for the ten millionth time why it is that my health has been so terrible for so long. And finally, towards dawn, I came to this conclusion, the only thing that makes sense: surely I committed some awful act or acts in a former life, and this ill-health is simply karma."

Angeline smiled and stroked his cheek. "You blame yourself? That is touching, my darling, but you know I do not share your belief in things such as karma or reincarnation so I will decline to comment. Now then. What would the best-looking husband in all of Castillac—nay, France!—desire for breakfast this morning? I am at your service."

Benoît looked at his wife. After a quick courtship, they had been married for twenty-some years. While Benoît would not admit to anyone (barely even to himself) that a certain depth of feeling was lacking on his part—in short, that he did not, to say it plainly, love his wife—he could not allow himself to regret the marriage. It's not as though we can expect perfection, he had told himself many times over the years.

At this glimmer of truth, a flood of guilt surged into his heart but mentally he firmed himself up and pushed it back. He mustn't throw stones; after all, he was not a good husband, that was indisputable. He was a drain, an endless black hole of need and illness, a husband who was not only no fun but negative fun. Sexless, jobless, pitiable, broke.

Benoît pushed those thoughts away too.

"I think I might like a hearty breakfast," he said, not especially hungry but knowing that she felt useful when she cooked for him. "A sausage? Eggs? Toast?"

"That peach jam from Madame Ferrand?

"Oh yes!"

Angeline left for the kitchen and Benoît's face relaxed. He took in a long breath; it wasn't smooth but caught several times along the inhalation, and then he breathed back out as slowly as he could manage. His shoulders relaxed and the muscles in his face let go. He closed his eyes.

Another June day in Castillac was just beginning. And Benoît LaRue was determined that it would be an improvement, somehow, in some small way, over the day before.

S aturday morning arrived with pouring rain.

"Ugh," Molly said. She pulled the covers up over her head.

"A bit of wet always makes for an interesting Changeover Day," said Ben, hopping out of bed. "I'll make the coffee, you make the list of what needs doing."

"Already done. Constance should be here by eleven. The Fogartys left late yesterday, so we can get into the pigeonnier and get that cleaning out of the way early. After Constance gets here, I'll make the run to the market."

"What about the...the...honestly, the names of our guests swim into my head and right back out again. The big family in the annex."

"Hmm, I don't think they've told me their plans. It's been nice having some young children around, hasn't it?" Molly looked at Ben with a brave expression.

"It has," said Ben. He turned and put one of his big hands along her cheek.

Molly blurted, "Do you think being an investigator and a mother would be a bad mix?"

Ben didn't answer right away. He got up and stepped into the shorts he had worn the day before. Ben had the trim body of the runner he was, with a brush cut and a handsome—but not *too* handsome— face. He made sure the window was tightly closed against the driving rain. "This might not be a satisfying answer— but I would say: maybe."

"You're right: not satisfying."

Ben shrugged. "It's no different from being a police officer. Or really, any job that requires some risk. One thing that's possibly helpful is that since we're independent, we can decide to mitigate those risks sometimes, by picking the cases we work while avoiding situations that might be dicey."

"Picking the cases?" laughed Molly. "As if."

"Those walkabouts you were doing in Aix, for example, you might have decided against if you were a new mother."

"And if you were still police chief, would you be making the same sorts of decisions if you were a new father?"

Ben kissed her forehead. "Thankfully, I am not chief of gendarmes any longer. I can honestly say I don't miss it at all. So tell me—is it Frances's baby that's got you thinking about this?"

"Well," said Molly. "I was wondering...oh man, my face is getting all hot. I...was wondering...and you don't have to answer this minute—just something to think about—if you were open to the idea of adopting."

Ben's eyebrows went up and he moved his mouth in the way he did when he was thinking about something.

"Seriously, don't answer right now. Take plenty of time to think about it. I'm not saying I am pushing for this, so don't feel pressure. I just...want to make sure we've considered all the options."

"Molly," he said, "I've been wanting to ask...listen, you're not that old. I know it's harder to get pregnant at your age, but it's not impossible. Is there some reason you feel so sure you won't?"

Molly ran her finger along the edge of the sheet, eyes downcast. "The biggest reason, and it's a whopper, is that I never used birth control while I was married to Donny. Years, you see. Never got pregnant."

"Maybe the problem was your husband."

"He got checked out. Wasn't him."

"And you must have seen doctors too. What did they say?"

"Very little hope," she said in a quiet voice. "And this was when I was in my late twenties, when age didn't even come into it. I don't mind at all your asking about this—and we should have had this conversation a long time ago—but believe me, when I say it's not going to happen, it's really not going to happen. All the doctors were in agreement on that point."

Ben kissed her forehead.

"I'm sorry," she said. "I know you—" Her throat closed up and she pushed her head into his shoulder. He put his arms around her and they stayed like that, not talking, for a long stretch of time.

Finally Ben said, "My information might be out of date, I will need to check—but I believe there are few French babies available for adoption. We would most likely need to look at other countries."

"Fine with me!"

He kissed her again, this time on the mouth, and she fell back on the bed and pulled him down with her.

AFTER SERVING Benoît a whopping breakfast on a tray, Angeline stepped into the garden. They lived on rue Simenon, a street with many grand houses, which theirs was not; it was a simple cottage, not grand in the least—but the garden, though small, was fit for a manor. She fussed over every detail, never shying away from the most work-intensive projects. A pear tree was espaliered against a brick wall (which nicely held the heat) with viburnums on either side. A palm was throwing out some new, bright-green fronds. A beehive was tucked by the side of the house. Just now the Zépherine de Drouin rose was in full bloom, spilling its pink blossoms over the wall to the street where passersby could get a good whiff of their perfume. Angeline liked to work on the street side of the wall and show people how that particular rose was thornless, and so a child could pick a flower without being pricked.

She went to the wall and looked over to see if anyone was walking by, but the street was quiet and empty despite its being market day. Tapping her fingers on her thighs, she ducked into a small shed on the other side of the garden from the wall. It was private, with only one small window for light that faced the back of the garden.

She breathed in the smell of sawdust and compost, hummed a tuneless hum. She tried to compose herself.

It was nearly time—that was the phrase that kept coming back to her. She had dragged it out long enough. Oh, the journey had been entertaining, quite amusing, no one would ever be able to change her mind about that. But nothing goes on forever.

She was nearing fifty years old, after all, though she didn't believe it for a second. In her heart—and comportment—she was still in her mid-twenties, still ravishing, still magnetic. There was —as she saw it—no end to the flattering adjectives that could rightfully be applied to her.

Yes, it was time.

＊ 4 ＊

L a Baraque was Molly's dream come true—a charming ramshackle collection of buildings she had bought on a whim at a moment when she had decided to toss her entire life in the air and move to France. She had made improvements over the years, so that she could support herself with guests who came for a week at a time. The pigeonnier was lovely and sought after, and she had a cottage to rent as well as an annex attached to the main house. The natural swimming pool was of course a hit with children and adults both. La Baraque was Molly's happy place—and now Ben's as well.

With her usual clatter, Constance arrived for Changeover Day with a long, complicated story about what her boyfriend Thomas may or may not have planned for their vacation in August, the history of her mother's gout, and worries about whether her sneakers were fashionable or woefully not.

Ben had had enough in the first ten minutes and faded out of sight, taking Bobo for a walk in the light rain. Molly sat on the terrace under an umbrella in a sort of stupor, listening to Constance go on and on, thinking that there was not enough coffee in the world to prepare her for Saturdays.

"And then—you'll never guess—Molly? I don't think you're actually listening. I can tell because your eyes are wide but you're not really looking at anything."

"I'm sorry, Constance, I'm distracted. I'm happy your mother seems to be doing a little better. I wanted to get this done earlier but I'm moving slowly this morning—let's get to the pigeonnier, shall we? Or would you rather I do the cottage while you do that by yourself?"

Constance might be flighty but she was not unperceptive. "I'll go alone," she said cheerfully, hoisting the vacuum up and heading down the path through the meadow.

Molly was glad Constance had taken the pigeonnier because it took less time to clean the cottage and she had some business in the village to take care of. Thankfully, the guests who had just vacated were neat and tidy, so in a little over an hour, the cottage was ready for its next inhabitants. It felt good to be home, to be doing her regularly scheduled chores at their regularly scheduled time. Not looking over her shoulder for murderers, as she had in Aix-en-Provence.

Molly changed into fresh clothes and headed out on foot. Rue de Chêne was full in the magnificence of early summer, the trees fresh and in myriad shades of green; the birds chattered like mad; a scruffy dog disappeared around the turn in the road ahead. Not for the first time—and despite the glut of murders that had taken place since her move to Castillac several years earlier—she appreciated how safe she felt, how docile were her surroundings in the best sort of way. A place where neighbors, dogs, birds, and all the rest lived in harmony.

Well, all right, she admitted, maybe that's verging on the ridiculous. But I love it here anyway.

The mechanic surprised her by not only giving her the keys to the scooter and saying it was ready to go, but charging her only an arm instead of an arm and a leg. With a wave she hopped on— grinning when the engine purred and she felt the familiar breeze in her face from driving a little too fast through the narrow streets, on her way to the antique shop owned by her friend, Lapin Broussard.

Her relationship with Lapin had started out poorly, as in those days Lapin had interacted with women mostly by leering and saying things better left unsaid. More recently, however, his girl-friend-now-wife Anne-Marie had given him a few signposts, and Molly no longer tried to avoid his company but could enjoy him for the lovable loon he was.

"Lapin!" she said, louder than any French-person would have, as she burst through the door to his shop, making the bells jingle.

Lapin was with a customer. He looked up and gave Molly a quick smile. "Be with you when I can, Madame Sutton," he said, all of a sudden Mr. Formality. The woman he was helping did not turn in Molly's direction. From the back, Molly did not recognize her.

She drifted down an aisle, looking at piles of china on the shelves, a chipped tureen, a few animals woven out of reeds, a tattered basket, a bowl of trinkets. The main way Lapin gained inventory was by the families of the recently deceased not wishing to go through every single bit of the dead relative's belongings, so they paid Lapin to come take it all away. Occasionally—perhaps not quite as often as he would have his customers believe—he found a valuable something-or-other hidden in the heap of junk. And so he was able to make a decent living, at what he called, to himself, the job of treasure hunter.

Out of habit, Molly listened to the conversation between Lapin and his customer. And as they spoke, Molly's eyes got wider and wider until she had to physically put her hand over her mouth to stop herself from jumping in.

"I DO UNDERSTAND, Angeline. The ring is beautiful indeed, and a fine example of its type. The condition is excellent. But I'm afraid that I cannot offer you more for it, simply because the resale value of these kinds of things doesn't justify a higher price. Trading it for the chest would be—regretfully, I cannot." Lapin shook his head. "Of course, you doubtless have feelings and memories associated with the ring, which makes it even more valuable to you. And those, alas, do not confer to a new owner."

Angeline LaRue scowled. She stared at the ring in Lapin's palm as though it had betrayed her.

"I know you appreciate the finer things," he said. "And so perhaps you can keep the ring and enjoy it?"

Angeline kept her eyes fixed on Lapin's and did not move a muscle.

Like a panther getting ready to strike, thought Lapin. He took a step back.

"It's not that I want to...to be ungenerous to you. If I could simply give you the contents of that chest you admire, you know I would. Out of friendship to Benoît," he added, wringing his hands. "But I'm afraid I must...I must adhere to the basic principles of capitalism, not to put too fine a point on it. Though in your case, I am loath to, believe me. I do hope you understand."

"It's just that..." she said, her tone like honey, "it's just that I've been unable to work at all these last years, because Benoît has needed me so. As you know, he was a good provider back when he was working for the post office, but..."

"I know, I know," said Lapin, in distress.

"I'll tell you, Lapin," she said, "if it weren't for the money his parents left us when they died, I don't know what would have become of us. Truly."

Lapin drummed his fingers against his thighs and licked his lips. "I know it has been difficult. Benoît is such a good man, and a hard worker, I know that once he gets back on his feet—"

"—that is not going to happen. I'm sorry to say."

"What? Tell me the latest! He is not doing well?" Lapin asked. "I'm afraid it's been too long since I've seen him. I think of him often, and miss him."

Angeline's face shifted, her expression softened to one of affection with an undertone of sorrow. "Not well, I'm sad to say. I'll tell you, Lapin—as one of his oldest friends—it might be a good idea to pay him a visit as soon as you can. I know it sounds dramatic, but I fear his last days might be upon us."

Discreetly, she wiped a tear from one eye.

"Oh no!" said Lapin. "This is—oh, this is terrible news! I thought he had stabilized? That he was out of the woods?"

Angeline shook her head. "No one has yet been able to tell us what those woods even are. Same as the others, the last doctor took me aside..." she paused, looking up at the ceiling. "I don't know if I should..."

"Oh please, *do* tell me," murmured Lapin, truly feeling for his old friend and also full of the usual desire of a Castillacois to know every bit of gossip there was to know.

"Well, since you are such an old friend...and since it does seem...to be near the end..." Angeline let out a strangled sob and took out an embroidered handkerchief with which to wipe both eyes, inwardly cursing the stain the mascara left on the linen.

"Take a deep breath," said Lapin, putting a hand on her arm. "You will get through this. You know you have my complete support, and the whole village will help you and Benoît through this difficulty."

"You are sweet," she said, peeking up at him through eyelashes glittering with tears. She nearly put a hand on his chest and began talking about his big, manly heart, but managed to stop herself. Whatever the next stop of her train was going to be, it was not going to be at the station of Lapin Broussard. So she might as well spare herself the effort in that department.

"All right," she said, taking in a ragged breath. "I will tell you. But please, out of respect for Benoît, keep this to yourself?"

"Of course," said Lapin emphatically.

"The doctors..." Angeline said, "they say...it's all in his head."

"*What?*"

"It's the sad truth. They say his illness—and I mean going all the way back to when these health problems began, so many years ago—they say it has all come upon him from his mind, from his psychological weaknesses."

"I don't believe it."

"Neither did I, Lapin. Not for a long time. But you and the entire village have seen how it has gone: first a mild sort of illness, not even worth going to the doctor over, but which kept recurring, and then when I took him to the doctor, there were so many tests and examinations. He met with this doctor and that specialist—it's been going on for years, as you and everyone knows—and not a one of them could find a physical reason for his problems.

"And that has happened over and over, even as the symptoms change and wax and wane, and I will tell you—I believe that early on, the first doctor gave up on him. You remember Dr. Vernay? Of course, his life took a nasty turn, but that doesn't mean he was a bad doctor. He was the first to tell me that Benoît's illnesses were psychosomatic, but others—a long legion of medical men and women, I must say, from as far afield as Bordeaux—have confirmed it."

"I don't know what to say. I've known Benoît all my life. He never suffered from any sort of psychological problems, not that I ever knew about. In fact, I would say he was always the most even-tempered and optimistic of men. I would pick him out as having superior mental health, better than most of us! So I can't... well...I'm sorry Angeline, I don't mean to be telling you what's what when I obviously don't know myself. All I can do is offer my warmest condolences, and please give my love to Benoît. I will come see him as soon as I can, perhaps as soon as this evening."

Angeline bowed her head. "You would not think an imagined

illness could be fatal, but the doctors tell me that it most certainly can be. That it most certainly *will* be, if nothing is done to shift Benoît's state of mind. I have moved heaven and earth to do just that, but with, I'm heartbroken to say, no positive result."

She stroked one hand through her blonde hair and let the hair fall gracefully back into place, curling again her chest. She could feel a rosy warmth on her cheeks and knew that she was looking, in that moment, as dazzling as ever.

"And by the way—if you ever do come across a marionette, like we discussed? Guinevere would be best, but I'll have a look at anything from that time period."

Lapin was put off balance by the abrupt change of subject. He simply nodded, smiled weakly, and watched—relieved—as Angeline left the shop.

❧

BENOÎT LAY STILL on the narrow bed, sunlight coming through slats on the unopened shutters. With enormous effort, he heaved his feet to the floor and stood up. Walked the few steps to the window and pushed open the shutters, letting the sun hit him in the face. He closed his eyes and listened to the birds, to the sound of a truck shifting gears, to a child shrieking a block away.

The June sun felt so wonderful, and wouldn't it be something if he could make his way downstairs and outside to the garden? It had been...let's see...probably more than six months since he had been outside. And wouldn't Angeline be amazed to come home and see him lounging in the garden without a care in the world?

Well, that last bit might be hard to pull off. But maybe he could try for it anyway. He rummaged in the armoire for some shorts and a shirt, sat down on the bed to get dressed, and staggered up again, holding on to the doorframe.

Easy does it, he thought, easy does it.

His legs were so stiff. It was as though his legs were made of

NELL GODDIN

wood and would not bend. But nevertheless, down the stairs he went, sort of rocking his way down on his wooden legs and unbending ankles, until he was through the kitchen door and into the back garden, heart pounding. There was no railing for the few short steps off the terrace, and with a burst of unearned confidence he sailed down those steps and tumbled headfirst into the grass.

He stayed very still for a moment, checking to see if he was still in one piece. And then—at the feeling of the grass and the sun on his skin, the feeling of breath heaving in and out of his chest, the feeling, simply, of still being alive—Benoît laughed and laughed until tears were rolling off his cheeks.

&

"WHO WAS THAT?" Molly asked Lapin, as soon as Angeline was back on the sidewalk.

"Angeline LaRue," said Lapin. "I'm sure you overheard—her husband, Benoît, has been ill for a very long time, and it sounds like he's taking a bad turn. Quite a sad story."

"Sorry to hear about your friend. That's the second Castillacois in two days who I've met, that I never knew existed before."

"It's not as though the village is so minuscule," said Lapin, with a bit of huff. "Angeline isn't a native. I have no idea why she moved to Castillac, but she did, oh what, maybe in the late seventies? And married Benoît right off. I think they were engaged the month they met."

"Hm," said Molly. She did not have a clear thought but was trying to pin down a funny feeling she had; it felt something like scanning past a typo in something you're reading—something not quite right, something just a bit off. Now where was it?

Just then her phone buzzed. A text from Ben.

Hurry home if u can. Throckmorton is here and oh boy

Molly laughed. "Doggone it, Lapin, I came to—eh, I'll tell you later. Ben needs me at La Baraque pronto. See you soon?"

"At your service," said Lapin, bowing, once again Mr. Formality.

Molly was on her scooter headed for home in a hot minute, curious and laughing about the new guest who had scared Ben.

1 *965*

FIVE-YEAR-OLD ANGELINE RODE atop her father's shoulders, her feet dangling down and bumping his chest as he galloped around the yard, her hands holding onto his ears.

"Giddyap!" she shouted, her little-girl voice musical, the syllables like quick notes played on a piano.

Her father took another turn around the bottom of the garden and then stopped, breathing hard. "All right then," he said, bending down so she could hop off. "Time for this horse to go back to the stable and get some oats."

"No!" said Angeline, not musical now. She let go of his ear and smacked her father on the shoulder. "Giddyap! Canter!"

With a sigh, he straightened and took several steps in a worn-out approximation of a canter.

"I need a crop," she said, digging her heels in under his arms. "Papa! Get me a crop!"

He reached up and lifted her off his shoulders, setting her

gently on the grass. "You know, jockeys are very light, so they don't overburden their mounts," he said. "You are growing up, and I think very soon, your riding days will be over."

Angeline glowered but did not speak. Another child, equally spoiled, might have stamped her foot and carried on, but Angeline was not like most children. She observed her father coldly, then smiled at him with all the warmth of a hundred suns. "Let's find a crop, shall we, Papa? I think this bush over here would be perfect." She ran to a hydrangea and pointed.

Her father did not want her to have a crop. He was not stupid and knew that she would be using it to hit him. He even knew, deep in his heart, that she would enjoy hitting him.

And yet, what did he do? He took a pocket knife from his pants-pocket, cut a slender branch of the hydrangea, and handed it to his daughter.

❧ 6 ❧

"These budget cuts are going to be our doom," said Florian to Matthias, who was leaning against his desk, broom in hand, gazing out of a window. Saturday was, like the fifty days preceding it, so far, a slow day for death.

"As I believe you have mentioned."

"Indeed. Because it is true. We already had to let Henri go, and you were very lucky that I could find a way to justify your position so you didn't get the heave-ho as well."

Matthias shrugged. "The Lord giveth and the Lord taketh away."

"Ha! Don't try to imply you have any religious sentiment whatsoever, Matthias de Clare. I know you well enough to know you are a heathen, through and through."

"Just saying that moving from a job where I got to sit at a computer all day and now I have to go out with a stretcher and handle dead people is not necessarily a step up, in my opinion."

"Opinions and paychecks are not handmaidens," said Florian. "I just thought that up, it's pretty good, eh?"

Matthias rolled his eyes.

"I would not be surprised to get word that more cuts are

coming," said Florian. "So perhaps you will be relieved of the stretchers after all and can move on to better things. It makes my blood boil, to be honest. All we do is serve the public. We are not padding expenses or performing useless, expensive acts that no one wants. The people of the village depend on us to do a job that many find distasteful but which needs to be done, day in and day out, whatever the weather, whatever anyone's mood. And yet we are the ones finding ourselves on the chopping block."

"Surely they won't cancel the office of the coroner altogether?"

"Not exactly. But they could easily get rid of this particular office and your position, and move me to Bergerac where I would have to work under that odious Peter Bonheur, and Castillac would simply be absorbed into that jurisdiction. Some parts of the world are getting richer and richer, to be sure, and at a galloping pace—but I fear local government budgets, of villages the size of Castillac, are not partaking in this blossoming wealth."

Matthias hopped off the desk and began sweeping again. He had an engagement that night that he was looking forward to, so he focused his thoughts on the dust under the desk and how pleasant it was going to be to see his friend and have a cocktail or two and talk to someone other than Florian Nagrand.

SELMA THROCKMORTON THREW back her unusually large head and brayed—there is no other way to say it—like a donkey.

It was unkind to think of her like that, Ben acknowledged to himself, but at the same time, agreeing with himself that *donkey* was right on the money. Except for her teeth, which were quite nice—straight, nicely shaped, and dazzlingly white. And—he liked donkeys.

"You're a funny man, Monsieur Dufort, just as wry as wry can be. So French!"

"I am that," he said, face frozen in what he hoped was an

expression of warmth of an appropriate degree. "My family has been French for as far back as the genealogists can determine."

"Oh, are you interested in ancestry? My father was quite big on it. Always seemed a giant bore to me, I must admit. Romanticizing the past, if you see what I mean. I'm interested in the *now*, Monsieur! In this very instant in which we are alive and breathing and standing here at La Baraque, looking at each other's faces and taking in the beauty of this country morning!"

Ben's mouth opened but no words emerged.

"It is my deepest, and I mean *deepest* pleasure to be in Castillac on this exquisite June morning!" Selma continued, with such emphasis that Ben thought he could see giant exclamation points pulsating in the air. Pink ones.

He had a bit of a headache. He glanced over at rue de Chêne, hoping to see Molly rounding the bend.

"If I may ask," he said, turning back to Selma, "how did Castillac become your destination? We do get a few tourists, since there are so many sites within a fairly easy drive. But I hope you won't be disappointed—it's rather a sleepy village, with little for entertainment. I was born and raised here and I love it dearly, but I don't expect strangers to feel so...passionately, as you seem to?"

Selma beamed at him. "It's got people in it, am I right? My experience is that if you've got people, you've got entertainment. Simple as that. And Monsieur Dufort," she said, her voice taking on a coquettish tone, "you have not complimented me on my beautiful French. It is very good, is it not?"

"Madame Throckmorton, my apologies, your French is indeed very good. By the intonation alone, I would not have guessed you are English."

"And you were the head detective at the gendarmerie, yes? So I will take that as an extra-shiny compliment. Now, in which of these charming dwellings will I be residing? I would like to settle in for just a moment, and then—let the par-tay begin!"

Ben's eyes widened and he looked to the road for Molly for

the third time. "The pigeonnier," he said, "please follow me." He set off on the path through the meadow with Bobo bounding in the lead. "It's quite roomy for one person but cozy at the same time," he said over one shoulder.

"I'm sure it will be glorious," said Selma. "I feel...I feel an adventure coming on," she said.

Once again Ben opened his mouth to reply but closed it when he realized he had absolutely no idea what to say to that.

❧ 7 ❧

Sunday morning was another perfect June day, the air soft and not hot, alive with bees and early summer bugs, rich with the smells of plants and earth. Angeline took all this in, standing on the terrace of her little house and surveying the garden. After the disappointment at Lapin's, she had worked in the garden all afternoon and not a blade of grass was out of place. It was, Angeline thought, perfect enough for anyone to envy, and especially that Madame Cartier who lived two houses down on rue Simenon and thought she was better than everyone else.

It had been Madame Cartier who had gotten Angeline interested in gardening fifteen years earlier. At a village fête, she happened to be seated next to Madame Cartier, who had gone on and on about her garden and been showered with compliments from the others at the table; Madame Cartier was so pleased with her garden and herself that Angeline vowed to bring the woman down a peg or two. It took five years and a considerable amount of money she could not afford, but she did eventually manage it. And on nights when she had trouble falling asleep, sometimes Angeline thought back to the dejected, beaten look on Madame Cartier's face when she saw Angeline's garden in the early summer of 1998—lush peonies in a profusion of white and pink, so many that the sweet smell filled the noses of anyone walking by; the bed of artichokes giving a lovely texture with their frosty, spiky leaves; the hydrangeas and viburnums of multiple types; and oh yes, the roses, the roses were enough to bring Madame Cartier to her knees...

She smiled, then turned and went inside to the foot of the stairs where she called up to Benoît to tell him breakfast would be ready soon.

In the kitchen, she did not make the usual French breakfast of coffee, toast, and jam, but laid out a spread worthy of the hungriest Briton or American—bacon, fried eggs, strawberry jam, butter, a pot of honey, a generous pile of fried potatoes.

"Here we are!" she said, bringing the tray in to Benoît, with a small glass vase containing a sprig of flowering rosemary in water.

"Oh my," he said, trying and failing to dredge up an expression of pleasure. He was exhausted and utterly without appetite.

"What, this doesn't make you happy?" she said, a knife-edge coming into her voice. "Perhaps if you hadn't gone flat on your face in the garden yesterday, you'd have more of an appetite. Or really, one would think such shenanigans would make you hungry, eh? Why can't you just do as you're told?"

Benoît's face crumpled. He did not answer but fixed his eyes on a tassel at the edge of his blanket and froze.

"You're *not* the one in charge," she said, with glittering eyes. "What if Lapin had seen you in such a state? He would think I was neglecting you most dreadfully."

Benoît did not move a muscle.

"Oh, darling," said Angeline, trying but not entirely succeeding to soften her tone. "It's only that I worry about you so. And if you try to get up and about when I'm not here, you see what happens—you're laid out on the grass with no one to help you get back to bed. And worse: what will people think, if they see you gamboling about the garden in that manner? They will think you are a faker. A *fraud*. They will think I am wasting my life catering to your every whim while you play me like a piano."

Benoît stayed immobile. He was like a bird sensing a predator, hoping if not a feather stirs, the fox will not see him and move along.

Inwardly Angeline chastised herself. She usually had more self-control, rarely allowing herself to say a cross word to her husband. But his impertinence—no, it was far worse than that, his *rebellion*—oh no, that was not going to be allowed. After all the ways he had failed her, rebellion would not be tolerated. She would put a stop to that, make no mistake.

She had told Lapin that Benoît's days were numbered. So perhaps she had already decided, in some part of her mind, that those days had run out.

❦

ONE OF MOLLY'S favorite village traditions was the meet-up at Chez Papa on Sunday nights. That particular night, it seemed as though half the village was there, including her closest friends: Frances was throwing her head back and cackling at something Nico had whispered to her, Lapin and Anne-Marie were arguing about politics, Lawrence was in a vintage sport coat drinking a Negroni, and Ben was on the stool next to her, after spending much of the day reading one of his naval histories.

"Ahh," said Molly, as Nico put a steaming hot plate of extra-salty frites in front of her. "My world is perfection at this moment." She took a sip of her kir and clinked glasses with Ben.

"It's been unusually quiet and peaceful of late. I would think you'd be mourning the lack of...mourners," said Lawrence with a smile.

"*Au contraire*," said Molly. "Call me a ghoul all you want, I am very pleased that Castillac is peaceful and calm. If my future holds no investigations at all, that would please me very much. It's high gardening season, you know, and I'm anxious to get going on it."

"Mm hm," said Lawrence, smiling and unconvinced. "The fact that part of your livelihood is tied to the poor people who get rushed to the finish line before their time, well, that's not your fault, is it? But yes, I agree—" he clinked his glass with hers—"it is indeed lovely for the village to have gone so long without a death. None of the elders have passed on, either, as far as I know, not for many months. Population growth is practically booming!" He gestured to Frances, who had gotten up to dance next to the bar, her long straight black hair swooping back and forth, her hands on her big belly. "You know, most of the small villages in France— and in other countries too, no doubt—get smaller and smaller, as young people take off for cities where they can make a living more easily. I hate to think of Castillac shrinking into oblivion. Frances and Nico are doing their part, at any rate."

"Indeed," said Molly, watching Frances dance and grinning. "Can you even imagine what a nut that baby will be, with those parents?"

Lawrence laughed. "He'll probably turn out to be a nuclear physicist or something, with no sense of humor whatsoever. It's funny how often that happens."

Molly laughed. "I called you last night and got sent straight to voicemail. Were you up to something interesting?"

Lawrence shrugged and motioned to Nico to refresh his Negroni. "A man should have a secret or two, lest the world become completely bored with him."

"Secret—or two? Oh do tell."

"Well, chérie, as I don't have to explain to you, of all people— if I told, it would no longer be a secret. Let a middle-aged man keep something private to cherish, how about it."

Molly wanted to ruffle his hair but restrained herself, knowing the care that Lawrence put into slicking it into place.

Ben's back was to the door, so he didn't see Selma Throckmorton come in to Chez Papa. Molly saw her but they had not met, so she barely noticed her. Who did notice Selma was Florian Nagrand, who was sitting at a table near the door, alone, nursing a Pernod and feeling sorry for himself. At the sight of Selma, however, he thought it was possible, even if infinitesimally so, that his fortunes had turned.

Frances was nearly six months along and had a nice little bump on her slender frame, and Nico never tired of coming up behind her and rubbing it with one hand. In Chez Papa, that meant coming out from behind the bar so he could get his mitts on her, which on a crowded night like that Sunday, did not go unnoticed.

"Ah, c'mon Nico, get back behind the bar where you belong and make me a margarita," said a young woman barely old enough to drink.

"Margarita? I'm out of limes," said Nico, hustling around the corner. "What else can I get you?"

A bit of hub-bub when several people called out drink orders at the same time. Frances enjoyed watching Nico as he moved quickly to fill them, all while keeping up his excellent bartender's banter.

"You scampered away yesterday before I could find out what you were looking for," Lapin said, having wandered over.

"I wish I could say I was looking for a gold ring with a ruby, or something equally exciting," said Molly. "But it's only that I need another armoire to put bed linens in. Doesn't need to be anything fancy."

"Ah," said Lapin. "Even practical items can be beautiful, *La Bombe*."

Molly grinned. "You haven't called me that in ages. It used to annoy me so much."

"Even among friends, we can admire beauty," he said, with a courtly bow.

"Oh Lapin, you are so full of it," laughed Molly. "Armoires can be gorgeous, for sure. When I first got to France, I hated having no closets. But I have adapted."

"This is one of your charms," said Lapin, with another bow.

"So that customer..." Molly began.

"You know I never discuss—"

"Ha! You don't gossip about your customers? Lapin—"

"Not that one," he said.

For a split second, Molly wondered what that meant. But her mouth was happily full of frites, the kir delicious as always, so Molly sighed and looked around the room once more. Her world was calm, delicious, and full of love—for the moment.

❧ 8 ❧

As Sunday wore on, Angeline did not calm down, did not find any way to divert her attention from the peasant's revolt staged by her husband, and her anger went from simmer to rolling boil.

The *audacity* of the man!

He could have had such a different life, if he had only been able to take the opportunities he was given. For so many things— really, all things with the one crucial exception—Angeline had been able to cajole, coerce, or fool Benoît into doing what she wanted. But in this one thing, he was implacable. And so, she thought, he sealed his own fate. She did not make the fatal decision, *he* did.

For years she had daydreamed about finishing him off. It had been one of the favorite cards in her mental deck, something she brought out when she was feeling low, when she felt someone had gotten the better of her, slighted her, or acted superior. But to actually, literally, kill him? She hadn't been sure, even as she took pleasure in thinking about it and planning the details, that she would ever take the step. In fact, one of the delicious parts of the daydream was the uncertainty, the not knowing exactly what would or would not happen.

But now that the end-game was finally in motion...somehow it made her want to throw everything into the air. It made her want to be careless, spontaneous, heedless of what others thought. Angeline was none of those things, not that day or any day before or after. And it was not clear why, on her husband's last day on earth, she felt a sudden compulsion to be someone she was not.

Whatever the impetus, it was not borne of regret, or self-doubt. The day's events had been planned and looked forward to for years. She licked her lips, bit them to make them red, and prepared for the long-awaited unfolding.

And then it was done. She had served her husband his final dinner with no ceremony. The smugness she felt at paying him back for his decades-long refusal was pleasurable and only undercut by the secrecy of her actions, since obviously if she told him the dinner was poisoned, he would not eat it. And so as she sat with him while he ate, her emotions swirling, she had to fight with herself not to tell him what she was doing so that she could squeeze that extra bit of victory out of the enterprise.

It turned into a long and messy night.

Now, in the brightening light of dawn, Angeline was out of spirits—the lead-up to the main event, now rapidly approaching, had not been satisfying at all, but instead made more work for her. Benoît had sweated monstrously, and that was the least of it: in addition she had had to sit close by to make sure the bucket was at hand for the epic puking, altogether disgusting, not to mention the bedpan duty. There was some anxiety that despite the dramatic result, perhaps the dose hadn't been large enough to do the job, but not long after daybreak, finally, the long-suffering Benoît LaRue breathed his last.

Just after, Angeline sat by the bed, holding his hand. She was, on the whole, disappointed. When you look forward to a thing for years and years, how can anything live up to that weighty expectation? Nevertheless, she blamed Benoît for not dying in a more satisfying manner, though she could not have said, in any explicit way, what that might have looked like.

The truth was that she expected to feel something—a release, some kind of relief, even a sort of joy—and none of those feelings appeared, or even any hint of them. So she ended up, on this day long anticipated and planned for, with annoyance being the dominant emotion. Not what she had been aiming for, it goes without saying.

At least I am free of him, she thought, trying to look on the bright side. I am unencumbered and ready for the next act of my life. It is going to be a showstopper, I can say that one hundred percent.

She dropped Benoît's hand and leaned back in the wooden chair, her mind filled with a dream of herself in a house at least as big and imposing as Madame Cartier's, a younger husband who was fit, handsome (and malleable), along with a bank account so large that the officers of the bank regularly called at the house to ask if there was anything, anything at all, that they might do to make sure she was pleased with their service.

With great effort and a serious strain to her back, she managed to get Benoît thoroughly cleaned up and into a fresh pair of pajama bottoms. She wanted to change the sheets but worried she might end up with Benoît on the floor which would take some explaining she did not wish to do, so she spot cleaned as best she could, and opened the windows for some fresh air.

She mopped the floor a second time—just to feel productive —washed out the bucket and put it back in the garden shed, and called the gendarmerie.

MATTHIAS HAD COME to work at the usual time on Monday. Florian was nearly always there before him, but not this Monday, and so it was Matthias who took the call from the gendarmerie and who hopped in the van alone to head to the LaRue's. He had performed this duty only once, since he had been moved from his desk job only about six months ago, and most of those months, as Florian moaned incessantly, had been entirely free of bodies needing picking up.

After pulling up in front of the LaRue cottage, he sent Florian a text telling him where he was and asking if he would meet him there, but got no answer.

When Paul-Henri called, he had described the deceased as chronically ill and said the death was a blessing. So it was not a situation for police presence or any sort of suspicion or urgency regarding cause of death.

Matthias sat for a few more moments hoping to hear from Florian. Then with a sigh, he unfolded his lanky body from the van. He was obviously not used to being the sole representative from the coroner's office; he wished he hadn't been so hasty and simply waited for Florian to arrive at the office. But now he was outside the LaRue's door, and probably Madame LaRue was looking anxiously out of the window, so there was no turning back.

Squaring his shoulders, he hopped up the few steps and rapped on the door.

No answer.

He looked for a doorbell and did not see one, so he rapped again, cocking his ear for footsteps.

No answer.

Hm. Have I got the wrong house, he wondered. He went back to the van to check his note scribbled when the gendarmerie called. 65 rue Simenon? This is it all right.

Matthias was not a man with social anxieties or a lack of confidence, but he hesitated about knocking again because why would three times be any better than two, and he was aware that whoever was inside was likely to be in a state of shock, with a loved one so recently passed.

He checked his phone to see if Florian had answered, still nothing. He put earbuds in and listened to music for a few minutes. A woman pushing a baby carriage went past, then two boys with a dog. Matthias was jumpy waiting in the best of circumstances, which this was not. He pulled out the earbuds, hopped up the steps again, and banged on the door like the fate of the world depended on it.

He heard a light sort of footstep, almost like dancing. He heard the steps and felt a funny feeling in his solar plexus. Then the door opened.

"Madame LaRue," he said. "I am Matthias de Clare, from the coroner's office. The gendarmerie sent me."

Angeline opened the door with a great sigh. "Yes," she said. "I've been waiting for you. These terrible moments come, and we don't quite know what we're supposed to do. I thought perhaps I should call *SAMU*, but why bother them when anyone could see that Benoît had gone. So then I nearly called your office, but it seemed, I don't know, a little...forward, if you understand me. That left me with the gendarmerie. The woman who answered was perfectly nice, so I won't say anything against her, but you know, who wants to call the gendarmerie for any reason? I certainly don't."

It did not put Matthias off, or surprise him, that a widow of only a matter of hours would talk some nonsense. People need time to find their footing, don't they?

They stood awkwardly in the front hallway for a few moments. Matthias was trying to figure out a sensitive way to ask where the body was when Angeline spoke. "He died in his own bed, which is just what he wanted," she said. She reached into an apron pocket and drew out a delicate linen handkerchief, then dabbed both eyes.

"Can you show me?"

"Oh yes, of course," said Angeline. "Please forgive me, this whole thing—it's just so much, emotionally, you understand—I'm scatter-brained. Come this way." She went up the short flight of narrow stairs ahead of Matthias, then pointed at the door to Benoît's room.

There was no doubt that the poor man had indeed passed. Matthias checked his phone again; no word from Florian. Matthias was a man with a mechanical sense to match his technological savvy, and so even though getting the corpse of Benoît LaRue onto the stretcher seemed challenging for one person, with the crafty use of bedsheets Matthias managed it easily.

Though he would never have said the experience was an enjoyable one. He missed his old desk job acutely.

And where in the world was Florian?

❦ 9 ❦

1979

Benoît LaRue was neither good-looking nor homely, and perhaps there was something to be said for holding that middle ground, Angeline Porcher thought as she carefully applied the reddest red lipstick, widening her mouth and stretching her lips as she expertly ran the lipstick around and around them without touching her teeth.

A knock at the door. She was irritated by his punctuality.

She made him wait.

"Bonsoir, Benoît," she said, eventually opening the door and demurely looking away from his eyes, which were taking her in with obvious pleasure.

"Bonsoir, Angeline! Are your ready for the fête?"

Village fêtes are *so* tedious, she thought. No one new, no one exciting, the same old sausages. "Delighted," she said, feeling color rising in her cheeks and knowing how flattering it was.

She took his arm and they left the run-down section of Castillac and made their way to the center of the village, where picnic tables were lined up in two rows in the middle of the

43

street, and Castillacois milled about doing what they loved best, eating and gossiping. Angeline had moved to Castillac only a few months earlier and already had a ring on her finger.

"Hola!" shouted an old man in a beret with a grand wave. "Good to see you both out this evening!"

Benoît grinned and greeted the man. Angeline once again looked away.

She sat at an empty picnic table while Benoît went off to get her a plate of sausages. Seeing his chance, Guillaume Toucher sauntered over with a *pichet* of red wine and a couple of glasses. "Bonsoir, little beauty," he said, dropping down on the bench beside her. He sat close enough that she could smell him, an animal smell that excited her.

"Bonsoir to you, Guillaume. You do know I'm engaged?" She held out her hand so he could see the engagement ring with the tiny, glittering stone.

Guillaume laughed. "I am not so much a man for words and promises."

"What are you a man for then?" She looked into his eyes, which were green, or blue, or maybe both.

He smiled a slow smile and ran those multi-colored eyes from her feet all the way up her body to her face and the top of her head, and then back down again. To Angeline it felt as though everywhere he looked, he left a trail of ice. Or fire. Maybe both.

She swallowed. Looked over to the grill to see if Benoît was coming. In a quick flash, she remembered her mother and father talking, remembered a string of words that meant little at the time—she was only five or six—but which had sparkled as she heard them. She could feel the intensity of her mother's feelings as she spoke, and the words gave off sparks, were electric somehow—so Angeline had tucked them away until later, years later, when she could understand them.

Guillaume was not a dullard and he knew when his efforts weren't likely to pay off, so he got up and disappeared into the crowd. Angeline sat, tapping her feet, anxious, wishing Benoît would come back even though he was so terribly boring and she had no interest in sausages.

Her parents had died two years earlier, killed by the same flu, which had given her the freedom to move to Castillac. Her childhood friend Hortense had followed, always grateful for any crumbs of attention Angeline deigned to toss her way. She craned her neck, then stood to see better, but did not see Hortense anywhere.

She thought that maybe she should not have chased Guillaume off so definitively; she should have allowed just a little bit of wiggle room, a way for him to believe there was hope, so that she could enjoy his attention and perhaps even the jealousy of Benoît as an added bit of icing on the cake.

10

"We finally had something to do! After all your moaning, where in hell are you?" Matthias knew that speaking to his boss in such a way was a misjudgment, but anger had gotten the best of him.

Florian acted unperturbed. "I'm sure you did just fine," he said. "Those new stretchers are a marvel of engineering, aren't they? Can practically do the job all on their own. Listen, I'm not going to be in for another couple of hours. Maybe not until tomorrow. But that's no problem since I have you to depend on."

Matthias looked askance and shook his head at the phone.

"So," continued Florian, "look, this is an easy one. Benoît LaRue was sickly and had been for years. Years! There's no need to run a hundred tests. Just do a basic post-mortem and call it a day." He looked over at the bed, at the shape of a sleeping woman tangled in the sheets, and felt such an uprising of emotion that he nearly burst into tears. With a huge effort he listened to what Matthias was saying.

"Florian. I am in no way trained to do a post-mortem as you very well know. Are you drunk? For God's sake, I was doing

NELL GODDIN

nothing but computer work a few months ago, I haven't even observed a post-mortem, much less performed one!"

Silence for a moment.

"Ah," said Florian, suddenly feeling as though Matthias could see he was naked. "You are correct, I don't know what I was thinking. All right then. I'll be in later in the afternoon, and I'll show you the ropes. Really, it doesn't take a great deal of skill in a case like this, but I can see why you wouldn't want to fly solo at this point. I'll try to get in before 4:00."

And then he hung up.

Matthias sat on the edge of his desk for a moment. Then he picked up and broom and started sweeping the clean floor. He was wondering whether he could get his old job back. Surely there must be some bureaucratic magic that could make that happen.

WITH BENOÎT OUT of the house—Matthias having taken care of his physical presence, however awkwardly with all those sheets and knots and who knows what else—gracious goodness, what has happened to the quality of civil servants these days?—Angeline had expected to feel marvelous, as though her new life started at the very moment her husband passed through the front door for the last time on that fancy wheeled stretcher. A life beginning not simply with a fresh sparkle but more like a thunderous burst of multi-colored fireworks.

But again she was disappointed.

She walked through the cottage, going into all four rooms and looking about, as though she had misplaced something.

She did not believe in spirits and so did not feel any presence of Benoît, in any form. The place was simply quiet, with dust motes spinning in the sun that poured through the windows. It was tidy. It felt unchanged.

Angeline went to the garden, hoping that the elusive

wonderful feeling would rush to her once she was outside. She wandered among the shrubs, smelling a viburnum, caressing the new velvety leaves of a lamb's ear beside the path.

She was unhappy. Not regretful—never that—but an expectation had fizzled and it made her very cross. Well, she did have the funeral to look forward to. Better hustle along and get that organized, she thought.

The sooner the better. Just to be on the safe side.

11

J ust two days later, on a balmy Wednesday afternoon, Molly
and Ben, holding hands and dressed in black, walked along
rue de Chêne on their way to the cemetery.

"Go home, Bobo!" Molly said over her shoulder, knowing
without seeing that Bobo was creeping along the side of the road,
hoping to join them without their noticing. "It just seems a little
funny to me, that's all. We just heard about Benoît's death yesterday. Doesn't the funeral feel a bit rushed to you?" said Molly.

Ben shrugged. "Why wait? I imagine a lot of people want to
just get it over with."

Molly didn't answer. They walked a few hundred yards in
companionable silence. They passed the Latours and saw that
their vegetable garden was coming along nicely. A black cat was
trotting along the ditch with a sense of purpose, as though late for
something important.

"So you grew up with Benoît?"

"Yes. At least in the way that everyone in the village grows up
together. We weren't the same age so we didn't have classes
together, but played in the same games sometimes during *recré*.
We weren't close friends, if that's what you're asking."

The cemetery was around the next bend and after a quick kiss, they got themselves presentable: Ben flicked some lint off his lapel, Molly pulled her black dress down and smoothed it over her thighs.

"And what about the widow," Molly asked. "Did you grow up with her too?"

"Woman of a million questions this morning," said Ben, giving her hand a squeeze. "She wasn't from Castillac. Knew who she was once she was married to Benoît, but that's it. Barely an acquaintance."

Molly wanted to ask Ben what he thought of her, but people were waving at them and they were at the cemetery gate, so she smiled at Ninette, the cashier at the *épicerie*, and forgot her question.

✿

MOLLY AND BEN followed the crowd under the iron sign that said *"Priez pour vos morts,"* nodding to some and cheek-kissing others. Castillac was small enough that when anyone died, whether they were popular or not, nearly the entire village turned out for their funeral. The priest stood at graveside, a few people—the family, Molly assumed—sat on folding chairs, and all around them, in the narrow pathways between graves, stood villagers who had known Benoît or his family, or simply wanted to pay their respects to another villager.

Angeline's parents were long dead and she was an only child. If the funeral had been divided like a wedding, with the groom's guests on one side and the bride's on the other, Angeline would have been sitting alone except for her hairdresser and a cousin who had driven over from Sarlat because she needed money and hoped that possibly in her bereavement Angeline might be feeling generous.

Molly could only see the back of Angeline's head. She noticed she looked freshly coiffed, the flossy blonde hair falling in soft curls.

Lapin waved from behind the priest, grinning as though he were at the circus.

"Oh, Lapin," Ben muttered, as Castillacois had been muttering ever since Lapin was a child. He watched with some trepidation as the big man shoved his way through the crowd on his way over.

Lawrence appeared next to Molly, dressed in an impeccably tailored black suit in a light wool. "You're looking sharp as ever," she said, kissing his cheeks.

"It's bad of me to say, but I do love funeral wear," he said. "The black dresses!" He kissed his fingertips like a chef. "And this suit always looks great since I never wear it except at funerals. Nary a Negroni has been spilled on it," he said with a wink.

"So, tell me about Benoît," said Molly, low enough that Ben wouldn't hear.

Lawrence shrugged. "I'm afraid I don't have much to tell you. I never knew him when he was well. By the time I moved here, he was already in decline. This has been a long time coming, I'm afraid."

"Mm," said Molly.

Lawrence gave her a sideways glance.

"And his wife—do you know her?"

"I do not," said Lawrence. "I'm not really the social butterfly you imagine me to be, you know."

"I guess not," said Molly, disappointed with his thin answers. "Do you happen to know who they were good friends with? Anyone in the crowd seem to fit that bill?"

They craned their necks and looked about. People were still crowding through the gates. The priest was riffling through a book and the people seated on the folding chairs sat patiently, not moving.

"Curiosity killed the cat, you know," said Lawrence.

"Just a mild question, that's all."

"Right." Lawrence brushed some imaginary lint from his sleeve. "You're barking up the wrong tree, *chérie.*"

"I'm not barking at anything," said Molly.

Lapin jostled up between Molly and Ben. "Well, she wasn't wrong," he said, too loudly.

"Ssh!" said Ben.

"Who? Wrong about what?" asked Molly.

"Angeline! It was just three days ago when she said Benoît was on his last legs, didn't you hear her? In the shop the other day?"

Molly looked at Lapin, thinking. Then she turned to look again at the back of Angeline's blonde head. She watched as the new widow ran her fingers through her hair and fluffed it up.

"And I'm very grateful she came in, because I went to see Benoît as soon as I closed up for the day...and obviously, if I had dillydallied, I would have missed the moment."

"I overheard some of that conversation, as you know," said Molly. "I nearly barged in to ask a bunch of questions once Dr. Vernay was mentioned. She was saying the doctors claimed his illness was all in his head?"

Lapin nodded. "Must have been some awfully dark thoughts he was having."

Molly spoke, eyes downcast. "I never met Benoît. But I...I can't help feeling a sort of kinship with him, because of that horrible time when I was suffering with Lyme. I understand, at least a little, how it feels to be isolated by illness, bedridden..." Molly shuddered.

Lapin craned his neck to see if the priest was getting ready to begin.

"People don't like being around sick people," Molly said, too softly for anyone to hear.

❧ II ❧

After skipping breakfast—she always ate or didn't eat with her figure in mind, and she judged that in her excitement she had eaten too much chocolate lately—Angeline worked in the garden for several hours, weeding the main flower bed and cutting several bouquet's worth of peonies and roses, which she arranged in antique porcelain vases she had gotten at a flea market. Then it was time to meet Hortense Depleurisse, whom Angeline called her best friend, not because Hortense was a friend in the sort of way most people understand them, but because doing so instilled in Hortense a sense of duty towards Angeline, even a devotion... and there was little that Angeline liked more than devotion.

Angeline and Hortense had grown up in the same village, about a hundred kilometers away from Castillac. Neither had been back for a visit, not once.

She spent some time looking through the armoire trying to work out the perfect outfit. She wanted to look good, of course. The trick was not to overplay the hand and appear overdressed for a simple chat over coffee.

At last Angeline settled on a cream skirt, just above the knee, which hugged her hips but not too boldly, a pair of loafers, and a simple white blouse. A gold chain around her neck that was not real gold. She wanted to add a belt and tried it and took it off three times before deciding the outfit was better without.

Hortense had suggested Chez Papa, not really a place for coffee, but Angeline had in that moment been playing the role of devastated widow and did not think it was the right time to get bossy about the meeting-place. But the fact that she had not wanted to go to Chez Papa but could not say so was an irritation still in her mind as she pushed open the door and saw Hortense, slumped at a table in the corner, dressed in her customary baggy clothes.

"Oh, Angeline!" said Hortense, jumping up and kissing her on both cheeks. "You poor sweet thing! Please tell me what I can do to help."

"I'm afraid there's nothing," said Angeline, dropping into a chair and allowing some tears to well up.

"He was your love. Your rock."

"I—I don't know what to say."

"You don't have to say anything," said Hortense. "I understand the depth of your loss...and how it must wipe the words right out of your head."

Angeline nearly burst out laughing. But then something unexpected: suddenly, Angeline wanted desperately to tell Hortense that she had killed Benoît. She wanted to tell her that it was not God or chance or bad luck that had taken him from this earth. It had been her.

All her.

She wanted to tell the whole, long, intricate story. Of Benoît's repeated failure to take certain actions she asked him to take— and how with that failure the die had been cast, even though it had taken years to cross the finish line. Angeline wanted to brag to Hortense about the wide reading she had done, the deep exploration into the realm of poisons. Of the various substances she had experimented with, and what their effects had been.

How she had never been one hundred percent sure, not until the last moment, whether she would take the final, irrevocable step. And how the suspense of that—would she or wouldn't she— had been the one thing that gave her life in this dreary village some razzle-dazzle.

Angeline imagined with satisfaction how shocked Hortense would be. And, Angeline believed, deeply impressed.

However, it must be admitted: Hortense was not exactly hard to impress.

"Are you going to order anything to eat?" Angeline asked, dispirited.

"The *frites* here are very good," said Hortense. "And I believe I'll get a *croque monsieur* to go with. You know, I'm so glad I moved to Castillac just like you did. I'm here to help you through this difficulty, for one thing. Plus people assume you're going to live in the same village you grew up in but I think it's smart to go make your mark in a new place. So thank you for leading the way."

Angeline was struggling to pay attention. She blinked and rubbed her eyes, smearing her eyeliner.

"Who's making a mark?" she said finally.

Hortense smiled. "Both of us, that's who! Now that you're free —and heavens, I don't mean to sound like Benoît's passing was a good thing, please don't think—"

"I don't think anything," said Angeline. "About what you're saying."

"Good! All I meant was, now you won't be emptying bedpans anymore but ready to start the next chapter. And as ever, I'll be cheering for you!"

"Mm," said Angeline. She glanced around the bistro, which was starting to fill up with the lunch crowd. That Nico Bartolucci (behind the bar) was a good-looking man, it was such a shame he had married that American witch. She tried to catch his eye but his attention was taken up by some workmen at the bar.

Hortense placed her order with a distracted waitress. Angeline declined to eat anything. She sat on the edge of her chair, tapping one toe and looking about the room. She felt an ever-increasing anxiety. Sitting on that hard chair in Chez Papa, with the chatter of people in her ears and Hortense looking at her with drippy solicitude—it verged on intolerable. Angeline felt as though she were waiting for something—but what?

Benoît's death was a door opening to her future...but when was it going to begin?

❧ 13 ❧

"Honestly, you look like you were made for pregnancy," Molly said to Frances as they were going for a short walk around Frances's neighborhood. "I guess because you're tall? I hope you feel as good as you look."

Frances didn't answer at first. They kept walking, maybe a wee bit slower than usual. She tucked her black, straight hair behind her ears and it immediately slid back. "Well, physically, true enough, I'm feeling great right now. Apparently it's the beginning and end of pregnancy that are the uncomfortable parts, and I'm sailing though the middle right now. Jaunty as hell."

They kept walking. Molly said, "So if it's not that...are you wondering...if your old bad luck is back?" She stifled a laugh. "I know it wasn't funny at the time, but remember when the Buckley's house nearly burned to the ground when you were housesitting?"

"That was *not* my fault."

"Of course it wasn't. And the interesting thing is, once you moved to Castillac, that long string of disasters stopped. Instead of cars getting stolen, dogs running away, and pipes bursting, you fell in love and your guy fell in love with you. Quite the turnaround."

"Right," said Frances, her tone lacking its usual gusto.

They kept walking. Molly waited. She sort of regretted bringing up the Buckley fire but was still snickering about it to herself.

"Okay Frances, there's a big fat single-T 'but' hanging in the air so just come on, out with it. What's bothering you?"

Frances groaned and squeezed her eyes shut. "Well, like you say, physically I'm going gangbusters. How I'm doing emotionally? Different story."

They went another half a block. "And?" Molly said finally, her patience tested to the limit.

"What if I don't like her?" Frances whispered.

"Don't like who?"

"The *baby!*"

Molly laughed. "I don't think that's an actual problem."

"Why in the world not? It's not like all children are lovable. Far from it. Children can be absolute monsters, even a softie like you would agree with that."

Molly considered. She shrugged. "Well, sure. They're little humans, and humans are...? Let's just say ...fallible. Imperfect."

"Right. And what if—what if those imperfections are things that just...that really, really set me off. Like—I know it's a little late to be thinking about this, but I'm...I'm afraid I'm going to be terrible at motherhood, Molly. That my daughter will pop out and I'll take an instant dislike to her and there'll be absolutely nothing to be done about it and I'll turn out to be one of those mothers nobody can stand, not to mention ruining my poor defenseless daughter with my ineptitude and antipathy—"

"Hold on, Frances, take the bit out of your teeth." Molly slipped her arm around her friend's waist. "Here's how it's going to be."

Frances's face relaxed before Molly even said anything more.

"When that baby is in your arms, you're going to feel so much love for her, it's going to be like nothing you've ever experienced before. And that will mean a lot, because then the times when the child is a little beast, you have that love to carry you through. Sometimes she will be a monster, it is true. And you will love her anyway. And she will love you, even though you're not a perfect mother. No one is."

"How do you know this?"

"It's just how it works."

"Most of the time."

"Most of the time."

BACK AT LA BARAQUE, Molly found Ben loitering around outside the pigeonnier with a carry-all of tools.

"Is something broken?" Molly asked, pointing at the carry-all.

"I remembered that I hadn't checked that rat-hole under the sink in months. And you know—"

"Oh indeed I do," said Molly with a shudder. "What about that divorce surveillance you got hired for, don't you have to get going on that?"

"My subject is on a business trip to Paris and the client didn't want to pay for me to go. I told her it was likely I could get some juicy evidence but she didn't go for it."

"Ah, too bad, I'd be happy to go to Paris with you for a few days! So—is Selma out?"

"That's the thing, I don't know."

"Did you knock?"

Ben looked sheepish.

"You are the funniest man," said Molly, leaning in to him and kissing him on the neck. "You can face down armed criminals without a second thought, but knocking on Selma Throckmorton's door does you in. It's eleven in the morning, a perfectly respectable time to knock." She rapped on the pigeonnier door.

They heard some rustling, two footsteps. Then silence.

Ben looked at Molly. "What does that mean," he whispered.

Molly shrugged. "Let's go discuss what to have for lunch." When they got halfway across the meadow, she said, "Look, people are...they're...you know this more than anyone! People are strange. Every last one of us. So, often a guest will be inside and just not want to talk. To anyone. It's doesn't mean anything. And I don't know this for sure but I expect being on vacation might make the desire for privacy even more pronounced—like part of the beauty of vacation is having no one peppering them with questions, or asking them to do anything, or having some kind of expectation. They want to be in their cozy rental and just *exist*. You see what I mean?"

"I guess. I haven't stayed in gîtes very often. We used to have a camper when I was a kid, and so we stayed at campgrounds, an entirely different thing. Or if you stay in a hotel, it's unusual for anyone to be knocking on your door. A violation of privacy, in my opinion."

They kept walking. Molly reached down and plucked a stalk of grass and chewed on it.

"So I have a few questions," she began, "about Benoît."

She saw Ben stiffen slightly out of the corner of her eye.

"He was sick for...how long, really? Like what age was he when the illnesses began? Did he ever have any kind of diagnosis?"

"He was a little sickly as a child, but adulthood is when things went badly wrong. No diagnosis that I knew of. Word at the funeral was that it was all psychosomatic."

"According to whom, Angeline?"

"Dammit, Molly."

"What?"

Ben squatted down to pet Bobo. "Don't go there."

"There? Where is there? I'm just asking for some details about the man's illness, for heaven's sake."

"You sounded like you might be sniffing around, thinking there was foul play."

"I'm not sniffing anything except this lovely June air," she said crossly. "If you're jumping to the conclusion that I think Benoît was murdered, that's ridiculous. But—I do think there's a *medical* mystery to be solved. I checked the coroner's report online and it simply says 'system failure,' which I think you'll agree is a bit of laziness on Florian's part—what death couldn't be put down to that? It's like he didn't even do an examination. Anyway, I'm curious about *what* killed Benoît—not who."

"He was sick for a long time. I want to emphasize that there is nothing whatsoever suspicious about his death."

"Did you listen to anything I just said? I'm not saying he was murdered, Ben! However, I will say something else: I don't believe psychosomatic illness even exists," Molly said, with an edge in her voice.

Ben's eyebrows flew up. "How can you say that?"

"Easily. I just did. I think it's what a bad doctor says when he doesn't know what's going on—he blames the patient. And honestly, it makes me want to start wondering whether Benoît's death *was* a murder because I'm getting so much pushback on the idea even though it's not an idea I've been entertaining!"

Ben opened his mouth but could think of nothing to say to that.

"And—and right now," said Molly, "I'm feeling like I'm about to boil over and I think it would be good for me to be alone for a moment. If you don't mind."

Ben glared at her and walked back out the French door.

Molly put her hands on her hips and dug her fingers in. She grimaced. She understood that her feelings about doctors not doing a good job had splashed over onto Ben, where they obviously did not belong. The boiling-over feeling passed quickly and now she just wanted everything to be good between her and Ben. She found him in the shed, and with a sly smile but no words, pulled him by a belt loop out of the shed, into the house, and back to bed.

14

1960

"Well, I'm getting older. We can't just sit back and let nature take its course, unless we don't care what that course is. We have to *act*. And this opportunity is better than having our own, anyway."

"Oh, Anne," said Artur Porcher, combing his fingers through his hair. "What are you talking about, better? Please don't feel so disappointed, you're still young! It'll happen, I'm sure of it. I wish you could have some faith in the future."

She made a noise—something in the vicinity of a laugh, but so markedly humorless that it chilled him.

"I'm just saying," she said, sweetening her tone, "that a situation like this doesn't pop up every day. It was a stroke of the most incredible luck, Artur! Like the hand of God! I've told you over and over, why do you not grasp it? It is like walking down the street and suddenly it's raining gold coins and all you have to do to get rich is fill your pockets and go straight to the bank."

"You don't know if it's true, though. What if the poor girl was delirious?"

Anne narrowed her eyes at him. "Don't you see? It doesn't even matter if it's true. It only matters if certain people think it's true. That's the crucial thing. And what do you think you know about it?" Her tone back to mocking, sharp-edged.

"I don't know anything about it at all. I don't *want* to know anything about it. I just wish…I just wish you could be happy with what we have, with what our life is, right now. We don't need to adopt, not yet. Just—please, darling—just have faith that when the time is right, you'll get pregnant."

"*Faith?*" Anne looked as though she had eaten something spoiled. She got up and walked to the small table in the small kitchen, and put her hands down on it to keep them from trembling. "I am destined for something better than this," she said in a low voice.

Artur felt a flash of fear run through him, not for the first time.

15

C hangeover Day sneaked up on Molly that week. What she really wanted on that lovely Saturday was to spend another languid morning with Ben (mostly in bed, with pastry breaks). But there was too much to do that could not be put off. Just after the guests in the cottage had departed, Constance arrived with the usual hubbub and hustled off to get started on the cleaning. Ben had gotten up early and gone for a run.

Molly glugged down the last of her coffee and made her way through the meadow to the pigeonnier, to see when Selma was heading out or if she needed help with transportation or luggage.

"What a blessed, *blessed* morning!" said Selma, throwing open the door before Molly could knock. "Just glorious, isn't it, Madame Sutton?"

"Oh, call me Molly, please," Molly said, making a move to come inside, but Selma blocked the doorway.

"I've got a question for you, my dear *Chatelaine* of La Baraque," said Selma with a wink. "I have enjoyed my stay in Castillac so much, I'd like to stay on. For at least another week, maybe two. Am I lucky enough that no one has reserved the pigeonnier for this week? If it is booked, I could make do with another accommodation, though I must say I have become quite attached to my home sweet pigeonnier."

"Happy to have you stay, and no need to move, no one has booked it for this week, though I do have guests coming the week after. I suppose I could shift them into the annex."

"Hip hip hooray!" said Selma, throwing her arms up in glee, or victory, or both.

Molly was not sure she had ever met anyone so...engaged with life.

"I'm curious, Selma," Molly said. "Of course we get our fair share of satisfied tourists, and I love the village beyond anything. But you...seem to be more enamored of it than any visitor I can think of. Are there particular things that you love about Castillac? Some surprise, some...detail I haven't yet stumbled across?"

Selma smiled the smile of the sphinx and shook her head slightly. "What's not to love. All right then, if you would leave me, it's time for my morning ablutions," she said, with a cheery wave. And the door closed before Molly could say another word.

WITH NO PIGEONNIER TO CLEAN, Molly set off on her scooter for the village, intending to get the usual bag of delights from Patisserie Bujold, and maybe pay a quick visit to Lapin to see if he had any armoires that she could put in the annex.

As she delighted in the breeze whipping through her hair as she sped down the rue de Chêne, she thought about how unlikely it was that she had moved to France simply to get over a divorce, and had ended up solving murder cases. She wondered if it meant something unsavory, that it was so easy for her to get into the mind of a killer.

Maybe if she were a decent sort, these kinds of acts would be unimaginable.

Well, she thought, they're imaginable to me, and that's simply that.

She took a side street to dodge the market traffic, avoiding the Place lined with tents and purveyors of all kinds of deliciousness, and pulled up in front of Lapin's junk—er, antique—shop. But she knew Lapin well, and it wasn't as simple as asking straightforward questions and getting straightforward answers. There was a game to be played, and she was willing—even delighted—to play it.

"Lapin!" she cried, enthusiastically (because the first step of the game was to butter him up).

Lapin held up a finger and winked at Molly. He was speaking with an older man, who was bent over as he looked at something in the glass case.

The man startled as Molly approached. He took off his glasses and rubbed them with a cloth he drew from his coat pocket. "I don't believe we've met," he said to Molly, with an expression that said perhaps it had been better that way.

"This is Madame Sutton, who runs La Baraque," said Lapin. "She comes in here all the time trying to snap up my best stuff and tell me it's nothing but trash. I wouldn't have anything to do with her if I were you." He winked at Molly.

"Pleasure to meet you," Molly said, sticking out her hand and hoping a handshake was the correct move.

"Delphus McDougal," he said, offering a damp, limp hand.

Molly smiled, taking note of his worn tweed sport coat, his stained trousers, his muddy tennis shoes. Delphus looked like an interesting man, but she did not think he felt the same about her.

And in fact, right away he put his shined-up glasses back on and left the shop, waving over his shoulder to Lapin.

"I don't know what's going on, all week I keep meeting citizens of Castillac that somehow I have never seen before in my life."

"You don't get out as much as you used to. Married life," sighed Lapin.

"How are things going with you? Is Anne-Marie..."

"Oh, she's fine. Dandy. I am learning that there are ups and downs to everything and one mustn't get hysterical at every little bump in the road."

"Wise words, Lapin," said Molly, still buttering him up, but meaning it. "Now, first order of business—I need another armoire. It's for the annex, for guests. It doesn't have to be especially nice—not valuable at any rate—it can be worn, but not sad."

"Lucky, lucky Molly," said Lapin, for a moment leaning his substantial weight on the counter and smiling his salesman's smile. "I've got just the thing."

They went down a narrow aisle to the back, where the larger pieces of furniture were kept in a jumble. Molly looked at the wide variety of things on shelves but saw nothing that caught her eye. Paperweights, chipped dishes, a million vases, porcelain figurines, objects that she had no clear idea what they were for.

"You get any good hauls lately?"

"It's been quiet, as you know very well. Castillac has had such a long stretch without any deaths that it's been quite unsatisfactory for my inventory. And of course, poor Benoît no doubt left everything to Angeline, not that he had anything much to leave, as far as I know. Anyway, I haven't been invited over to do an inventory."

"Angeline strikes me as a person who likes nice things," said Molly.

But Lapin merely grunted a noncommittal grunt. "Here you are," he said, sucking in his belly to squeeze between two massive armoires. "What size are you looking for? If it's for guests, I suppose they're not bringing their entire wardrobe so you could go a little smaller. Something like this one?"

Molly wanted to step back to get a better look but the armoire was jammed in between two others, the aisle was narrow, and there was nowhere to step. It was deco, with rounded edges and some triangles inlaid along the cabinet doors.

"How much?"

"Ohh...for you? Eight hundred euros," said Lapin, wiping his brow and feeling rather claustrophobic in the tight space.

Molly just laughed. Part of the game.

She walked down the row, looking at all of them, stopping to open cabinet doors or try a drawer.

"I'm so glad you got to see your friend right at the end. I'm sure it gave him some comfort."

Lapin looked up at the ceiling and sighed. Molly could see he had something to say, and that he was going to drag it out as long as possible.

Some of the traditions of Castillacois gossip were set in stone, and one could not budge them, no matter how high-flown one's intentions.

"I'm glad I made it in time, but truthfully, that's more for me than for him. I guess we had a pretty jolly half hour, all things considering."

"Jolly?"

"Well, I'll tell you, Molly, since you're always one for death-related details—I came away from that visit not thinking for a moment that he was on his last legs. Not at all. Benoît and I had a couple of good laughs, he had a nice bit of color in his cheeks, didn't seem to be suffering from any symptoms..." Lapin shook his head. "I mean, I scurried right over after Angeline made it sound so dire. You were here, you heard her! I expected him to look dreadful, not altogether perky and ready to joke around like always. And I guess...well, he did die, after all, so what do I know. I'm just saying..."

"You didn't expect him to go so soon, once you got a look at him?"

"*Exactement.* Maybe your experience with death is all post-mortem? But I myself have seen a number of people in their last days. I know, of course, there are mysteries that no human can penetrate, I'm not claiming to be some kind of soothsayer —but

I'll tell you, it was clear as a bell to me that those people were going to die soon. You could feel it. You could see it."

"And Benoît...?"

"No." Lapin shook his big, shaggy head. "I mean—all right, he did not look like an Olympic pole vaulter about to win a gold. He did not look as though he was going to go skiing in the Alps. But dying before the next dawn? No, not remotely. I thought Angeline was a hundred percent wrong. And I made sure to tell her that as I was leaving. I thought it would bring her comfort, but then the next morning when I heard, I worried that I gave her false hope." Lapin made an exaggerated shrug and knocked his broad shoulders into an armoire and a standing mirror and winced.

"I guess the path of dying isn't necessarily linear," said Molly. But of course, her mind was off to the races, thoroughbred intuiter of murderous mischief that she was.

PATISSERIE BUJOLD WAS ALWAYS PACKED on Saturdays, and this was no exception. Molly shoved her way in and got a spot next to the case where she could inspect each pastry on offer, checking in case there was some new seasonal creation she'd never tried before.

"Molly!" said Edmond Nugent, the proprietor, having to raise his voice to be heard over the chatter. "You'll see the apricots on the far right!"

Molly's mouth watered as she anticipated her very favorite of all, the *oranais aux abricots*, with the apricots slightly blackened, the pastry crisp in some places and soft in others, the layer of pastry cream, the whole wonderfully buttery and sweet and absolutely magnificent. They were not available year-round which of course added to their desirability.

"Hello, how I've missed you," Molly said, speaking directly to the first apricot pastry in the row, and then standing up straight and pressing her lips together so as not to demonstrate any further eccentric behavior in the middle of the crowded shop.

Eventually the crowd thinned, along with Edmond's inventory, and he, Molly and one other customer were all that remained.

"Paul-Henri," said Edmond, "have you decided?"

"Oh!" said Molly, "I didn't realize it was you!" And then, seeing that she had probably put her foot in her mouth, she managed to stop herself from clapping a hand over her mouth and tried to pass it off as swatting a nonexistent fly.

Paul-Henri Monsour, junior officer at the Castillac gendarmerie (bachelor, aged forty-two) had gained quite a bit of weight since the last time Molly had seen him—fifty pounds at least.

"Maybe you heard, I was in Aix-en-Provence for quite some time," she said to him. "What have you been up to, haven't seen you in an age."

Paul-Henri squinted at her as though perhaps he didn't recognize her either. He pulled down his tight uniform jacket and Molly saw that the brass buttons were all well-polished as usual; Paul-Henri was always a man for details, especially in appearance.

Their relationship had always been a bit...competitive.

"Castillac has been blessedly quiet," he said, with an expression that dared her to disagree. "I have returned a few dogs to their owners and given quite a few traffic tickets. But that is about all."

"I have not quite forgiven you about that trip to Aix," said Edmond. "I know very well you were fraternizing with all manner of patisseries down there. I cannot stomach the disloyalty!"

Molly laughed. "You've got nothing at all to worry about," she said. "Don't even get me started on those wretched calissons."

Edmond threw back his head and laughed. Molly complaining about bad cookies from inferior bakeries was the stuff dreams were made of as far as he was concerned.

"Are you going to get my order or should I have it sent to the gendarmerie?" said Paul-Henri.

"Now, now, don't get yourself out of sorts," said Edmond. "Molly is always such a distraction, isn't she? But a sweet one," he added, with a little smile.

Paul-Henri rolled his eyes. "It's the turkey sandwich, napoleon, and—"

"I'm on it, I'm on it," said Edmond, with another smile at Molly.

A short but awkward silence.

"So," said Molly to Paul-Henri, "How's Chantal doing? Going stir-crazy from lack of anything to do?"

"We at the gendarmerie are nothing but grateful about the peacefulness of the village," said Paul-Henri, lifting his nose in the air.

"Oh of course, of course!" said Molly, trying not to laugh. "The only mystery I see on the horizon is what killed poor Benoît LaRue. Not so sure 'all in his head' is a real diagnosis. Heck, maybe Angeline's been poisoning him all these years!"

"Oh, Molly," said Edmond.

"Oh, *Molly*," said Paul-Henri. "For the love of...all that is holy... do *not* try to stir that particular pot. There is such a thing as *case closed*, you know. No matter how desperate *you* might be for what you call excitement."

"I was joking, fellas, get a hold of yourselves." Molly had instantly regretted her offhand remark but of course there was no snatching it back. "I just meant that there seems to be something of a medical mystery. 'It was all in his head' seems like such a cop-out, don't you think?"

"Medicine is outside of my bailiwick," said Paul-Henri, lifting his nose even higher in the air.

"People die, Molly," said Edmond. "Unfortunately for us all, there is no mystery about that."

❧ 16 ❧

It was an important meeting. So Angeline spent more than the usual amount of time getting dressed before going out—which is to say, quite a long time—involving several complete wardrobe changes and indecision over hairstyle. Finally she settled on a simple low ponytail, which she hoped was flattering and also conveyed that she was so overwhelmed that she couldn't manage anything more complicated. The shoes were more of a problem; she tried simple black flats and then a pair of faux snakeskin kitten heels she had snagged at a thrift store before deciding on a plain sandal with a low heel.

Her makeup was nearly perfect: a light foundation, barely noticeable, pink blush, mascara, and a stick shadow on her lids, beige with a hint of gold. The whole was so artfully done that the effect was that she did not look made up at all, but rather years younger, glowing with good health, beautiful skin, and lovely features; she never overdid with makeup. However, now she did not look woeful or sad, which was also part of what she was looking for.

Presenting herself as a grieving yet beautiful widow was turning out to be much more difficult than she anticipated.

The perfume...so tricky to decide on. Alluring—as all perfumes should be—but not sultry. Not flowery. Not...*joyful*. What does that leave me, she thought, extra-cross.

All in all, it was quite tiresome, this new reality. Angeline wanted to look (and smell) breathtaking, and also: grieving, worthy of sympathy, suffering deeply. She had failed to consider in advance how these two states had only a slim potential for overlap between them. Irritated, she tossed aside the tight bright green skirt that fitted her exactly right, and put on a looser black skirt with a hem below her knees. It made her look frumpy, and seeing herself in the mirror by the front door, Angeline felt a surge of fury and her fist flew out and smacked her reflection with force.

The mirror cracked. But it did not shatter.

She stared at herself while rubbing her sore knuckles. Angeline was not used to losing control and did not have ready means to pull herself together. It was not just an important meeting but a *crucial* meeting, and if she screwed it up, then murdering Benoît would almost be for nothing.

Well, she thought, that's only leaving out how interesting—she could almost say entertaining—the process had been. It had taken years to work up to it, and in the end, she had summoned the courage to do it, and how many people could say that? That should count for something, she thought, taking one last look at herself in the cracked mirror before setting off.

ANGELINE PAUSED for a moment outside the insurance office, smoothed her skirt and then her hair, took a deep breath, and went inside to the tinkling of a bell.

"Bonjour, Leon," she said, allowing her voice to catch just a little.

"Angeline," said Leon Garnier, jumping up from his chair and using the soft tone Angeline had learned was *de rigeur* when talking to the bereaved. "How *are* you doing?" Leon had something of a paternal aspect about him that came in handy in his business; you felt, from his tone and his gracefully silvering hair, that he was going to be there for you, to make sure you had support for whatever calamity had befallen you (as long as you were insured against it).

"How I wish we were meeting under other circumstances," said Angeline, delicately pulling a lace handkerchief out of her handbag.

"Indeed, chérie, indeed. And really, there was no need for you to come in so soon. You must be right in the thick of it, the most difficult part of your mourning. The shock can't have worn off yet." He ruffled some papers and gave her a sympathetic look. "It's quite something, isn't it—I mean, like the whole village, I was aware of Benoît's fragile state of health. And yet, when the final moment comes? We're stunned. One cannot prepare, emotionally—that's the fact of it."

Oh, what a fatiguing, boring man, thought Angeline. She dabbed her eyes with the handkerchief and nodded.

"As for the business before us...the wheels of the insurance world do turn rather slowly, I'm afraid," Leon said with a genial chuckle. "I wish I could write you a big, fat check this very instant! But you know how it is."

Angeline did not know how it was. But she kept all indication of that out of her expression. She turned a three-hundred watt smile at Leon and spoke softly. "I'm just...if you could only give me some reassurance...I feel so alone, Leon, so alone in this world..."

Leon jumped up from his chair and came around to comfort her. "Of course you are not alone, Angeline! You have the whole village to support you during this difficult time. And you specifi- cally have me and Amiable Insurance, backing you every step of the way. Benoît may not have been the biggest earner in the

Dordogne, but he understood the value of insurance and has provided for you very well."

If you only knew how much wheedling and outright threats it had taken for him to reach that understanding, thought Angeline.

"Is there...I understand these things take time...but is there any way you could let me know the timing? Just so I can plan...you understand. I am of necessity on a strict budget and only hoping to know...obviously, now that I no longer have Benoît to take care of, I am free to find work, so of course that will go a long way, if I am lucky enough to find something..." She bent her head and twisted the handkerchief in both hands.

"Ah," said Leon, "let me track down the particular policy and have a look. As I said, Benoît did the right thing by you and I think you should be very pleased. Of course, no one wants to profit from the death of a loved one. But we here at Amiable Insurance like to believe that the payouts do bring a comfort that is meaningful and even necessary to a person's life, after losing a loved one."

Angeline looked at Leon. His hair is thinning on top and he doesn't even know it, she thought, careful to keep the sneer from her face. And then, in a moment of unusual introspection, she wondered why she had this surge of negative feeling towards a man who was going to be giving her at least a hundred thousand euros, even if he wasn't handing it over that second.

Curious, she thought, looking at Leon and continuing to feel a physical distaste for him. She imagined slapping him across the face but the fantasy did not bring her much satisfaction.

I want the money now, she thought. *Now.* She sat back in the chair, thinking, trying to come up with a way to make Leon understand this, and to take care of her as he should.

"I'm sure...I'm sure your company wouldn't want..."

Leon waited, head cocked. He had learned not to jump in to try to finish people's sentences.

"I'm sure your company wouldn't want beneficiaries to...to

starve to death while waiting for the settlement," she blurted out, and grimaced at the ham-handedness of it.

Leon laughed. "Certainly not," he said. He stood, and Angeline understood she was being ushered back to the street with no check in her hand. "I will be in touch. I'm sure all the bureaucratic hurdles won't take too long, and neither will your settlement from Amiable. I very much wish I could give you a date, but am sorry to say it just doesn't work that way. It will come! I can reassure you on that score."

After she was gone, Leon sat down with his elbows on his desk, tapping his foot. He was, on the whole, a pleasant, warm-hearted man, who indeed genuinely took pleasure in paying settlements to people, especially when the money made a dramatic improvement in the person's life. But with Angeline—he couldn't put his finger on why, but he felt a sort of resistance, an unfamiliar unwillingness.

He shoved her paperwork on the bottom of a pile and leaned back in his chair to contemplate what to have for lunch.

ANGELINE, meanwhile, was walking home in the uncomfortable cheap sandals, deep in a foul mood brought on entirely (she thought at first) by the bald spot on the top of Leon Garnier's head. And then, with a flash, she realized why she was feeling so out of sorts. It was the same as it had been when she was with Hortense, only more so.

She, Angeline LaRue, daughter of a midwife's aide and a laborer, had succeeded over eleven years in fatally poisoning her husband. She did not judge this to be a negligible accomplishment. She granted that anyone is capable of poisoning another person, as long as they have some access to them. The logistics are not that difficult. The world is full of toxic chemicals, plants, vapors, on and on. The fatal agent doesn't have to be expensive or exotic. There is no dearth of choice when it comes to poison.

So that part of it, securing the toxin and the physical act of administration, was not the accomplishment. No—what she has done, her superlative achievement—is that she has *gotten away with it.*

The entire village came to Benoît's funeral. They treated her with the respect any widow deserves. They shed tears for their friend. And none of them ever suspected that Benoît was in the casket because of her. *She* did it. And no one had the slightest clue.

And therein lies the reality she had failed to anticipate: who is going to admire her for what she has done, if a necessary—even innate—quality of her feat is that no one knows about it?

She was not so deluded as to think she would be receiving accolades, in any case; Angeline did understand that murder was not everyone's cup of tea. But that would only make the awe of the villagers more delicious, that she had gotten away with something they did not approve of, even believed to be odious.

A blister had popped up on the inside of her ankle and she was four blocks from home. She tried to think about the insurance money to make herself feel better. A valiant effort that failed.

17

"You're not usually one for indecision," said Lapin, grinning at Molly.

"I know. And it's not like this armoire is the centerpiece of anything. It's just utilitarian, for the guests who stay longer and need more room to put stuff away. Or for extra sheets. Anyway, show me again? I promise this time I'll pick one and we'll close the deal."

They moved down the narrow aisle to the back of the store. When they passed the old chest with the fancy china, Lapin stopped. He wanted to tell Molly of Angeline's obsession with it; he opened his mouth, then closed it again. He knew it was ridiculous, he shamed himself for feeling it—but standing there by the chest, he felt the dark presence again. As though Angeline had, what? Put some kind of curse on it? Shuddering, and without saying a word, he followed Molly to the row of armoires along the back wall.

She looked at each one, complimented this or that feature, seemed at moments to be so taken by all of them that he thought she might buy more than one.

"You seem to be in an awfully good mood," he said. Warily.

"And why not?" said Molly, moving back to look at the second armoire again, opening and closing all its drawers and giving it a thorough once-over.

Then a shadow passed over Lapin's expression.

"What?" said Molly.

"Oh, it's nothing." Lapin waved his hand. "Are you decided? It's this big one? The cheapest of the lot, I note."

"No really, what bothered you just then? Did you get some bad news?"

"Oh heavens no, it's not that. I just...I had a little flash of Benoît. Like a short little movie in my head, of the last time I saw him. I guess my brain is still trying to process it."

Molly considered this, remembering the dissonance between what Lapin expected to see and the cheerful Benoît he did see.

Lapin frowned. "In fact, I came away thinking that despite what Angeline was reporting, maybe he was beginning to recover. His spirits were very good—as they always were—and as I told you, he had some color in his face and did not seem troubled by any symptoms. And I...I can't seem to let go of this. My mind keeps going back to it, around and around."

Molly chewed her lip. "And just to be sure of the facts—that was the same night he died?"

"It was. I was completely stunned when I heard the news."

"And you were—except for Angeline—the last person to see him alive?"

Lapin nodded, looking distressed. "As far as I know."

She chewed her lip some more.

The bell at the door tinkled and Lapin craned his neck to see who it was.

"It's Delphus McDougal again," he said quietly to Molly. "Never buys a damn thing. But he comes nearly every day to wear me out with a lot of questions."

Along with gossip, Castillacois thoroughly enjoyed complaining about everyday nuisances. It was not meant as actual complaining, but more of a minor bit of theater for the listener to enjoy and express sympathy with.

"I think this is the one," she said, patting the piece that was more worn than the others, which she thought gave it character... and the cheapest. Lapin nodded and hustled to the front of the store where Delphus had already started in on the list of things he wanted Lapin to bring out to show him.

18

The office of the gendarmerie, that Monday morning in June, was as quiet as a tomb. Paul-Henri was using a cloth to shine up a mirror on the wall next to his desk. The Chief, Chantal Charlot, was shopping for a mandoline online. Nothing—no crime, no lost dogs, no wandering folks with dementia, not even any traffic violations—had transpired to disturb the calm of Castillac that morning.

"I've heard newspapers do very well for cleaning windows," said Paul-Henri.

"There has to be some way of sharpening the blades," said the Chief. "Otherwise, the whole thing would become useless before long."

"That's how they get you," said Paul-Henri. "The thing is cheap but I bet the replacement blades cost an arm and a leg."

"Mm."

A beam of sunlight showed the dust on the Chief's desk and Paul-Henri eyed it. He went to the broom closet and took out a rag. The Chief could be prickly and he didn't want to give her any reason to snap at him, but the sight of the dust on her desk was more than he could stand and he had to speak up.

"Might I?" he said, as delicately and unobtrusively as he could, holding the rag up and nodding his head at her desk.

"What? Oh. Whatever makes you happy," said Charlot, eyes on her computer screen as she scrolled through another set of mandolines.

"I heard a little something on the street the other day," said Paul-Henri. "Our beloved Molly Sutton is at it again," he said with a chuckle.

Charlot looked up. "At what?"

"Asking a lot of questions. About Benoît LaRue."

Charlot leaned back in her chair with a smirk. "Sutton/Dufort Investigations is just limping along, isn't it?" She laughed a mirthless laugh. "No doubt bills are starting to pile up. I don't know how they think they're going to stay in business in a village this small. I heard Ben's spending his days doing cheating-husband surveillance, if you can believe a man of his talents has fallen that far. And as for Benoît, as I don't have to tell you, Sutton/Dufort or Dufort/Sutton, whatever the heck it is—they're barking up the wrong tree."

"No doubt. If ever there was a natural death, Benoît LaRue was it." Paul-Henri finished the dusting and went back to his desk, wondering what in the world he could find to fill the rest of the day.

Nico slid a beer down the bar to Ben. Chez Papa was otherwise empty, the dead hour after lunch and before aperitifs.

"Well, you know how Molly is," said Nico. "She's got something of a restless streak. More level-headed than Frances, that's for sure—but still..."

"I am perhaps the least restless person in all of France."

"You can be a little jumpy."

"Not the same thing at all."

Ben took a long pull on his beer. "It's just that—I know her, Nico. She's saying she's only interested in Benoît's medical history and how the illness developed—a medical mystery, she calls it—but I...I see what's right around the corner. And it feels like I'm in the middle of the highway waving my arms with a tractor-trailer bearing down on me.

"Funny."

"Yeah. Hilarious. See how I'm dying from laughing over here." Ben grimaced. "I just don't want the entire village thinking she's drunk on the idea of murder."

"Now who's jumping to conclusions? Molly is—as you most certainly know—a treasured part of the village. People respect her. If she thinks there was foul play, maybe there *was* foul play."

Ben glared.

"Or not," continued Nico. "But either way, I think the village would hear her out instead of getting annoyed or drawing conclusions about her character. She's earned that much, and we're not so capricious. And plus—maybe she's telling the truth about only being interested in the medical angle. It's not like she has a history of holding back her real thoughts from you, right?"

Ben nodded. "I know you're making sense. Everything you say is true. And yet...why would I have this strong feeling that there's more to it than that?"

Nico shrugged. "It is uncomfortable to disagree strongly with someone you love and are close to."

Ben's eyes got wide. He drummed his fingers on the polished bar and looked up at the ceiling, thinking this over. "You didn't answer my question," he said finally.

"Because I don't know the answer," said Nico with another shrug. "And honestly—here's some four o'clock in the afternoon wisdom for you: the older I get, the more I realize there aren't ready answers for most questions."

The two men looked into each other's eyes as they thought about this.

Slowly Ben nodded and finished the beer. "What about the baby?" he said.

"What about it?"

"Speaking of questions..."

Nico let out a guffaw, almost a bark. "I'll say I've got questions! And all of them are in the unanswerable category. Top of the list: will I be a terrible father? Can't say I had much of a model to follow, if you follow?"

Ben nodded. He put his elbows on the bar and leaned on them. Nico got out a clean rag and buffed the already shining walnut of the bar.

And they took comfort in sharing the unanswerable questions with each other, and in not trying to make up answers to fill the silence.

19

1964

A nne stood at the window, her back to her husband and child. The paint on the sill was chipped. Outside, it was snowing. The room was very cold and spikes of frost glittered on the wallpaper.

"Cherie," said Artur.

"Don't plead," she said, not turning around. "The sound of it makes my skin crawl."

Little Angeline squatted, picking up a battered marionette, a *chevalier* with a silver helmet and a shield. She ran the puppet across the floor as fast as she could, bumping its feet on the wooden floor and saying "Bub-bup-bup," quietly to herself.

When her mother turned around to face Artur, her face was blank, emotionless. "Figure out a way to get more money," she said. Her tone sounded offhand but Artur heard the menace underneath.

"I will," he said. He looked away.

But the sound of his voice was like fingernails on a blackboard to his wife, who turned back around to watch the snow fall, shivering slightly even though she was willing herself not to. "Put another sweater on your daughter," she said to him. "Can't you see she's freezing?"

20

M olly was tucking into an early lunch, a *salade Périgourdine* at the Cafe de la Place, joined by one of her best friends in Castillac, Lawrence Weebly.

"I know it marks me as an utter Philistine," Lawrence was saying as he smeared some rillette of duck onto a round of toasted baguette and then put a thick layer of softened butter on top of that, "but the idea of chicken gizzards just does my head in. I absolutely cannot."

"You are silly. You eat *foie gras*, don't you? Why is one body part any grosser than another?"

"Well, of course it isn't. I know it's silly. And yet there it is and I stand by it entirely."

"Sometimes our head knows a thing is true but the rest of us does not go along."

"Indeed," said Lawrence, with a look.

"I didn't even bring it up."

"You don't have to."

"I wasn't even thinking about it."

"Fibber."

Molly laughed. Then she felt so tickled she threw her head

back and roared, and the one remaining couple lingering over lunch glanced over, not amused.

"Okay, busted," she said. "I'm ninety-nine percent solely interested in how Benoît LaRue died, and I mean medically. You know I have a soft spot for the chronically ill, and I've got heaps of opinions about his doctors without knowing any actual facts to base those opinions on."

Lawrence just looked at her. The look of an old and dear friend who knows you're blustering.

"Well all right, if you're going to be that way about it," she said, with a faint smile. "This is just between you and me, now? For real?"

Lawrence nodded, all ears.

"I've got an inkling of a whisper of a notion about Benoît LaRue's death not being on the up and up. And the inkling is not, the more I look into it, fading."

Lawrence busied himself with his rillettes, working very hard not to shout "I knew it!"

"Do you know Angeline? I can't help wondering...a man has such a variety of symptoms over the course of his adulthood that the doctors just throw up their hands and say it's in his head. What if those symptoms were caused by quite specific things. Things given to him by his caretaker."

Lawrence looked very serious. "That's a whopper of an allegation."

"I'm not alleging it. Just...ruminating. Considering possibilities. I'll tell you though. One thing that's been giving me pause?"

"Yes?"

"It's simply this: how many times have I heard the news about a murder from you? Not from Ben, even when he was still Chief. Not from Madame Tessier or any other random person passing along gossip in the village tradition. No. Time after time, it's been a text from you alerting me to the latest corpse. I did rather miss that when I was in Aix," she said, remembering the long list of victims in that lovely city.

"Anyway—with Benoît LaRue? I got no text. Now, I don't know whether all along you've been in cahoots with all the murderers?"

Lawrence grinned.

"I've come to depend on those texts. So in the absence of one, I think it's likely there was no murder." She looked carefully at her friend to see if he seemed to be holding something back. "It's a Castillac mystery I have never made the slightest progress in solving, how you got so high up on the information pipeline."

She waited. She took a bite of salad. Lawrence took a bite of rillette.

"You're not going to tell me, are you?"

"I think not."

Molly stared at her friend—well, she glared at him, to be honest.

"It could be," said Lawrence, "that you got no text about Benoît because you have spent the last few days trying to turn a natural death into something more interesting, when the true and unassailable— if boring—fact is that his death was commonplace and not violent and only sad, the way most deaths are. Everyone dies, Molly! And most of those events are going to be relatively peaceful and expected and without nefarious underpinnings."

"Sure, that last bit's true enough. But...you can't know, Lawrence. Even if your track record has been a hundred percent so far. You can't *know*. Nobody knows. Including me. I'm only saying—why not look a little more into it, just to make sure?"

"Do we have to perform a lot of tests to make sure the sun will come up in the morning?"

"That argument is beneath you, really it is."

Now she was annoyed, and she did not like feeling annoyed with Lawrence, not at all. Especially when she and Ben were a little off already.

She admitted to herself that she would be happier if Ben and Lawrence weren't pushing back so hard about Benoît LaRue's death, or failing that, if they merely made some room for her questions without pretending they knew all the answers. But she was not a woman who arranged her thinking so as to produce the greatest amount of agreement. And so instead of changing her mind or arguing, she talked about the best tomato varieties and a new end table Lawrence had found at Lapin's shop, hidden in a back corner for what might have been decades, and which might turn out to be quite valuable, and even if not, a gorgeous addition to his living room.

The funny thing was: Molly really had been only interested in the medical mystery and not been privately ginning up a case for Benoît being murdered. At least until Lapin told her how Benoît looked the night of his death. But everyone assuming she was so set on murder had only encouraged her to give the idea some attention.

§

HE ROLLED his big body to the edge of the bed, letting the sheet fall away, and peered around for his shoes.

"I don't want to sound petulant. It wouldn't be attractive at my age," Selma made a little hoot, a sound he had come to love. She sat up in bed, naked, her skin rosy. "But if there were some way I could make your office disappear into a sinkhole so you wouldn't have to go back to it? I would make it happen." She fell back on the pillows with a moan.

Florian rolled back towards her and put his hand on her cheek. "*Ma petite chou*," he said in his raspy voice. "Believe me, if there were a way for me not to go..."

She grasped his wrist and brought it to her mouth and kissed it. "It's really the most bizarre thing. I know I keep telling you this and I don't know why I am compelled to keep telling you, over and over. But when I was trying to decide where to go on vacation, I felt drawn, inexorably, to this village I had never even heard of before. At first I dismissed it. But the urge would not go away."

"And here you are," he said, throwing a leg over her leg and leaning in to kiss her neck. "And I would like to show you again exactly how happy that makes me."

$\maltese$ 21 $\maltese$

B ack at La Baraque, Molly sat down at her computer to see if the coroner's office had made any additions to the report on the LaRue case. It was short and unchanged and she read it through quickly. She sat staring out the window, tapping her fingers on the desk, wondering. She kept picturing this man she had never met, as Lapin described him: color in his cheeks, joking around. *Jolly*.

With low expectations, Molly googled Angeline's name. She had no idea what she was looking for, but had long experience with searching with no specific thing in mind. It was liberating, that kind of search—nothing was out of bounds, nothing was limiting her thinking, and she did her best to stay open to stray thoughts, to bits of information that looked like nothing but were momentous if you did not give in to the impulse to throw them out too quickly.

Really, detective work is just being a glorified trash sifter, she thought. Well, maybe not even glorified, depending on whom you ask.

Angeline did not appear to have much of an online presence, which was not a surprise. She found some innocuous messages on facebook, which had only recently been opened in France. A mention in a Castillac newsletter about winning a prize for her roses, some posts on an alternative health yahoogroup asking about what Molly assumed were some of Benoît's symptoms. Which Molly made a note of, though the symptoms seemed rather generic at first glance: heart palpitations and dizziness. Could be from a million things, she thought, but it was a start.

She tried Angeline's maiden name, Porcher, and came up empty. She saw that Porcher meant *swineherd* and that made Molly laugh out loud—she was sure, without knowing her, that Angeline would absolutely hate that. LaRue must have been much more to her liking.

Angeline LaRue, thought Molly, leaning back in her chair and thinking about the widow, seeing her at the cemetery and at Lapin's shop. Molly closed her eyes and remembered, seeing the scenes like little movies in her mind.

Angeline LaRue. Not the first name for a swineherd, Molly thought, smiling. A name for a woman who wants more. More than a cottage in Castillac, she guessed. More than what Benoît was able to give.

She stood up and stretched, glanced out to the road to see if Ben was coming. Then with a shrug—knowing it was impulsive but doing it anyway—she hopped on her scooter and headed to the coroner's office.

🐌

"WELL, LOOK WHO IT IS," said Florian, looking up at the ceiling with an expression of unutterable fatigue. His jowls looked saggier than usual and his eyes were bloodshot with dark bags under them. "I believe you were just here. Mere moments ago, was it not? No, no one has died since then, Madame Sutton, it grieves me to have to tell you. And may I point out that this office does not exist to report deaths for your convenience?"

"Bonjour, Florian," said Molly, unperturbed. "And bonjour Matthias," she said. He waved from his desk and looked back at his computer screen.

"I'll just jump right to the point," she said.

"That would be best," said Florian.

"I've been thinking a little. About Benoît LaRue."

"So I gather."

"Gracious, news travels fast. The speed of Castillac gossip can be shocking. But listen, Florian: I want to make clear from the start, I'm not focused on foul play. But I *am* quite curious about what actually killed him. I think the concept of psychosomatic illness is rubbish, to be honest."

"What does it matter? If the disease began in his mind and then affected his body, or started in his body and affected his mind? It's really six of one, half dozen of the other, wouldn't you say? And further—I don't mean this to be rude, you know I have some affection for you, Madame Sutton, somewhere, though it tends to get lost from time to time—this conversation falls squarely under the heading of Idle Ruminations and I just cannot. Not today. Not with the kind of sleep deficit I am burdened with." He stood, walked to the door, and pulled it open.

Molly sat down in the chair next to his desk. She turned to give Matthias a wink but he was looking very intently at his computer screen, though Molly suspected that was something of an act.

"I saw the report. 'System failure'? That's it? And I don't mean to be wagging a finger at you, Florian—I have affection for you too, it goes without saying—but it does look a bit like on that particular day, contrary to your usual punctiliousness, you just phoned it in? Didn't really give the case your usual thorough effort?"

Florian narrowed his eyes at her and gripped the door handle tightly.

Matthias held his breath.

"Madame Sutton, you have no idea of the amount of pressure this office is under. If you had met my boss, Peter Bonheur, and seen the malignance in his expression, perhaps you would understand. My point is that I get more than enough criticism from him and have not the slightest interest in getting it from you, who has no standing what-so-ever to be making judgments and commentary on the work of this office, behind which Matthias de Clare and I stand with confidence. Good day to you."

Slowly Molly got up. She glanced at Matthias who was still staring at his computer.

"Good day to you, Florian. One more question. Can you tell me who Benoît's doctor was, here in Castillac?"

"There are only two," said Florian. "I believe you can take it from there. Though I would offer the most warm-hearted advice to let this entire subject drop and find something else to entertain you this summer."

AFTER GIVING MOLLY enough time to be out of sight on her scooter, Florian made an excuse to Matthias and left the office. Quickly walking to the Place, he climbed without a word into Christophe's taxi.

Christophe, who had been enjoying a bite to eat at Chez Papa at a table by the window, scrambled outside with a napkin still tucked into his shirt. "Are you in a hurry, Florian? I've got a bowl of *sobranade* in front me and I've got a few spoonfuls left—"

"Yes, I'm in a hurry!" Florian said. "Office of the coroner business! Chop-chop!"

Christophe did not think to ask why Florian wasn't driving the usual white van. Nor did he think to ask why Florian asked to be let off on a part of rue de Chêne out of sight of any houses.

Christophe was thinking about his sobranade and how deeply good it was and how it reminded him of his grandmother who used to slip him chocolates when his mother wasn't looking. He would ask Nico to heat it up for him if he got back and it had cooled off, surely he wouldn't mind. And he would stop by the Presse after, and get the biggest bar of chocolate they had. Not skimping on quality, it went without saying.

2 2

M olly had started for home after talking to Florian, but then pulled over and turned around, back into the village. It was the classic situation of an angel on one shoulder telling her to go home and weed the peony beds, and the devil on the other telling her to go talk to Charlot at the gendarmerie... just to see if Charlot had any of the same inklings Molly was having.

As it often does, the devil won.

"WELL, no, it didn't go well. Now don't look at me like that, I didn't expect it to go well, that wasn't the idea at all. I just wanted...to see what she was thinking. And perhaps...to plant a seed. And I believe I accomplished that."

Ben scowled. "The seed you planted—and fertilized, and watered—might be 'Molly Sutton is a crank' instead of whatever it is you intended. Chief Charlot was the last person you should have gone to with this."

"It's nice to talk gardening with you. I noticed Angeline's roses are spectacular this month."

"Don't tell me you've gone to see her too?"

"No. I do, however, stroll about the village. Exercise is good for one, you know."

"Not funny."

Molly took a deep breath and stopped herself from saying anything else sarcastic. "I'm sorry. Truly. It's just—I'm so *annoyed*, Ben! It feels like you of all people should give me the benefit of the doubt. Yet you're calling me a crank. A crank, really? Is that what you think of my investigative instincts?"

"I did not say that. I said Chief Charlot might think it."

"Same thing."

"Not at all."

Now it was Ben's turn to take a breath. He was correct on the minor point of what he had just said or not said, and he was sure he was right on the larger point of whether Benoît had been murdered or not. But being right isn't always what it's cracked up to be, he thought, putting a hand on Molly's shoulder.

"All right. I can see how you might think I just insulted you. I didn't mean that at all. I'm only very protective of our reputation, so if either of us is doing anything that could possibly damage that, I'm going to get...disconcerted."

"You're not disconcerted, you're annoyed."

"Yes. Right along with you."

"Correct."

Ben let his hand drop and the two glared at each other.

"Just listen for one minute," said Molly. "I know this is not what you want to hear. But please."

Ben nodded. Rather curtly.

"First of all, the coroner's report is sketchy. Lists 'system failure' as cause of death which you know is nothing but blah-blah-blah. Yes, the man had debilitating symptoms for years—but no one has made much of an effort to determine why. Second, Lapin was the last person to see him alive other than Angeline, and he reports that Benoît seemed in high spirits and looked good. Those two facts prevent me from simply accepting the situation at face value. I could do what you say and spend my time pruning the roses and mulching the irises...but I just can't. All I'm doing here is trying to offer some possible explanations. So that we understand what really happened."

Ben nodded again. "Go on."

"What if poor Benoît was sick all those years because someone was making him sick?"

Ben's eyebrows went up but he said nothing.

"What if Angeline is not the long-suffering Florence Nightingale she appears to be, but more Guilia Tofana?"

"Who in hell is Guilia Tofana?"

"Do they not teach you any history in gendarme school? Tofana was a famous professional poisoner. She sold poison to women so they could kill their husbands. No, I am not making this up. She worked in Palermo and Rome and died peacefully in her sleep in 1651."

"Sometimes you take my breath away."

"I hope you mean that in a good way."

He snorted. "Every way, to be honest. So you think Angeline killed Benoît. Why? He didn't have any money. I believe they just barely got by with what his parents left them, once he wasn't able to work."

"Maybe you've heard of insurance. Maybe she despised him for reasons unknown. Maybe she enjoyed torturing him. These are all questions that need answers, I agree wholeheartedly on that point. And besides, you know perfectly well that motive is always the least of the legs holding up the table. What I tried to tell Charlot—though to say she was unreceptive is an understatement —is that a simple exhumation would answer most of these questions. He hasn't been in the ground five minutes."

Ben opened his mouth and closed it again. Then passed a palm over his face. "Oh, Molly," he said.

✤ 23 ✤

The following morning, Molly and Ben lingered contentedly over breakfast. They had talked into the night, and at last Molly had received, if not his blessing, at least his acceptance of her beginning to work the Benoît case, even though Molly admitted it was not actually a case at all. (A project, she called it now.)

In other words, he had agreed to shut up about her activities and she had agreed to stop trying to convince him she was right. She would find out it was a dead end soon enough, Ben rationalized, before any real damage was done. So, now that his divorce surveillance subject was back from Paris, Ben was off to spend some boring hours watching him. Molly took off on her scooter for the village, for the office of Dr. François Boulet to be precise, former doctor of Benoît (at least one of the many).

At the doctor's door, she paused for a moment. As it should be, doctors were unwilling to discuss their patients with other people, especially people who had no relation whatsoever to their patients, and it was going to be tricky to get this doctor to open up. Well, tally ho, she thought, hoping she would figure out a strategy on the fly, once she met the doctor.

A small woman sat behind a counter just inside the door.

"May I help you?" she asked.

"I'm wondering if I could speak to Dr. Boulet? I'm sure he's quite busy, but I was hoping he might be able to fit me in for just a moment or two."

"What is the matter?"

"Excuse me?"

"You are not well? You have a complaint?"

"Oh no, it's not that."

"You can tell me," the woman assured her. "It's helpful if I can give the doctor a head's up on his schedule, you understand. Your information is completely confidential, it goes without saying."

"Maybe I should schedule an appointment."

"Depends on what's bothering you. If it's something pressing, we can try to fit you in. I can't tell you how many lunches Dr. Boulet has skipped over the years!"

"He sounds very dedicated."

"He most certainly is!" The woman's cheeks reddened and Molly wondered what their relationship was. Perhaps she was his wife? Or...?

"Has he been in practice long?"

"Well, he's no newcomer, if that's what you're asking. Dr. Boulet was in Bordeaux previously, but found that village life suited him more than city life did. So he moved to Castillac about five years ago."

"And how long had he been practicing in Bordeaux?"

"My gracious, you ask a lot of questions! Usually it's the doctor asking the questions, not so much the patient." She smiled, apparently thinking this was amusing more than objectionable.

Molly looked around the small waiting room. There were several old paintings on the wall, landscapes in gilt frames. A potted plant that looked like it could use some water. A leather-bound ledger on the counter, the appointment book, Molly guessed.

"So sad about Benoît LaRue," said Molly.

"Oh, yes," said the woman. Her smile was fixed and her expression one of routine, impersonal condolence, like a card from the drugstore.

"I'm Molly Sutton," said Molly, reaching a hand over the counter to shake. "I run the gîtes over at La Baraque."

"Ah, it's a pleasure to meet you. I am Renée Gobel. Now, would you like to schedule an appointment? What was your complaint again?"

My complaint is that I can't get anyone to talk to me, thought Molly. "Well," said, "it's nothing too specific. Just feeling sort of...um...sort of blah, overall. How soon can you fit me in?"

&.

"YOU WERE JUST HERE five minutes ago," said Florian, just arriving at the office himself as Molly cruised up on her scooter and hopped off to follow him inside.

"And you're so glad to see me again!" laughed Molly. "I thought maybe there was some, uh, professional activity? I saw you driving down rue de Chêne in a taxi yesterday on my way home. Thought maybe someone..."

Florian rolled his eyes. "Can't a fellow go for a drive in the country without comment? Is every single waking moment in this infernal village open to scrutiny?"

"Oh, Florian, for crying out loud, I was just wondering, not asking for a minute-by-minute accounting of your movements. Okay, so the Castillac death count still stands with only poor Benoît LaRue added. Hey listen—the new mechanic at the shop on rue Montclare is a dream. Did you hear how my dear little scooter purrs?"

Florian did not care about scooters. He pushed open the door, nodded to Matthias, and sat heavily in the chair at his desk.

"I just have...only an idle question or two," said Molly, reaching for a quick handshake with Matthias.

"Idle. Sure," said Florian, with an eye-roll worthy of the stage.

"It's about Benoît."

"Of course it is."

"I really need to know: what did you mean exactly by 'system failure'?"

"I'm flattered to know that this office's bureaucratic documents get such attention from the general public." He heaved a sigh and reached for his cigarettes. "I would imagine the term to be quite self-explanatory."

"It wasn't exactly fascinating reading," said Molly cheerfully. "Seemed like it was a bit rushed. But so...*which* system? In what way? From what cause? The determination seems a little...vague."

Florian put his hands flat on his desk and heaved a gargantuan sigh. "Molly," he said. "I have not slept well of late and do not have the wherewithal to indulge you this way. To sum up: Benoît LaRue had been ill for many, many years and his death was a surprise to no one. If I may give you a bit of advice, *again*, which I urge you this time to heed: I would tell you to find some other way to keep yourself busy than trying to stir up trouble over this. The poor man is finally at rest. And I can say with some confidence: that rest was well-deserved and a long time coming."

"What do you mean, 'well-deserved?'"

Florian put his forehead down on the desk. "If there were ever a good reason to smoke a cigarette," he said. "Its name is Molly Sutton."

24

The next night, the main street of Castillac was transformed, as picnic tables were dragged out, a line of grills set on the sidewalk, banners and streamers hung, as the annual June village fête got underway. It was one of Molly's very favorite traditions: the entire village all in one place, eating, drinking, and ready to chat.

Surely, she thought—not mentioning this to Ben—surely, if Angeline has poisoned her husband, somebody at the fête would have some information about it. Either Angeline couldn't resist taking someone into her confidence or she had shown her hand in some other way. It was simply a matter of finding that person or persons and getting them to talk.

At least, if you had any luck at all.

Molly kept thinking back to the first time she saw Angeline, in Lapin's shop, when Benoît was still alive. Angeline's face had turned pink when Lapin refused to buy her ring. What was that about, exactly? Was she in desperate need of funds and the pink cheeks a sign of emotion at Lapin's door closing on her? No doubt she and Benoît were under some financial pressure since he hadn't been able to work for so long, but...was there more to it than that? Did she have debts, possibly debts to someone unsavory, who wouldn't be understanding if she didn't pay on time?

Molly shook her head. Her imagination could get out of hand and it was time to get some food and enjoy the party. Ben was already at the grill with two plates and she hurried to join him.

He leaned in and kissed the side of her head and she grinned at him.

"There's Frances," he said, gesturing with a plate.

Molly laughed. "I cannot get used to her looking so round. She has always been a sort of giraffe, you know? All skinny legs, slim as a rail. And now…"

"A whale," said Ben.

"Benjamin!"

"I mean that in the fondest way, you know that."

She kissed him on the lips. "I think maybe we should make up again tonight," she murmured in his ear.

"I support that idea one hundred per cent. I suppose we'll need to have a disagreement first then?"

"To make it real. Yes."

They moved up in the line. Ben caught a glimpse of Chief Charlot holding out her plate while Alphonse, owner of Chez Papa, put a sausage on it. "Okay, I'll throw down this gauntlet. How about you go over to Charlot, all easy-breezy, and pass the time of day without once mentioning the LaRues or poison or murder?" he said.

Molly scowled. "I'm not sure I like the flavor of this disagreement."

"I'm on your side, chérie. Just go chat her up to put her off the scent. She'll think you've given up the chase and that will give you some breathing room to continue with your investigation."

"So you're saying…you think there's a chance I might be right?"

"I never, ever count you out, Molly."

His saying that made her happy deep in her soul, no exaggeration. She nodded. "Okay. If you don't mind—grab me a plate and I'll meet you at the table?"

Ben did not mind and Molly melted into the crowd, touching an arm here and kissing hello there, making her way to where Chief Charlot was now sitting with Paul-Henri at her side.

"Beautiful night!" said Molly.

Charlot smiled faintly. "What have you been busying yourself with, Madame Sutton? Knitting booties for your friend's impending circumstances?"

Molly laughed. "You mean Frances's baby? Sadly, I don't know how to knit. Do you? Maybe you could give me some lessons?"

Paul-Henri sniffed and looked away.

Molly desperately searched for a subject besides the weather but came up empty.

"I did hear of your success in Aix-en-Provence," said Charlot. "I congratulate you. It sounds like you did quite a job."

Molly smiled and thanked her but she wondered what Charlot was up to. Perhaps she was taking the same route Ben had suggested—talk about nothing, toss in a smattering of flattery—to distract Molly from....from what?

At a total loss for any scrap of chitchat—unusual for her—Molly said *à tout à l'heure* and moved on, having gotten a glimpse of Chloe, who ran the herb shop in Bergerac. "How *are* you?" she said with enthusiasm. "I haven't seen you in an age." They hit the conversational ball back and forth over the net a few times before Molly said, in a quiet voice, "You know, I've been thinking about something. Well, poisons, to come right out with it. Obviously, plants can be such powerful medicines, and I wondered whether anything in your shop could be used for...for nefarious purposes?"

Chloe looked pensive. "That is a long conversation, Molly. Involved. I would ask that you drop by my shop so we can really dig into it." She sipped her wine and waved at someone behind Molly, and Molly sighed and kept walking.

Hortense sat at the last table in the row, by herself, watching the other villagers. She saw a redheaded woman talking to the herbalist from Bergerac. She looked in vain for Angeline. Something was bothering her but she could not determine what it was. It was as though she felt something noxious in her body, as though she were about to fall ill...but she did not think she was going to get sick. It was something else. Something wrong. Something sick, but the sickness did not belong to her but to someone else.

"Molly!" said Lapin, far too loudly, clapping Molly on the back. "You're in a brown study."

"Haha, perhaps. Just observing my beloved village," she said.

"You're a troublemaker in your heart," he said with an uncertain smile. "Are you enjoying the fête? I know you appreciate a good sausage."

Molly smirked. "Hilarious, Lapin. Listen...step over here so we can talk a little more privately..." She took him by the elbow and walked until they were a little distance from the crowd, just outside Chez Papa. "It's about Benoît—"

"Oh, believe me, I've heard. You think Angeline poisoned him." Lapin started to laugh. "I don't know why I'm laughing, it's actually not funny, Molly."

"You told me he looked in good shape the night he ended up dying."

"Well, sure, how many times do you want me to tell you? But the crucial thing is: what do I know? Maybe I had just been anticipating that he would look really awful and it wasn't quite that bad. Really—don't you know not to take me seriously, Molly? On antiques, yes. But medical matters? Not one bit."

"You do affirm that he was lively, had some color in his cheeks, did not—to your uninformed, ignorant mind—seem at all to be on the brink of expiring?"

"For the ten thousandth time, Molly, yes, that is what I thought in my ignorant mind. But my telling you that was not an invitation to—"

"Understood, Lapin, understood."

"—and I would really rather, I mean, it would just be better, overall, in a general sort of way...if you wouldn't mention to anyone what I said. If that could just...be private. Between you and me."

"I already told Ben. What you said—it's quite mild, Lapin, nothing to be worried about. And look, you'd already heard I suspect Angeline, I can't even imagine how that news got around the village already, I've barely even had the thought much less actual conversations. So the idea of 'private,' in Castillac? Not sure that's a thing."

"Well, Ben knows how to keep his mouth shut, at least. I don't like the idea of my random words being spread out all over the village for anyone to hear, when I wasn't talking to everybody when I said them."

"All right," said Molly, but she looked at Lapin curiously, trying to work out what he was worried about.

"And now, let me at those sausages!" He patted her shoulder and took off.

Molly looked for Ben and saw him sitting with Pascal and took a step in that direction. And then—a sudden, acute pain in her leg—a little boy had ridden his tiny scooter straight into her, then thrown his arms around her leg to stop from falling.

"Oh la la!" said Molly, smiling, but with tears springing up because the pain was so sharp.

The boy apologized, got his balance, and took off.

And all of a sudden, far worse than the sensation of the scooter ramming into her shin, she felt a pain in her heart about the children she would never have, and it felt so out of nowhere, so completely encompassing, that she thought she might sink right down to the sidewalk outside of Chez Papa and never get up again. She was utterly and unexpectedly overwhelmed.

She did not sink down to the sidewalk, though she wanted to. Instead she held on to the little tree trunk of the scraggly tree that was hung with a limp strand of lights, and tried to pull herself together.

All she ever wanted was a family. And now she had one, most of one, with Ben—and she knew she should be happy for that and contented with that.

And she *was*. But also—deeply sad. She didn't want to share this sorrow with Ben, or Frances, so it was a lonely kind of sadness. She patted the scraggly tree and wiped her eyes. Ben was finding out about adoption and that seemed like a wonderful step in the right direction. Maybe she would look back on a night like this and see how ridiculous she had been—or not ridiculous, but simply unknowing of all the happiness that was waiting to come but had not come yet.

❧ 25 ❧

Friday morning. A quiet day in Castillac, as some nursed headaches after carousing at the fête longer than they should have. A few tourists passed through on their way to somewhere else. There was little foot traffic and Lapin was startled to hear the tinkle of the bell and hurried from the back of his shop to see who it was.

"Angeline!" he said, trying hard for warmth but missing the mark just slightly. "How have you been doing?"

"Bonjour, Lapin." She sighed. "I didn't go last night, I was feeling too bereft, and the idea of attending a fête without Benoît, who loved them so..." She bowed her head and sniffled.

Lapin took a big breath in before speaking to try to calm himself. He felt his nerves activate as though his body had just been plugged into a socket. He glanced out to the sidewalk hoping another customer would come by. "Ah, Angeline," he said, patting her shoulder. "It's always hard, the first celebrations and holidays without a loved one. And you're right, Benoît would have been up there as Chief of the Grill, passing out sausages all night long." He tried to chuckle but it came out as a kind of strangled gasp.

"It's been difficult, trying to figure out how to fill my days, now that I'm no longer on call 24/7."

"It's quite a transition, no doubt." He looked out to the sidewalk yet again, with little hope.

"So I just thought," said Angeline, walking down the central aisle of the store and trailing the fingers of one hand along various items as she went, "I just thought I would come in and look at the chest, if you don't mind. I won't disturb anything. Just to look."

Lapin agreed because he almost never knew how to say no to anybody, and Angeline had done this many times before. Besides, what was she going to do, put an entire china service for thirty under her shirt and try to sneak out with it? He bustled to the back of the shop and to the corner where the large leather chest sat on an old table he had rescued from the side of the road on the outskirts of Bergerac. The chest had leather straps and brass buckles and appeared to be quite old.

Angeline breathed a little faster as Lapin worked to loosen the straps. Her arms were down by her sides and she wiggled her fingers, smiling a tense smile, eyes pinned on the scratched-up lid.

"It's a real wonder I ever acquired this," said Lapin. "Did I ever tell you the story? The de la Chabelles, as you must know, are not from around here. Up north, maybe as far as the Charente—no, farther, probably Normandy or Brittany. I had driven up to Angouleme for a show. Some real beauties at that show, I'll tell you— a Louis Quinze commode that was a real gem. Not by one of the *ébenistes*, you understand, but even so, those 19th century copies can be altogether stunning. Well, you wouldn't call that one stunning, exactly, it was probably from the servant's hall and didn't have any ormolu or anything of that sort. But still, a lovely piece all the same. I got outbid on most of the things I wanted. There was this one guy, a real shark he was, had a good eye, I'll give him that much...anyway, I didn't want to come home empty-handed after driving all that way, and so I bid on the chest without even knowing what was in it. That was a condition of the sale. And you know how it is, the bidders have to follow the rules or we're out, we don't have any say in how things are handled. Well, like I said, I didn't even open it up until I got it home.

"No idea there would be something like this inside. I mean, what are the chances?"

He shook his head in wonderment. Angeline was paying no attention to him, but staring into the chest, fluttering her hands with the effort of not reaching in to touch, to caress the plates, the dishes, the cups, all packed in wood shavings and smelling of cedar.

"Maybe I could take out just a few pieces?" she whispered.

"Let's...well, just the one on top. Do you like to give big dinner parties? I can't think of the last time I went to a dinner that had thirty people. Well," he laughed nervously, "I never have. Maybe that's me with a paltry and impecunious set of friends," he chuckled. "I suppose if you were a de la Chabelle and had the chateau to go with the title, this service would be only a small part of what would be on hand for entertaining."

"But I *am* a de la Chabelle," said Angeline.

Something in her tone made Lapin step back. He thought she was trying to make a joke, and it simply fell flat, as jokes sometimes do. But that was not all. He was not a superstitious man, but he suddenly felt a dark presence, he would even say a demonic presence, not that he would ever tell anyone because it made him sound as though his imagination had entirely run away with him, and worse, a man with no courage whatsoever—to be afraid of a tiny little cupcake like Angeline LaRue!

But he was, and he knew it without a doubt.

MOLLY AND BEN had made up—again—and so the day had gotten off to a slow start, with several pots of coffee and a big plate of eggs and bacon, and neither getting dressed until nearly ten o'clock.

"We are living the life of Riley," said Molly.

"Who is this Riley?"

"Huh. I never considered. Apparently, a fellow who enjoyed himself."

"I've got surveilling to do so I better get a move on. I'd complain but the pay is good. And you? What's on your docket for today?"

"I thought I would drop by Florian's office and get on his last nerve."

"Mm," said Ben. "Before I go, I'll try to get into the pigeon-nier to check on that rat-hole. For all her professed love for Castillac, Selma doesn't get out much."

"Maybe she's keeping the rats away by staying in."

"From what Constance described, this is not a rat who would be put off so easily. He might come out of his hidey-hole with a boater and cane and do a little soft-shoe across the floor in broad daylight."

Molly cracked up. They kissed, again, and before anything else got started, Molly sped over to Florian's to see if she could rattle his cage and get something out of him.

"Bonjour, Matthias," said Molly, coming straight into the office. "Is Florian out on a case?"

"Ah, no. No deaths, Madame Sutton, that I know of."

"Call me Molly, please." She plopped down in the chair in front of Florian's desk and did not miss the crestfallen expression on Matthias's face as she did so.

"It's quite unusual, isn't it, for Florian not to be at his desk on a Friday morning, if there is no out-of-the-office business? There is no autopsy to be performed, no body to pick up, no death certificate to sign. He has told me many times that he is swamped —practically drowning—in bureaucratic busy work. With the

terrible eyes of Peter Bonheur tracking his every move. And yet...
he is not here."

"Hm," said Matthias, looking at his computer screen and
clicking with the mouse.

"Quite curious."

"Is it?"

"I wonder if you might have any idea where he is?"

"Me?"

"You."

"He didn't tell me."

"Mm. But perhaps you know, nonetheless?"

Matthias stood up quickly. He cracked the knuckles on both
hands and stretched his neck from side to side. "Madame—Molly,
I wish I could help you. I honestly do. But Florian is the head of
the office and I am just an underling. I take my orders from him,
if you understand me." He looked at Molly and did not look away.

Maybe just maybe...there is something going on.

"Isn't it funny that I've lived in Castillac all this time and we've
only recently met?"

"Funny?"

"Well, not ha-ha funny, but odd. Castillac is so small and I
figured I'd met nearly everyone by now."

"I'm a private sort of person. I don't go out much. And I only
got this job recently."

"What were you doing before?" Molly knew that in France it
was considered rude to grill people about their work, but she
pressed on anyway.

"Same department, different office," he said, sitting back down
and putting his hand on the mouse. "I'm sorry, I really must get back
to work. I could...would you like me to text you if Florian comes in?"

"Yes!" said Molly. "That would be really helpful." She paused at
the door. "I don't mean to make a pest of myself, and I know
that's exactly what I'm doing. It's only that...I like a sort of neat-

NELL GODDIN

ness when it comes to death. Not a bunch of lingering questions, maybe this or maybe that, loose threads all over the place. It might be a sign of some kind of mental instability on my part—I freely admit it—but I very much like certainty when it comes to bodies and how they came to be dead. And so, in my longwinded way, I humbly ask for your forbearance."

Matthias nodded though his expression was strained. "À tout à l'heure, Molly."

Well, she thought as she got back on her scooter, it was better than *au revoir*.

❧ 26 ❧

Changeover Day dawned sunny and cool. Constance arrived on foot, full of reports of who Molly was annoying with her suspicions about Benoît LaRue's death.

"Look, Molls, you know I'm your biggest fan, and in my ever-humble opinion you've got a track record nobody should set aside." She slung a bag of cleaning supplies over one shoulder and then hoisted up the vacuum cleaner. "Some people are just jealous, you know? You have a talent they don't have, so they feel like they gotta run you down. I'll take the pigeonnier, by the way, if it's okay with you. Anyway—the Latours? All they can talk about is how the American—that's what they call you, hilarious, isn't it? *The American.* As if there's only one of 'em. Anyway, yeah, they talk about how *The American* waltzes into the village and tries to stir up trouble among people who have lived here since birth, whose parents and grandparents and on and on into genealogical infinity—well, to sum up, according to the Latours, if you've lived in Castillac forever you're allowed to have an opinion, otherwise —no."

Molly blinked. It was never easy trying to keep up with

Constance. "You're saying...uh...public opinion is going against me?"

"Well, it's only the Latours, to be honest, so I wouldn't go that far. But people are...you know. Dumb. I mean, why would anyone run around defending Angeline LaRue, anyway? Nobody likes her. She didn't grow up in Castillac anyway! She's tried for years to make out like she's this long-suffering angel but I never bought that for a half-second. There's something...not quite right about her, is what I'd say."

"How do you mean?"

"Oh, nothing. Don't mind me. Well, you okay with doing the cottage?"

"Sure," said Molly, wondering what had come over Constance, who usually liked to luxuriate in all the details of her opinions. "No one's been staying there so I'll just do a quick dusting and once-over. Got a new couple arriving later. From Sweden."

"Oh! Tall and blond?"

"Haven't met them, can't say," said Molly.

"See? Spoken like a true investigator," cackled Constance. "No assumptions, am I right?"

Constance walked quickly through the meadow to the pigeonnier. She had been glad to have all the village gossip—and gossip about Molly herself, even better—as a diversion, since it was important that she get the pigeonnier as her Changeover Day job and not Molly. Florian had offered her a fat tip if she cleaned instead of Molly, and of course it was way better for that to happen without any explanation, since secrecy was exactly what Florian was paying for.

WHEN MOLLY FINISHED with the cottage once-over, Ben was waiting in the kitchen with a fresh pot of coffee.

"I've got something to show you," he said, and Molly could

feel...she wasn't sure what...a sense that her life was about to change, dramatic as that sounded.

"Is something wrong?" she asked.

"No no no, not at all. It's about adoption. I've done some looking around online and made some calls. I didn't want to ask anyone in the village because that news would travel like wildfire and I figured we didn't need to be dealing with the commentary that would bring on before we even know what we're going to do."

"Good thinking," said Molly. She saw the steaming cup of coffee Ben had set out for her, and a folder next to it. "I have to tell you—I'm nervous. It's like...just opening the door a crack? Like we might get to have a family after all? It's...it's...well, *whew*. Happy, absolutely, and also terrifying. To hope."

"Not the effect I was going for."

Molly put an arm around him, then sat at the table and sipped the coffee. "Okay, show me what you've got."

"Well, as we've talked about, there aren't many French babies available for adoption. We could get on a list, but we might wait and wait and never get a chance. So I think that leaves us with two options. We can adopt from another country—and here are some brochures from places that handle that—or we could sign up with an outfit that places children who are unable to live at home in temporary care."

Molly opened her mouth and closed it again.

"I know that second option isn't exactly the typical family you might have been dreaming of. I only mention it because it is an option and I know you have a serious urge to help, which this particular group of kids really needs."

She looked out through the French doors to the meadow and saw Constance lugging the vacuum. She took another sip of her coffee. For some reason, she resisted looking at the brochures because they would obviously have photos of children in them and she felt already on the verge of tears and did not want to start bawling.

"Don't you want to look," Ben said, gently.

"I do," said Molly, not moving a muscle.

He kissed the top of her head. "Just know, Molly—one way or another, we will have children in this house. It might not look the way either of us thought it would, but it will work out just fine. For all of us."

She opened the folder and began looking at the first brochure. The photographs were exactly what she expected and she squeezed her eyes shut for a moment. It wasn't that she was reluctant to cry in front of Ben, it was that it felt as though if she let the tears start, they might never stop. Not from sadness, or relief, or happiness, or gratitude for Ben—but all of it together.

"Look at this nut," she said, pointing at a small boy wearing a shirt with a dinosaur on it. He was grinning from ear to ear, holding a half-eaten banana.

"Cute," said Ben.

"Thank you so much for getting all this together, the prospect is...*so* exciting. Overwhelming, in a good way! But give me some time to think about all this."

"Of course. And you have plenty of time, because to be eligible as adoptive parents we have to have married for—um, I think it's two years? So there's no need to rush into anything."

Suddenly Molly stood up from the table, her eyes looking a little wild. "Oh my gosh," she said, putting her hands on either side of her head.

"What? Are you all right?"

"It's just—I had a flash right then. A *thought*. What if—what if the reason I've been so stirred up about this case, about Benoît LaRue—what if the whole reason isn't the merits or my intuition or *truth*—but instead to distract myself from...from *this?*" She pointed to the boy in the dinosaur shirt. "It's been hitting me hard lately. The sadness. The prospect of adopting goes a long way towards fixing that, don't get me wrong. But still...there is some sorrow that will never, ever go away. I think you understand about that."

Ben looked at the photograph of the boy in the dinosaur shirt, and then at Molly. He nodded.

"But see...maybe I've been using poor Benoît as a way to focus on something else, to feel like I'm doing something, like my life has purpose?" She sat back down and bowed her head. "Maybe I've been seeing evil where there was none," she said softly, and Ben put his big hands on her shoulders and stood there for a long while as they thought this over.

🐚 27 🐚

1966

"Pretty as a princess," said Anne, adjusting the plastic tiara on little Angeline's head. She smoothed the girl's blonde hair away from her face.

The costume was cheap and the rough fabric irritated Angeline's arms, but she was willing to put up with it because it looked fancy. She skipped over to a mirror her mother had propped against the wall and gazed at herself.

"Pretty as you are, you could be a real princess, if you play your cards right," Anne said. "Little girls grow up and get married. It's simply a matter of choosing the right man."

"A prince!" crowed Angeline.

"If he has enough money, the title doesn't matter so much."

"I want to be a princess! Or a countess. That's good too, right?"

"A countess would do. Even a baroness in a pinch. Though, like I say—and listen closely, daughter—money without title is fine. Title without money—forget it." That lot won't want you anyway, she thought, but didn't want to overcomplicate the morning's lesson.

Angeline was too little to understand what her mother was talking about. The costume came with a wand that had sparkly strands dangling at the end of it, and she waved it around and admired the way the light caught it.

"You are meant for something better than this," Anne said as she scanned the room with its broken-down sofa, the kitchen table littered with breakfast crumbs and some dirty plates, the two small windows smudged and not allowing in much light. "Much, much better than this," she repeated.

She turned to her daughter and took her hands. "What shall we play? I will be the monster and you will be the witch, how's that?"

Angeline clapped her hands. "I like being a witch way more than a princess!" she shrieked, and waved her wand through the air, and in a moment of inspiration, whacked her mother on the leg with it.

That was the last time she ever got an idea like that in her head.

Anne grabbed her by the wrist and leaned her face close in. "You're going to be very sorry you did that," she hissed.

"But you're a monster!" yelled Angeline. She had felt a thrill when the wand hit her mother's bare skin and was interested in repeating it.

"You got that right, I *am*. Just you watch. Just you watch and see."

"The Swedes couldn't be nicer, they're all settled in, and they're newlyweds—so the last thing they want is attention from me," laughed Molly, as she and Frances were out on a Sunday morning walk.

"That whole gîte thing has turned out better than I ever thought it would," said Frances, and clapped her hand over her mouth. "I didn't mean to say that out loud."

"I really do enjoy the guests, at least most of them." Molly threw her arms out and breathed in the sweet June air. "I feel such a lightness, all of a sudden. A joyfulness. Just looking at those roses over there—the beauty, the freshness—"

"What in hell has gotten into you?"

Molly, still laughing. "Well, probably...it's that I'm not thinking about Benoît LaRue anymore."

"But I thought his wife—"

"Right, I *was* thinking...and then I realized...it doesn't matter. Why always swim against the tide, I ask myself? I've let it go. And I've got super big news. The biggest."

"Lay it on me, sister."

"Keep this under your hat, for now, would you? Ben and I are going to adopt."

Frances took Molly's hand and did a quick jitterbug, spinning her short friend under her arm and singing a song she made up on the spot—which Frances was quite good at, being a jingle writer by trade.

"I know it's totally selfish of me, but the idea of both of us having kids at the same time—well, it's a million trillion times better than doing it alone! So tell me all the deets—will it be soon? How old? How does it all work, is it like in old movies where you go to an orphanage and pick out a child? Because that seems fairly horrible, at least for the children. Oh my Lord Jesus, this is the best news ever!"

"Um..."

"Sorry. Got a little overexcited. Just...come on and tell me, I need more than just the headline."

Molly took Frances's hand as though they were schoolgirls. "It'll be awhile. There's some rule about how long you have to be married before you can adopt jointly. But Ben is on the case, he'll work it all out, and before too long I'll be joining you at the sandbox and on the playground."

"Gotta say, I haven't seen you look this good in an age."

"I think there's an insult in there somewhere."

"Yes! Your face was looking sort of haggard. Your color wasn't good even though here it is June when people look their dewiest. I mean, pale is one thing. But now? Glowing, my friend, absolutely glowing."

"Must be the hormones," said Molly, deadpan, and Frances howled with laughter. "So, you're still feeling good? How's Nico doing? Looking forward to fatherhood?"

"He's a wreck," said Frances with a huge smile. "It's adorable, what a wreck he is."

"How about you guys come over for dinner? Tonight?"

"Since when can you throw together a dinner party on the same day, when there's no market?"

"Okay, Chez Papa then?"

Frances leaned her head on Molly's shoulder, which took some doing given their difference in height. "You have made me the happiest whale in Castillac," she said. And the two old friends walked for a long time in companionable quiet, daydreaming about the children they had not yet met.

❧

CHEZ PAPA WAS PACKED, as it often was on Sunday nights. Nico manned the bar and was kept hopping by Lapin and Anne-Marie, Molly and Ben, Frances, the Swedes from the gîte, Paul-Henri Monsour, and various other villagers coming and going, laughing at jokes, teasing each other, full of the optimism that a warm and sweet-smelling June evening can bring.

"Surprised to see you here," said Paul-Henri to Molly. "Isn't there investigative work to be done?" He smirked.

"Is that—are you being sarcastic? It's beneath you, Paul-Henri," she answered, and breezed past him to Lapin, kissing cheeks with him and Anne-Marie. A kir appeared on the bar in front of her and Nico gave her a wink.

"Ahh," said Molly, leaning back against the bar and looking out at the tables, nearly all full. "I do love this place."

"Uh," said Lapin, and tugged at his collar, which felt suddenly tight.

"Just tell her," said Anne-Marie. "She's your good friend and you can't keep it from her."

"Uh oh," said Molly.

"Well," started Lapin, but just then Ben came over and gave him an excuse to interrupt himself. "Benjamin! What do you have to say for yourself this fine Sunday?"

"Very little," said Ben. "I spent half the day reading about a battle, the British Navy versus the French, Battle of Diamond Rock in 1805—" he caught Lapin's eyes beginning to glaze over "— and I managed to check the patch on a rat-hole, and a few other such fascinating pursuits. Bobo caught a baby rabbit but kept her mouth soft and didn't hurt it, so that was a happy ending."

"Good for Bobo," said Anne-Marie. "Lapin?" She dug an elbow into his impressive girth.

Lapin heaved a mighty sigh, worthy of the *Comédie Française*. "It's only...Molly, I don't like ratting anyone out, but in this case... So here goes. You know how it is in the antique business—people like to drop in and have a look around even if they're not in a buying frame of mind. Some people have favorite items they aren't ever going to buy, they don't have the money and won't ever have the money, so they come in just to visit with a treasured piece. I have this one customer, well, you can't really call him a customer if he doesn't ever buy anything, can you? And every Tues—"

"Lapin!" Anne-Marie gave him The Look.

"Oh, all right. I feel like this is none of my business but here goes. I don't think you should be sniffing around Angeline LaRue, casting aspersions."

"What's that word," said Molly, whose French was really very good but not perfect.

"*Critical suspicions* will do in this case," said Lapin.

"Molly hasn't done anything wrong," said Ben. "She's not talking to the press or accosting Angeline on the street or really doing anything at all beyond thinking. Maybe having a word with a few people she's close to. Surely that's no crime, and no worse than what everyone in the village does, day in and day out? And why in the world do you think you have any right to tell Molly what to do, anyway??

Molly was so touched by Ben's instant and strong defense of

her that tears welled up. None of them had spied Angeline, who was at Chez Papa as well, tucked away in a corner.

"I don't think you've done a thing wrong either," said Anne-Marie, rubbing Molly's arm. "It's not about telling you what to do, exactly... it's more...how to put it..."

"We're worried for you," murmured Lapin.

Molly laughed. "Worried? That's silly. Besides, I've moved on anyway. And since when do you feel compelled to come to the defense of—?"

"—I don't want to be in the middle of any trouble, either way," said Lapin. "It's bad for business."

"Not everything is about money," murmured Anne-Marie.

Lapin's expression was tortured, which Molly noticed, and wondered about.

Just then she heard a familiar gravelly voice and turned to see Florian Nagrand standing by a table talking to someone she only knew by sight. "Back in a sec," she said, going straight to Florian.

For a moment she forgot she wasn't interested in Benoît LaRue anymore, and opened her mouth to begin some friendly pestering. But mid-syllable she realized her intentions had changed, and out came a garbled sound that was not French, nor any other intelligible language.

"Pardon?" said Florian. His friend seemed to draw back in his chair as though he didn't want to be too close to her.

"I just—came over to say bonsoir and hope you have a lovely evening!" She scurried back to Ben and her friends, her cheeks reddening.

"I am an idiot," she murmured in Ben's ear.

Florian's eyes were on the door. He drank a beer slowly, the bags under his eyes enormous from lack of sleep.

Paul-Henri dropped by his table. They exchanged greetings, and Paul-Henri started to sit in the empty chair but Florian glared at him so harshly that he stood back up again. Then Paul-Henri saw Angeline at a table in the corner with that woman whose name he could never remember, and he headed their way.

"Angeline," he said, kissing her cheeks.

Angeline noted that he was using the gentle *I'm talking to the widow* voice, which was extremely tiresome and she wondered when people would cut it out. She told herself to put her annoyance aside; it was important to stay in Paul-Henri's good graces no matter what a fool he was.

"Allow me to present my friend Hortense Depleurisse," she said, then regretted sounding so formal. She didn't know Paul-Henri well at all and had no sense of how to operate with him.

"Bonsoir, Hortense," said Paul-Henri. He started to sit, watching the women to see their reaction. When they didn't look averse, he settled into the chair. "Sunday night—it's always packed in here, but sometimes it's just what one wants, some company on the night before the week starts up again."

"But your work isn't really divided by weeks, is it?" said Angeline. "Aren't you virtually on call at any time, to keep the grateful citizens of the village safe and sound?" She smiled at him and tried to put some warmth into her eyes.

"Indeed, you are correct," said Paul-Henri, sitting up as straight as he could. He wished he were wearing his uniform since he believed it had a good effect on the ladies. He tried to suck in his newly expanded belly but with only moderate success.

A silence fell. Hortense looked down at the table. Angeline was still smiling but her eyes had cooled.

"I'm so glad to run into you tonight," Paul-Henri said finally. He leaned his arms on the table and said to Angeline, "There's something I've been wanting to tell you. It's about...Molly Sutton. You know who I mean?"

𝕾 29 𝕾

First thing Monday morning, Angeline was waiting outside the office of Aimable Insurance before it opened. She looked at her reflection in the glass, tilting her head this way and that, smiling at herself. Then turned around to look for Leon Garnier, whom she irritably thought should have been at his desk by now.

As he walked to work, Leon saw her from a block away and veered into an alleyway. He stood by a garbage can, out of sight, for more than a moment. He wiped his brow, adjusted his belt which was suddenly one hole too tight, and tried to work out his next step. Eventually, distasteful as it was, he realized that even if he could avoid Angeline right then, she would be back; there was going to be no getting rid of her until he wrote her a check. And so he was stuck—wedged, most uncomfortably—between two things he did not want to do—*strongly* did not want to do.

He sighed and combed his fingers through his thinning hair.

Just be a man about it, he thought, and straightening up, strode out of the alleyway and towards his office.

Angeline had seen him duck into the alley, and she understood that it was not a good omen on the subject of the check.

NELL GODDIN

"Bonjour, Leon, it's lovely to see you on this fine morning!"

"Lovely to see you as well, Angeline. Come in, come in, I'm afraid I got off to a slow start today. Still recovering from the fête the other night." He unlocked the door and ushered her inside. "I didn't see you there, were you feeling all right?"

"Well, I don't like to complain…"

Leon gave her an expression of warmth and concern that he did not feel.

"…but the idea of going to a fête without Benoît, in the end, was just unthinkable. I had planned to go, of course, my friends were waiting for me…but I'm sure you can imagine, I was just too sad. When you're broken-hearted, it's better to keep to yourself, don't you think?"

Leon was chuckling to himself about Angeline's "friends," whom he doubted existed anywhere but in her imagination. In his years as an insurance agent, he had gained quite a depth of understanding about people, having worked with liars, deeply greedy people, and fraudsters, along with the genuinely kindhearted and the clueless. He didn't need any whispered stories about Angeline LaRue to tell him who she was; he already knew.

"So, of course I know why you have come to see me, and I wish I had better news. As I said, the wheels of insurance do grind rather slowly, I'm afraid. I can promise you that the minute the money arrives, I will let you know. I have your phone number and will call you straightaway."

Angeline bowed her head. She was thinking very fast, running through various scenarios and judging their effectiveness: should she throw a tantrum (she had always been quite good at that)? Or try seduction? Bullying? Threats? Tears?

Finally, none of those options appealed to her and she simply fixed him with a cold stare, allowing her gaze to go up to the top of his head where the bald spot was, and she thought but did not say, *you are going to give me that money, Leon Garnier. Within the week. Or you will be very, very sorry.*

꙳

ANGELINE STARTED to go home but then brightened as she turned toward the center of the village, to the gendarmerie. Paul-Henri Monsour had dropped some hints at Chez Papa the night before which she wanted to follow up on right away. Paul-Henri, obviously, was a horse's behind, as her mother used to say, but when was it not useful to have a friend at the gendarmerie? She had flirted with him until she couldn't stomach it anymore, but it had been worth it: she had his cell number, and an invitation to text him if she needed anything.

There was plenty she needed; that would always be true no matter what she was given.

She stopped about a block from the gendarmerie, smoothed her skirt and her hair, and texted Paul-Henri that she was nearby and if he had a minute maybe they could get together? She had in mind the tone of a teenager texting a boy she liked. And she laughed to herself to see, seconds and not minutes later, Paul Henri shooting through the door of the gendarmerie like he was a fireman headed to a fire.

Angeline—still holding on the teenager idea—leaned her back against a wall and pushed her hips forward, one knee up with the foot against the wall. She smiled and then looked away when he got close. His face was pink and she could see the junior officer was in a state of some agitation.

"Why, Paul-Henri, are you feeling all right? You look a bit feverish," said Angeline, her voice silky as she turned towards him.

"Right as rain," he said, standing up straight with military stiffness. "I'm glad you got in touch. I didn't want to say anything in Chez Papa, not with all those ears listening for any nugget of information I might drop. And Molly Sutton herself, just a few meters away."

"Who is this Molly Sutton?"

"Surely you know her. She runs a gîte business out on rue de Chêne. Also she married Ben Dufort, who was Chief?"

Angeline shrugged as though she had never heard of any of these people, which was not even a little bit true.

"Well, you *should* know her," said Paul-Henri darkly. "And I'll tell you why, now that we can speak in private. Shall we walk along while we talk?"

He held out his arm and she took it.

"I'll get right to the point. Molly Sutton—whom you don't even know—has been running all over town telling people she suspects that you poisoned Benoît. If you can believe such utter ridiculousness. The audacity of the woman!"

Angeline missed the next few sentences because an uncomfortable chill went up her back hearing the words "poison" and "Benoît" and "you" in the same sentence, and it felt as though the shock had frozen her brain.

"—of course she's just fantasizing, the investigation service she and Ben started is going nowhere and this is just a bald attempt to get some publicity, to drum up some business—"

Angeline missed yet more because she was suddenly remembering the terrible night of Benoît's death, how he had vomited for what seemed an eternity, and how she had wondered if another poison might have been a tidier choice.

Focus, Angeline, she said to herself. *Focus.*

"—I shouldn't be telling anyone gendarmerie business, but just using common sense instead of the rulebook—if you're being falsely accused, you rightly should know about it, that's how I see it. Chief Charlot told her in no uncertain terms that she was riding the wrong horse and had better get off, full stop."

"This—this Molly Sutton—has talked to Chief Charlot about me?"

"She has," said Paul-Henri, daring to put his arm around her and squeeze her shoulder. "Sutton actually marched right into the gendarmerie last week and even started blabbing away about an exhumation—"

Exhumation?

Angeline's breathing sped up and her heart along with it. What is this disaster appearing out of nowhere, before she'd even got the insurance money? She had had no idea this Molly Sutton was so dangerous.

"Paul-Henri," she said, her voice quavering (which for once was not an act), "is there any chance the Chief took any of her accusations seriously?"

"No. Of course not. We both told her plain as can be that Benoît had been ill for a long time, that he died of natural causes —and that you had been an angel, selflessly taking care of him for years on end."

Well, maybe they hadn't said that last part. But he had thought it.

Angeline continued to struggle to pay attention to what he was saying. "No chance at all?" she repeated, her voice sounding a bit strangled.

"None," said Paul-Henri, and taking more license than he ever had in his life, he leaned over and kissed the top of her blonde head.

Angeline did not notice the kiss. Her thoughts were fractured and ungovernable. Her mind was filled with various headlines, in dark block lettering like a newspaper:

EXHUMATION.

WIFE CONVICTED.

LIFE SENTENCE.

§ III §

❧ 30 ❧

"I'm *not* pouting. *Au contraire!* I am simply speaking my mind. Not the same thing at all and I must say I resent the implication," said Selma, tightening the sash on her silk kimono and glaring at Florian.

"Oh, my darling English dumpling—I meant no implication, none at all. You are drawing an entirely false conclusion. You think that I want us to stay private because I am...what? Not proud to be seen with you? Some silly notion like that? No, no, no," he said, pulling on her sleeve and bending down to kiss her on the lips.

"No," he murmured, kissing her more ardently. He felt her body start to relax, then it stiffened again.

"I do not think it is asking too much to share a meal in a restaurant, in public, with my lover," she said. "It's not as though you're married."

Florian looked at the floor, his shoulders slumped.

"*Are* you married?"

He laughed. "Heavens no." He ran his hands down her arms then attempted to pick her up, but alas, the years of sitting behind a desk, smoking, and avoiding any sort of exercise like the plague had left him without enough strength. "Get back in bed," he said, "and I'll explain everything."

"This better be good."

"Well, I wouldn't say *good*, but hopefully you will understand. And see that there is no insult intended what-so-ever."

Selma settled herself in bed, sitting up against the pillows, arms crossed. Florian slid in beside her and awkwardly put his hand on her thigh.

"I haven't said anything before now, because...because it's... well, it doesn't put me in the best light. And of course I want you, of all people, to think well of me."

Florian stopped talking and stroked her thigh. He sighed. "You see, there was such a long stretch with no deaths in Castil-lac, which meant—I *am* the coroner, you understand—that I had plenty of free time, as long as I got through the usual bureaucratic nonsense early in the day. Matthias, my assistant, and I were at the point of doing sudoku and crossword puzzles to pass the time. We were bored out of our skulls."

"Wishing someone would die?"

"Well, it's not like that. Just wishing to be of service, to do our jobs. Not, by any means, hoping anyone would go before their time."

"Do you believe in the afterlife, Monsieur Coroner?"

Florian paused. "That is quite a big question. I would have to say no. Though I freely admit that I am ignorant, on questions of that scale at least, so my answer means...pfft." He shrugged, then sighed again. "Now, if it's all right, let me finish. On the very day after we met—a happy, lucky day, to be sure!—it happened that a villager did die. It was not unexpected, not a surprise, though of course we rarely know in advance which day such an event will take place."

He stroked her leg some more; she did not respond.

"The call was answered by Matthias because I was out of the office. I was here, in the *pigeonnier*, with the most beautiful and sensuous woman I have ever met, experiencing a joy which—" He leaned in for a kiss, which she tolerated, only just.

Another Herculean sigh from Florian. "Matthias is capable enough, when he is doing what he knows, which happens to be technology. Put him in front of a computer and he is nothing short of a wizard. Corpses, maybe not so much. It's a matter of experience, really—like any job, a person has to do it and do it and do it, and that's how they begin to get an understanding of how the thing has to be done. You can't explain over the phone how to collect a body and do an autopsy. He wasn't trained for it. He has none of the necessary qualifications."

Selma cocked her head, starting to get interested. "So you just left it to him, is that it?"

"In a nutshell. And it was so profoundly unprofessional of me that words cannot express. I have never done anything like this before. Not to shift blame—really—but you have addled my brain, Selma Throckmorton."

"And so? You said the death was expected. So what's the problem? Did Matthias manage to mess that up, something so routine?"

"Well, it's not so much Matthias that's the problem. All he did was fill out the paperwork giving cause of death—I told him what to write and he wrote it. It wasn't a lie. Benoît LaRue had been sick for *years*, Selma. It was hardly a stretch to think that his body simply gave out at last."

"But...so what? Who's gonna know? Spell it out for me, I still don't see the problem."

"It's...Molly Sutton."

"The Molly Sutton who owns this gîte?"

"The very one."

"For God's sake, Florian. What does Molly have to do with anything?"

"She has the gîte business and also is half-owner of Sutton/Dufort Investigations. Or Dufort/Sutton, I never can remember.

Anyway, she's a detective, self-styled. Now, I don't have a problem with her, I've worked with her on several cases and she's...she's not stupid. *However*."

Florian trailed his fingertips along Selma's leg, hoping against hope that she would accept the invitation.

"However what?"

"However, Sutton has been sniffing around Benoît LaRue, insinuating—even suggesting outright—to more than just me— that there was foul play. The same death where I handed everything off to Matthias, who was not, to say the least, equipped or qualified to handle the job. If it came out that I was rolling around in bed with you instead of doing my job...well...you can just imagine. I won't bore you with the stories of Peter Bonheur, my boss in Bergerac who's an absolute monster and who would be gleeful to hear of my lapse. Suffice to say—I do not want to give Sutton any reason to think that the aftermath of Benoît LaRue's death wasn't handled appropriately. I don't want her to know I wasn't in the office, doing everything as I always have."

"I'm still not...I don't see why Molly would be coming after you? You obviously didn't kill the man."

"It's not that she's coming after me. If the rumors of what she is saying are true, she thinks he was poisoned by his wife. She hasn't mentioned it to me yet, thank God—but the clear next step would be an exhumation. I've been living in dread, knowing that's what's coming. It's a surprise that she hasn't demanded it already."

"Wouldn't it be too late?"

"Depends on the poison. Those tests could show something, if he actually was poisoned." He paused. "And if it *was* poison, and that was missed because I was out of the office when I shouldn't have been, you can see..."

They sat in silence for a few moments.

"Do you think he *was* poisoned?" asked Selma quietly.

"I wish I knew," said Florian. "I wish I knew."

M olly made the usual stops on the way home: first, importantly, she dropped by Patisserie Bujold to see Edmond Nugent and buy some items from his always impressive selection of bread and pastry. She burst through the door and was glad to find the shop empty so she and Edmond could have a chat without feeling rushed.

"Bonjour, Edmond!"

"Bonjour to you, Molly," said Edmond, making only the briefest eye contact.

Molly was taken aback. Edmond was usually the warmest of friends, sometimes a little too warm. But not now. Not chilly, exactly—but noticeably cooler than usual. She chatted him up, making a few jokes which she thought were pretty good but which did not get more than a token chuckle. She asked about any new pastries he was working on, a subject he usually relished, and got little back.

"Something on your mind?" she asked finally.

Edmond took a moment to answer. He looked uncomfortably about the room like a trapped animal. "Well," he said, and then "Hold on just a moment," and disappeared into the back.

People are endlessly strange, thought Molly.

He reappeared with a lopsided pastry, a circle of puff pastry with a filling of what looked like pistachios. "This was just a practice version. Taste it, tell me what you think?"

Carefully Molly took the fragile pastry and bit into it. "Mmm!"

Edmond couldn't help himself, he beamed.

"Quite delicious! The pistachios give such a different taste than the usual walnuts. I mean obviously, it's a different nut. The flavor of the honey really comes through, but it's not too sweet. Also I rather like the greenness of it. Does it have a name, this pastry?"

Edmond had put his palms on the counter and was pressing down on them, clearly troubled about something. "It does not," he said after a long pause, shaking his head. "Listen, Molly."

She listened. He did not say anything.

"*What?* Just come out with it for heaven's sake."

"Well, you know I don't like to put my nose in where it doesn't belong."

"Why do Castillacois say this all day long when it is exactly the thing they most love doing?" Molly laughed.

Edmond looked grim. He passed a hand over his face, rubbing his eyebrows. "Molly, you know I adore you above everything, have since the day we met. I understand that you are an independent woman who makes her own decisions and all that, but...."

Molly waited. "Yes?"

"You've got to leave Angeline LaRue alone."

Instantly Molly felt defiant. "Why do people act as though I have been bullying her? I have not."

"It's not a question of bullying. It's a question of...well...it's some things I've heard...Angeline LaRue is not a person you want to trifle with. If you had a watertight case against her and could let Charlot take over, then by all means, be my guest. But if you're doing what you usually do, poking around and asking a lot of questions and going places you have no business going, with no formal support of the gendarmerie—then I urge you, as my dearest, most beloved friend—don't. Just don't. Leave her be."

"What things have you heard? Tell me."

Edmond pressed his lips together until they were white. Again he leaned both hands on the counter and bowed his head.

Molly was mystified.

"I think it is better if we just leave it at that," he said finally. "I hope you understand. Just—for the love of pastry—keep your mind entirely off of Angeline LaRue."

Molly cocked her head. "I'm not on the trail of Angeline anymore, but nobody seems to believe me. When I had the slightest idea of suspecting her—that news whipped through Castillac like wildfire, but when I dropped it, no one seems to have heard a word about it."

"Well, to be fair, when have you ever just dropped a case before it was resolved? Letting things drop is not exactly the kind of thing you are known for. Quite the opposite, chérie, quite the opposite."

❦ 32 ❦

1971

It was a very cold January, the afternoon already dark. Anne sat rocking in front of the fire—the small house had no other form of heat. Her face was set; it looked nearly frozen, the corners of her mouth turned down, her skin dull and beginning to sag.

Her husband was a man of habit and Artur came home from his job at the village mechanic's every day at the same time. You could set your watch by his regularity. He would enter the house with some hesitation, never knowing what kind of mood Anne was in. Once, he had just stepped inside when a glass jar whizzed past his head and crashed into the door before he could close it. Or she might be singing a Broadway show tune and want to dance around the living room with him. Or she might be catatonic in bed, unresponsive to anything he said.

There was no telling. No anticipating what might set her off. Sometimes it was obvious enough—any special occasion would do it, a birthday, or God forbid, Christmas. But it seemed as though at least as often, there was nothing he could point to, no rhyme or reason. Anne would be filled with rage and someone would be the target. It was usually him, which was, to his mind, preferable to when the target was young Angeline. When Anne focused on Angeline in that way, there was no stopping her, and any attempts to distract were met with renewed vigor and even more viciousness.

That January, early evening, he came inside and Anne did not move from her chair by the fire. She did not look over, did not speak, was as still as the soup pot sitting on the kitchen table. She was so still that for an instant he wondered if she had died, sitting up with her eyes open.

"Anne?" he said, as gently as he could so as not to startle her.

"He could have been ours," she said, not lifting her eyes to him but continuing to stare into the flames.

Artur sighed. They had been around and around on this topic so many times, and when she got started on it, it never ended well. Not ever.

"I told you all about it that night when I got home. There was a brief moment when we could have acted, could have chosen a different sort of life. It was practically given to us on a platter, a *silver* platter, and that's no figure of speech. It was pure luck that I happened to be working that night, pure luck that the midwife stepped out of the room right as that girl was on the brink of death, and felt an urge to unburden herself—pure, unadulterated, incredible luck that the girl told me everything, the whole sordid story, and all before the nurse or the doctor returned so I was the only one who knew. *The only one who knew*—do you see now what that could have been worth? What that could have meant for us? For Angeline?

"I've tried to explain to you, Artur, that when you lift your eyes from the regular working life...of milking cows and fixing cars and such...when you raise your sights and begin to operate on a higher level—that's when information is currency. It's when knowing some things most people don't can be very, very valuable."

She stopped talking and Artur knew from experience not to drop his guard. He wanted to change the subject but knew if he tried that too quickly she would react badly.

"I held that baby in my arms," she said bitterly. "And you made me let him go and would not hear of getting him back. You did that, Artur. And yet you come in here every night after going to your stupid job expecting to find a happy family waiting for you. That's all you want, isn't it? A wife who kisses you when you come in, a daughter who smiles when she sees you. That's it. Well, I'm here to tell you, if you still haven't figured it out: you can't make a life out of that. Not if you have any respect for yourself at all."

Artur had heard it all before. He bowed his head and prayed she would run out of steam before too long.

He did not make excuses for his wife. He knew, more or less, what she was. But he did not have the strength (or the courage) to get a divorce. First, because he knew she would take Angeline away and he would never see her again—Anne would do this out of spite, he had not the slightest doubt of that.

And second, because he was afraid of her. Not afraid of lacerating words, or even a beating. Afraid for his life.

Anne had never killed anyone, not that Artur knew about. She never claimed to have killed anyone. But Artur believed she would have no qualms about doing it, and he trusted that belief implicitly. He could sense it, and that sensing was as real to him as if he had witnessed her cut someone to bits right in front of his eyes.

$\mathscr{H}$ 33 $\mathscr{H}$

M olly arrived back at La Baraque feeling a bit befuddled. What was Lapin, and now Edmond, going on about? Such dire warnings, as though I've been stalking a gang of axe murderers, she thought. With some effort, she pushed all thoughts of them and Angeline out of her mind, sat at the table on the terrace with an iced coffee, and made a list of what needing doing for the rest of the week.

The list was short. Actually, there was not even one thing on it.

The adoption could be over a year away, there was no need to rush around preparing for that. Dufort/Sutton Investigations had no investigation. The gîtes were humming along just fine: La Baraque had no pressing problems, the roofs weren't leaking, the faucets weren't dripping, no rats to be seen, the guests seemed happy...

There was nothing to do but kick back and enjoy life. Which, Molly was finding, was a rare enough state that it wasn't neces- sarily so easy to do. All kinds of thoughts bubbled up unbidden: what exactly had Edmond and Lapin heard that made them so nervous? Why had she not done whatever investigating she felt she had to do in private, before going to Charlot, of all people?

And most of all, the question humming along underneath all the others: would she be a good mother?

She had spent so many years wishing to be a mom, she had never had any space to wonder about how well she could do it if it happened. It wasn't easy, anybody knew that much.

"Madame Sutton!" came a loud voice through the viburnums.

Molly hopped up. "Yes? Selma?"

Selma rounded the corner of the house, her face flushed.

"Is everything all right?"

"Oh yes! Right as rain. Allow me to tell you for the umpteenth time what a delight the pigeonnier is? I just adore the tiny windows that make rectangles of sunlight all across the floor. I could sit there still as a statue all day and just watch those rectangles move with the sun."

Molly grinned. "I like that too. So tell me, what have you been up to? I'm afraid Castillac is lacking in things to do and see, in a tourist sort of way. But there are plenty of interesting places not too far away—have you thought of going to see the caves in Lascaux? Amazing. Those prehistoric people really knew how to draw! The animals come alive on the walls of the cave, not exaggerating."

"I'm afraid I'm something of an oddball when it comes to traveling habits," said Selma. "Going to see this or that—it just isn't my cup of tea. What I like to do is immerse myself in a place, get to know the locals, that sort of thing."

"I understand," said Molly. Then, impulsively (once again), "I was thinking about having an *apèro* this Friday, would you like to come?"

"Oh yes indeed, I would *love* it," beamed Selma, though in the midst of her excitement she was hit with a pang of anxiety, wondering whether Florian would be invited. It seemed potentially dangerous either way. She stayed on the terrace chatting with Molly for another fifteen minutes, thinking that no matter what, having Molly as a friend or at least an ally couldn't hurt. And perhaps, if she and Florian were lucky, a moment would present itself where Selma could, in the most subtle manner of course, suggest to Molly that laying off Angeline LaRue would be a very good idea for everyone.

I mean, Selma thought, ever pragmatic, if the woman did kill her husband? He was dead now. There was nothing to be done to save him. Might as well protect the living.

❧

ANGELINE WAS PRUNING the roses again, and if roses had feelings, they would have been very unhappy.

Leon Garnier is bad enough, she thought, wrenching a long cane out from the fresh June foliage and tossing it behind her on what was developing into a large pile. I've got Leon twiddling his stupid bald thumbs instead of writing me a check. I've got that idiot Lapin Broussard who won't part with the china service even though clearly I should have it.

And now, on top of it, here comes that horrid Molly Sutton, to top everything off. Quite the cherry on top of this *merde* sundae, Molly Sutton is.

Angeline could not stop thinking about Paul-Henri telling her that Sutton was pressing for an exhumation. She wished she had some other friends, other sources of information, in the village. Had Florian Nagrand brushed her off? Why would he listen to this random American who didn't even know Benoît?

I wonder what she said to Charlot. I wonder...what does she know. Well, she doesn't *know* anything.

But what does she *guess?*

It wouldn't do to have Sutton running around causing mischief without my even knowing about it. But now I know. And I will take care of Molly Sutton, you can bank on *that*.

Well, there's only one thing to be done. Molly Sutton will have to be stopped. One way or another—she will have to be stopped. And lucky for me, if there's one thing I've proven: I know how to stop people.

And not get caught.

34

Lapin groaned and let his big head fall against Anne-Marie's shoulder. They had just eaten a big meal she had spent most of the day making, even though it was only a nondescript Monday and there was nothing to celebrate. But sometimes one gets a craving for *boeuf bourguignon*, and when that happened with Anne-Marie, she did not hesitate but went for it, all out.

"My lovely," said Lapin, snuggling in and delighting in the smell of Anne-Marie, her usual lemony earthiness with a touch of the powdered sugar from the beignets he had brought for dessert. "I want to pick you up and carry you into the bedroom but I'm afraid I am too full to even sit up straight. What a meal that was. You astonish me!"

"It *was* good," said Anne-Marie, satisfied. She patted her husband's shoulder and kissed the side of his head. "I'm not ready for the bedroom either. Digesting that meal might take a few days...maybe a month." She laughed.

They sat in silence for some time.

"I sort of wish it were January and we could have a fire," said Lapin.

"Mm. Ok, I think I've waited long enough," said Anne-Marie. She gave his shoulder something between a pat and a smack.

"For what?" said Lapin.

"To hear what's troubling you. Clearly it's something. I've been waiting for days, getting on to weeks, for you to open up. I swear, Lapin, don't you trust me yet? It's not as though we're newlyweds, after all."

"Now, don't go making this about us," said Lapin.

"All right. What is it about then?"

"How do you know I have something on my mind?"

Anne-Marie just laughed. Then laughed some more.

"Oh, all right," he said. "I didn't want to talk about it because...I don't want you mixed up in it. It's...and plus, I don't even know the facts. That's the thing. How can you talk about something when you don't even know what's true and what's just...a muddle of feelings or unfounded gossip or maybe even runaway imagination?"

Anne-Marie cocked her head and did not answer this rather rhetorical question.

"It's about Angeline LaRue," said Lapin, lowering his voice nearly to a whisper even though they were alone in their house.

Anne-Marie's eyebrows went up. "That is not what I expected."

Lapin's shoulders sagged. "I wish it were about anyone but her."

They sat in silence for another long stretch, Anne-Marie having the patience of a saint.

"You know that Benoît was a good friend of mine. More so before his marriage. He was a funny fellow, always getting up to silliness to make people laugh. Not a serious bone in his body, really. Kind-hearted. So friendly to everyone. But once he married Angeline, it was like...his personality got turned down, like she somehow turned the dial allll the way down, from an 8 down to 1. He didn't seem unhappy, really, but he was no longer...fun. No longer jolly. Now, I know it's commonplace for a friend to marry someone who isn't your favorite, and you just figure out ways to muddle along. I'm not claiming any of what I just said is out of the ordinary. Not really."

"But...?"

"But...this isn't anything Benoît ever said to me, because he was not that kind of man. He wouldn't have said anything against his wife behind her back, no matter what." Lapin sighed again. "I miss him. I mean the him from before his marriage."

Anne-Marie nodded. She took her arm from around him and held his hand.

"I mean, it's not that I *know* anything, really," he said. "Not factually. It's more...what I..."

And then he broke off, shaking his head. He tried to complete the sentence, to communicate the thought to Anne-Marie, whom he did trust and who was waiting to hear it—but in the end he could not force the words out of his mouth, not about that part of it anyway.

"Edmond told me something," he said finally. "About something Angeline did when she was still a kid, maybe around thirteen or so."

"Are we really going to hold teenage hijinks against people once they've grown up?"

"I'm not talking about hijinks."

"What, then?"

He took a deep breath. He made her swear six different ways that she would not breathe a word to another soul. And then he told her what Edmond had heard from Hortense Depleurisse one day when she had come into his shop to buy a large box of éclairs.

❧ 35 ❧

At La Baraque, Tuesday had begun much like the preceding days, with Molly and Ben enjoying a sort of second honeymoon and staying in bed way past the rising hour of good citizens.

"I could get used to this," said Ben, as Molly came back to the bedroom with a tray, her bathrobe scandalously open.

"I *am* used to it," said Molly. "I don't know why in the world we got in the habit of hopping out of bed so early when we could have been enjoying ourselves."

"You know, a baby will get in the way of this rather dramatically."

Molly chewed on her cheek and considered. "Then we'd best keep these hours until the very day the baby arrives!" She poured their coffees and slipped back into bed. "Do you think—we'll get a baby? I mean, will there be a choice between baby and an older child? I don't think I care one way or another. I mean, I would *love* a baby of course, but—"

"I don't know. I would imagine these things fluctuate and it just depends on the moment who is available." Ben sipped his coffee and leaned back into the pillows. "I have to say, maternity suits you. Your cheeks are so rosy!"

Molly grinned. "Frances was kidding me about that too. She's so excited for us, of course. Ahhh," Molly let out a big sigh as she fell back on the pillows next to Ben. "What a lovely, beautiful morning this is! I'll tell you, Benjamin—I am so relieved to have let go of that whole Angeline LaRue thing. That's probably why I look so much better—it's like a weight has been lifted, you know? And...I'm sorry I didn't listen to you right at the beginning."

Ben had the good grace to merely say, "Mm."

"Do you—is it paranoid of me to wonder if my intuition has gone off somehow? Gotten stale?"

"Yes."

"Yes it has gone off, or yes I'm paranoid?"

"The latter. Why don't you wait until we have a real case and then you'll see, soon enough."

"I've been thinking about that—wondering if you're okay with doing these bread-and-butter investigative jobs you've been doing —the insurance scams, divorce surveillance stuff? I know it must seem tedious after being Chief of the gendarmerie."

Ben shrugged. "It pays the bills. I don't have the expectation that my work life is thrilling every single day. Sometimes it's not a bad thing to saddle up and do the simple things day after day."

Molly dove under the covers, while Ben with an athletic move grabbed the tray to keep coffee from going everywhere, as Molly tickled the backs of his knees with muffled giggles.

"Molly!" said Ben. "There's someone at the door!"

BEN QUICKLY PUT on his running clothes so as to open the door with something on. "Angeline! Bonjour! Please come in."

Odd, he was thinking. They were acquaintances, of course, but of the barest kind. Not what he would have described as friends. Definitely not 'drop-in-unannounced' friends.

Molly came out looking reasonably put together and her

eyebrows flew up when she saw who it was. "Bonjour, Angeline," she said, and Ben thought he heard the slightest meekness in her voice, a faint tone of apology.

"If you'll excuse me," said Ben, "I'm off to a job. I'll see you both later."

Molly knew he thought she and Angeline needed to clear the air and it would be best if he weren't there. But that didn't mean she wanted him to go.

"Can I offer you—let's see, what time is it? 11:00. Would you like some coffee? A croissant?"

"No, no, Maggie," said Angeline. "Not necessary. And I'm so sorry for barging in like this unannounced. I have no manners at all!" She smiled at Molly. "I only—I've been practically shut in, you see, for years...and so I'm making an effort to get out more, to see people...I don't mean to intrude."

Molly got the slightest little tickle in the back of her skull. She shook her head.

"I'm glad you came," Molly said, and she meant it. "I wonder if you would talk to me a little about Benoît, if it's not too upsetting? I've found that so often, when someone dies, people don't want to bring them up because they worry about upsetting the family and close friends. But the family and friends are already upset, they're thinking about the lost loved one all the time!"

"Oh, you *do* understand," said Angeline, putting a small manicured hand on Molly's arm. Molly startled, just barely.

"Well, a little. I'm not a widow and no doubt no one can really understand how that feels unless they've experienced it. Anyway, tell me about Benoît. What kind of man was he, what did he care about, how did you meet?"

For a moment, Molly considered making a direct apology for suspecting Angeline of poisoning her husband, but only for a moment. She led Angeline over to the sofa, and then changed her mind and walked through the French doors to the terrace, which was shaded at that time of day and very pleasant.

NELL GODDIN

"Oh, Benoît, Benoît," said Angeline, taking a seat and folding her hands in her lap like a schoolgirl. "He was...well...what can I say? Truly a believer in *Liberté, Egalité, Fraternité*—which—if you knew where he came from—" she stopped short. She had never told the whole truth to anyone and why in the world would she start with Molly Sutton, of all people?

An odd thing to say, Molly thought. Would the first thing you had to say about your spouse just after they died be about their politics? If they weren't a politician?

"I know he had many friends in the village," Molly said. "Including a close friend of mine—Lapin Broussard. Lapin's rather a complicated man, don't you think? But he has a big heart, and I know he cared very much for Benoît. So please, Angeline, tell me more about him—what did he like to spend time doing?"

"Oh, you know," she said, "this and that." She waved her hand in the air as though to brush away Molly's question. "Alas, he was sick for so long. And now he's dead."

Molly blinked. The tickle at the base of her skull was more insistent. "Was Benoît ever able to work? I know that in France it's not polite to ask about that, but maybe it's all right if the person has passed?" She made a rueful smile but Angeline did not smile back.

"He worked for the post office. If you don't mind," the widow said, bending her face towards her lap and dabbing at her eyes with a handkerchief, "let's talk of something else. Sometimes...I just get overwhelmed."

"Oh of course," said Molly, not believing her for a second.

"How did you end up in Castillac?" asked Angeline.

"Just chance," said Molly. "It was La Baraque that drew me. Obviously, I didn't know anyone in Castillac. Not a soul in all of France, actually, so I had no ideas about where to go or anyone to see once I got here. The photos of La Baraque on that real estate website...I don't know, it sounds a little crazy, but the place called to me."

Angeline was staring at Molly. She didn't nod or murmur or make any indication that she heard what Molly was saying.

"Anyway," said Molly, standing up, and using the tone that everyone knows means *it's time for you to leave now*. "It was good to see you and I'm glad you dropped by."

Angeline did not stand up. She watched Molly, looking to see her reaction to a guest who was missing her cue. She wanted to see Molly uncomfortable, wanted to see what she might do next. Did she get angry easily? Was she a pushover? Angeline tapped her fingers on the edge of the table, cocked her head, and finally met Molly's eyes.

Molly felt something inside contract as she looked into Angeline's eyes, which were a startling blue and cold as ice.

She poisoned her husband, Molly thought. Simple as that. I know it. And she knows I know it.

Molly did not look away as Angeline stared at her. With effort, she kept her body relaxed, her gaze unemotional, but not chilly.

Molly waited.

After quite a long time, Angeline suddenly jerked her head back and blinked quickly several times.

"Thanks again for coming by," said Molly, and she went inside and closed the door, leaving Angeline on the terrace.

Molly would have told Ben she was back on the case but he was still out doing surveillance and there was no telling where he might be, most likely in a parked car pretending to read a newspaper. There would be plenty of time to have that conversation, she thought, her mind racing ahead. When she returned to the terrace, Angeline was gone.

A fresh sheet of paper on the notepad, pencil nice and sharp... and the list of what to do next, in the matter of Angeline LaRue, appeared in Molly's mind as though she had never stopped thinking about it.

Intuition is a funny thing, she thought, after finishing the list and quickly eating a half-stale croissant on her way to the scooter. People talk about it like it's silly, as though it's nothing more than people wishing or pretending in some way. But Molly knew different. She had learned that when the quiet inner voice tried to get her attention, it was never wrong. She didn't think her inner voice was special—everyone's inner voice was not wrong. But many or most of us—for a million reasons—tune it out and do not listen.

She flipped through the notepad and saw she'd completely forgotten that she had an appointment with Dr. Boulet for that very afternoon. Perfect timing, she thought, it's like everything is falling into place now.

Next on the list—baby steps—was having a private word with Matthias, Florian's assistant. He had always seemed willing to help, and more than that (intuition again) she had the feeling that he might know more than he was willing to say in front of Florian. So she was going to stake out the coroner's office, silly as that sounded, and see if she could catch him leaving the office for lunch. She guessed that he and Florian did not eat lunch together very often; their relationship did not seem that collegial.

She hoped Matthias hadn't left for lunch already. After a quick trip into the village, Molly parked outside Chez Papa and was locking up the scooter when Florian Nagrand burst through the door with a self-satisfied expression on his face, which disappeared when he saw her.

"Bonjour, Florian," she said, coming over to shake hands. "Early lunch?"

"Well, that's no crime is it?" Nervously he patted his pockets as though searching for something.

"Not in my book," said Molly. She considered. Was it unusual for Florian to have an early lunch at Chez Papa? There was nothing on the face of it that was out of place. People get hungry. Chez Papa has excellent frites. And yet...

Florian glanced quickly behind him and then took off down the street in the direction of the coroner's office. "Have a lovely day," he said over his shoulder, which was so unlike him Molly stared at his back as he walked away.

A lovely day? A usual farewell from Florian was more along the lines of "stay out of trouble, if that's humanly possible," or "for the love of God, leave me alone," or even "goodbye and shut up."

What in the world had gotten into him?

While she let Florian get ahead, she peered into Chez Papa. There was Nico manning the bar as always. A fellow in a worker's blue jacket seated at the bar, talking with his hands. Selma

Throckmorton was taking a last sip of wine and then standing up from a table.

Molly turned and followed. It was just past noon, most of the village was settling down to lunch, and the streets were empty. Florian walked quickly and Molly didn't catch up to him before he was already back in the office. Might as well go in and give it a go, she figured.

"What I'd like to know is," she said to him, not wasting any time, "under what conditions would you consider digging up a body in order to perform some new tests? And also—who decides whether the body can be dug up? Whose call is it? Do family members get a say or is it exclusively a police matter—or is it completely under the coroner's purview?"

Florian let his head drop to his chest. He let out a wheezy sort of moan. "Madame Sutton, you might as well put that idea right out of your head this instant because it is not. going. to. happen. The bureaucratic hurdles for such an operation are immense— this is France, after all! Exhumation is never an action undertaken for simple curiosity and random 'what-ifs'. It is only carried out when there is a solid reason to believe evidence was missed that cannot be gotten any other way, evidence that matters a great deal."

"Do you not think that knowing whether or not Benoît was poisoned matters a great deal?"

"I believe, in logic, that that is what is called a straw man. And I will not be rattled by it." With a sigh, he closed the door and sat back in his chair. He rubbed his thumb along his forefinger, wishing a cigarette were resting there. "This is really none of your business," he said, "but I will fill you in on some of the context you are missing. You want to see this potential exhumation as an isolated event with one goal. But that is not how the world works, Madame Sutton. This office is but a sub-office of the main office of the department of the coroner, which is based in Bergerac and headed by the odious Peter Bonheur. Doubtless I have mentioned him before, he is the bane of my existence. He is always, but always, looking to strip the sub-offices of any self-determination, let me tell you, being more concerned with consolidating power than in performing his job, which is to make sure the citizens of the department get the services they need in a timely manner. I'm sure this sort of thing is not unknown to you—bureaucracies and corporate structures are full of such people."

Molly summoned every bit of patience not to interrupt and urge Florian to get to the point.

"And so," he continued, "we here at the Castillac sub-office have a particular interest in...shall we say...not doing anything that could possibly bring the attention of the main office, because that attention never—absolutely *never*— has a positive outcome. An exhumation, of all things, would entail review of all our protocols, it would invite snooping into every detail of our work here, no matter how insignificant. And it is expensive, for another thing, which is one hundred percent guaranteed to bring criticism, even censure."

Molly chewed on her lip. "But Florian. Surely the whole point of an exhumation is to correct an error—which is not to say that the error was made unwisely? In this instance, in particular—the error was completely understandable, as I said. I don't believe anyone would fault you or Matthias for it."

"You don't know Peter Bonheur."

"But if the exhumation did show that the cause of death was not what was first thought—wouldn't your office get credit for correcting the error?"

Florian shook his head. "Again, Madame Sutton, you don't seem to have any grasp at all on how the world works. Errors, in my world, are always, and I mean *always*, a very bad thing. It doesn't matter if you're making them or correcting them. Any association with them, in any way at all, covers you with bureaucratic toxic slime that you cannot wash off."

"What a wonderfully vivid way to express that," said Molly.

Matthias snickered in spite of himself.

"And—just to make sure you understand that this matter is closed, one hundred percent *shut*—our office does not have the funds to proceed with an exhumation even if we wanted to. You have no idea of the crippling budgetary pressures we are under. It's a wonder any work gets done at all, it's a wonder that we have a roof over our heads and a van to pick up bodies—"

Molly could see that Florian had wound himself up to such a degree that she would make no headway with him. At least, not on that particular Tuesday.

She would continue looking for evidence, since so far the tickle hadn't gone anywhere. And, she thought, waving as she left, she had quite a list of leads to follow before coming back to the coroner and pressing him further on the exhumation.

Out on the street, Molly shook her hands at her sides to release some tension. She crossed the street to smell the Chenault's roses, which were spilling over a low stone wall in the most abundant way, pinks and apricots. She was just inhaling their heady aroma when hallelujah, Matthias de Clare came out of the office and closed the door behind him.

Perfect. Things falling into place.

She nearly called out to him but for some reason did not. All Molly wanted to do was have a word with him without Florian around, and she thought that being out of the office might make him a bit more talkative. She had no particular guesses about what he might have to say, only the sense that there was something he was holding back.

Matthias rounded a corner, and Molly walked a little faster so as not to lose him.

At this point she should simply pick up the pace and catch up to him; there was no reason having a chat on the street wouldn't serve her purpose. But curiosity about where he was going kept her from doing so. He was not walking toward the Place, where most of the restaurants were, but instead to a less-traveled part of

Castillac, where as far as she knew, there were only houses, and no shops or places to have lunch or buy any food at all.

Matthias turned down a narrow street and then cut though an alley. If was as if he knew he was being followed—but Molly was almost certain he did not.

At last, he stopped at a very small house, one-story, with an ancient door, painted a deep green. Molly closed in, thinking she would call out to him before he went inside.

As Matthias put the key in the lock, the door opened. And who to her wondering eyes should appear—none other than Lawrence Weebly.

The men embraced. Molly's mouth hung open. She managed to step behind a van so they couldn't see her while she tried to collect her thoughts.

OK, now hold on a minute, she thought. It felt literally like the world as she knew it was tilting, and she put her hand on the side of the van to steady herself.

Lawrence knows Matthias.

Matthias works in the coroner's office.

All those texts, over the years, when Lawrence knew about a death before she did, before anyone in the village did...well, anyone except the coroner's office, she thought, with a feeling of such satisfaction that this small mystery had finally, finally, finally been solved.

And wait—was Matthias Lawrence's boyfriend? *Longtime* boyfriend?

Castillac was charming, quaint, beloved to her. And a source, apparently, of infinite secrets.

MOLLY CONSIDERED KNOCKING on the green door of what she guessed was Matthias's house, but decided to file away this new knowledge until she had a better idea of what to do with it. And she didn't want to be late for Dr. Boulet. Quickly she walked to his office on rue Montclard, which was the front room of his house, and his assistant let her in.

"Bonjour, Renée," Molly said, "I'm here for my appointment?"

Renee flicked her eyes at Molly and consulted the appointment book without returning the greeting. "He will be ready for you soon," she said, and busied herself with a stack of papers that was she was using as a prop and not hiding that fact.

Oh boy, thought Molly.

She waited. Her stomach growled. Her appointment had been for 12:30, which she realized was smack in the middle of lunchtime and why had she been given this slot when the doctor was almost certainly eating his lunch, and being French, not at his desk and not rushing through it?

A half hour went by.

Did they think she was there to cause trouble for the doctor? To yell at him, make accusations? Maybe Renee figured she would give up and leave. And little as Molly wanted to give her that satisfaction, when she thought through what she was hoping to accomplish, she realized this appointment was never going to give her what she needed. The doctor, unless he was very sloppy or unethical, was not about to reveal the symptoms and diagnoses of his patient, even if the patient were no longer living—and certainly not to her, who had no standing whatsoever to ask those sorts of questions, or any relationship with the doctor either.

What in the world had she been thinking? Molly made an excuse to Renee and went back onto the street, blinking in the bright sunshine and suddenly starving.

Not for the first time she wondered if maybe she was losing her edge. Of course the doctor wasn't going to talk to her, and how had she convinced herself otherwise? At least she had left before embarrassing them both by asking a lot of questions he would refuse to answer.

Molly felt sure—though even in her own mind, she acknowledged it was a guess, with no evidence to back it up—*yet*—that Benoît's years of symptoms were caused by a variety of poisons Angeline had administered. She imagined writing out a diagram with arrows going from the poison to the symptom, on a timeline of his illness. Neat and clear, evidence that Florian and any other bureaucrat would find impossible to set aside. So who else could tell her about those symptoms and when they occurred? It was agonizing to think that everything she needed was most likely in the records at Dr. Boulet's office. But without a court-ordered injunction, she was never going to get her hot little hands on those records.

For a moment, but only a moment, she considered enlisting Renée, Dr. Boulet's assistant. But realistically, Renee would be loyal to her employer, whom she clearly respected, unwilling to breach his trust even if Molly convinced her the cause was just.

She would have to find another way.

❧ 37 ❧

"I know, I know, *I know*," said Molly, reaching across the table to hold Ben's hand. "I said I was done with it. And I was actually happy about that decision, I would even say at peace with it. I didn't make it because of pressure. It felt like, okay, maybe everyone is right, and I'm imagining something evil has happened just...just because...well, the reasons don't matter. So many people I trust—well, *all* the people I trust: you, Lawrence, Lapin, Edmond, Frances...all of you said I should let it go, that the poor man died a natural death and why was I so unwilling to believe that?"

Molly took a deep breath, her long speech not over.

Ben, to his credit, did not interrupt or appear to be readying himself with what he wanted to say, but was simply attentive and listening to Molly.

"And I value your opinions. I honestly do. I wasn't just ignoring all of you and blithely going on my merry way."

"I know that. You're very stubborn. But not *that* stubborn."

"Mm. Well," Molly laughed. "But here I am, ready to dive back in. It's just—I *have* taken what you said to heart, but...something has changed. I'll explain in a sec, but before I continue on the subject of Angeline, let me say first that I am absolutely thrilled about our adoption plans and none of this has anything at all to do with that."

Ben nodded and squeezed her hand.

"Ok. So. This morning." She took a deep breath. "Angeline shows up here, at La Baraque. Why? You're not friends with her. I'm not friends with her. *Why?* There is no reason I can think of for her to arrive unannounced, with no believable reason given. The only thing that makes any sense is that someone told her I suspected her, and she wanted to come...to...well, threaten is maybe too strong a word. Wanted to come make it known that she knew I suspected her. To put me on notice, for whatever that might mean."

"Surely there could be some other reason, maybe something you wouldn't have any way to know?"

"Of course that's possible. I don't think so, but it's possible. What I'm about to tell you might not sound very convincing. But it is to me. Her coming here—it was a kind of gauntlet thrown down, between me and Angeline. She wasn't here long. After a bit of small talk that was losing steam, I stood up and thanked her for coming. She did not budge. She stared at me and I swear on a plate of almond croissants, Ben Dufort, her look was...well, it was like poison. Full of hate. Absolute *hate.*"

"You can't blame her for taking a dislike to you. Given the circumstances."

"Sure, I get that. But this was...*way* more intense than that. I could feel a sort of chaotic, animal energy coming from her. It's hard for me to describe. As though she might suddenly lunge across the table and bite me."

Ben's eyebrows went up. "*Bite* you?"

"Well, she didn't. But I felt like she might."

"Molly..."

"Look, I know how it sounds. I'm jumping back into investigating her without a single new shred of evidence to convince you that I'm on the right track or even possibly on the right track. All I can say right now is this: I knew in that moment, when all she did was look at me on the terrace, that she had killed her husband. And she knew that I knew, and wanted me to know that she knew. Without either of us saying a word, the cards were on the table."

Ben licked his lips and rubbed his brush cut with one hand. He looked out at the meadow and then down at his feet, wanting to give Bobo a pat. "This is all based on feelings, and unspoken feelings at that," he said finally. "Where's any...not even proof, but facts that could be building toward proof?"

"I know," said Molly. "It sounds flimsy. I don't like it either. But all I can do is tell you how it is. That woman killed her husband, I am dead certain of it. She was practically taunting me, showing her utter disinterest in him. I kept asking her to tell me about him and she couldn't be bothered. She was showing me, *on purpose*, how he was nothing to her. And—it's possible that I misheard, but I think she called me Maggie."

"What?"

Molly laughed a dark sort of laugh. "She's just trying to mess with my head."

"Good luck to her," said Ben, shaking his head. "Now listen, did I tell you I picked up some prunes stuffed with foie gras yesterday?"

Molly made a little shriek of happiness and threw her arms around him. It wasn't every man who could handle having his advice ignored, and she felt so grateful for him. Plus prunes stuffed with foie gras are truly food of the gods, and having them in the house was cause for celebration.

❧ 38 ❧

The next morning, after stuffing herself silly with those prunes, Molly gave Ben a kiss and told him she was heading to the herbalist's shop in Bergerac. "I want to ask for information about plant poisons. Since Angeline is such a talented gardener, seems like a reasonable place to start."

Ben started to warn her to be careful, but stopped himself. "Please give Chloe my warmest regards," he said. He had gone to her years ago for help with anxiety, and she had given him some tinctures that had brought him through some rough moments.

Molly set off on the scooter, going much too fast, humming to herself. She kept thinking about Angeline's visit, and that bone-chilling stare. Clearly it was meant to be intimidating—the stare was not covert but intentional, out in the open, *pointed*. It was as though the whole situation was a game to Angeline, and she was actually pleased that someone wanted to challenge her. Almost as though she'd been waiting and hoping for that challenge. At least that is how it seemed to Molly, who, it must be admitted, rather relished challenges herself.

But what I am describing is a dangerous person, Molly

185

thought. This is not a game, and Benoît was not a chess piece for his wife's amusement.

Molly shuddered and the scooter wobbled for an instant.

Angeline looks so angelic, Molly thought. The glossy blonde hair, pink lips, so petite she didn't look capable of hurting a fly. Angeline didn't look the part of a stone-cold murderess, so she must not be one? We are all so vulnerable to assumptions, thought Molly. And the worst part is—they are unconscious, happening without our even knowing it, all the time, all the damn time.

The herbalist's shop was on a tiny street, barely bigger than an alley; the cobblestones were uneven and Molly bumped along until she found a place to lock up the scooter. The bell tinkled as she walked into the shop; she was not sure if Chloe would remember their conversation at the fête, but Chloe was nowhere to be seen and Molly began looking at the bottles and jars on the shelves.

Jars and jars filled with plant matter. Dark blue glass bottles. Handwritten labels on some of them. Molly breathed in through her nose and the smells were intense, so many different ones competing—spicy, earthy, licorice, sweet, floral...

"May I help you?" said Chloe, popping up from behind the counter. "Oh bonjour, Molly! Are you looking for something in particular? I remember you had some specific questions..."

"I do," said Molly. "Since you are the expert on plants and their effects. If you wouldn't mind?"

Chloe nodded. "You want to know about poison," she said matter-of-factly.

"Yes. Plant-derived poisons. That could...kill a person."

"You believe Angeline LaRue killed her husband. Maybe you think she might have bought the means for it here, in my shop?"

"No, no, I'm not suggesting—"

"Good. Let's get that cleared up right away. I'm not in the business of selling poisons, quite the opposite, in fact."

"Of course! I didn't for a moment think that—I only wanted to ask—and before I forget, Ben Dufort sends his warmest regards, he says you gave him some help when he was having a bad time..."

Chloe shrugged and looked away.

"How did you know..."

"About your suspicions?" Chloe laughed, a deep laugh from her belly. "Everyone in Castillac is talking about it. It doesn't take long for news to get from there to Bergerac, when it's juicy enough. I would guess the postman knows. The children on the playground. Angeline and her dog, if she has one. *Everybody* knows, Molly. There are no secrets in Castillac, don't you know that by now?"

Molly made a weak little laugh. "I know people love to talk. Good Lord, they *love* to talk. But all right, since I've come pre-announced, as it were, is it all right if I ask a few questions?"

"As long as no customers come in, fire away."

"Thank you! So...I know there are some plants that are used medicinally in a low dose, but can be fatal in a higher dose. Do you have anything like that in your shop?"

Chloe nodded. "You're thinking about something like belladonna?"

"Tell me about it."

"I don't sell it. But a powder made from the roots and leaves can be used to treat asthma, colic, and an excess of stomach acid."

"And if you take too much?"

"Oh, the usual—dilated pupils, rapid heartbeat, a number of other symptoms, then coma and death. Which is why I don't sell it. You send a thing home with someone who wasn't listening when you told them to be careful, and, well, you can see where that might end up. I don't want that on my conscience even if I did everything I could to warn people. People don't listen."

Molly laughed. "No, they don't. But so...belladonna would grow here, in this part of France?"

"It is not a difficult plant to grow. If you could get seeds, I don't think growing it here would be a problem."

Molly had taken out a small notepad and scribbled some notes as Chloe was talking.

"And what else?

Chloe looked up at the ceiling as she thought. "I take this enterprise—herbal medicines—very seriously. Perhaps to a fault. I cannot say with one hundred per cent certainty there is nothing like you describe here, but I have taken great pains to keep my products safe. Even for people who don't listen. I certainly don't want to be in the business of providing murder weapons, even accidental ones.

"Now, that's medicines. If you want to talk about poisonous garden plants, that is another matter. There are so many of them, and most people—I would venture to say even most gardeners—have no idea how poisonous some common plants are. Rhododendron, oleander, castor bean—the list goes on and on."

"Interesting list. I'd call myself more of a gardening dabbler, but I had no idea—rhododendron is so popular where I come from, it's all over the place. So tell me, are the symptoms of these poisonous garden plants very different? Would it be possible to back-solve the agent by looking at the symptoms?"

"Tricky. There is, unfortunately for that project, a fair amount of overlap. There are broad categories, though—for example, plants that cause heart arrhythmias and plants that cause the heart to slow way down."

"Oh, that would be really helpful," said Molly. "If you don't mind, let's dig right into that."

Luckily for Molly, no customers showed up. She and Chloe talked for several hours, until Molly felt as though her brain was so stuffed with facts she couldn't take in even one more, and her notepad had not a single blank page.

A dangerous gardener, she thought, climbing back on the scooter. She imagined all the evidence melting into the compost heap, wondered if it might be possible to trace purchases of seeds, but how far back? All the way to Castillac, her mind was whirling, trying to see how to get the goods on this dangerous gardener with the glossy blonde hair and the stare of death.

❧

"AND DID you know that Egyptian women used belladonna to make their pupils dilate, which was thought to be beautiful?" say Molly. "You know, you've always had a sort of Egyptian look about you. Maybe it's the haircut. Wasn't there some dude in college who used to call you Cleopatra?"

Frances cackled. "Howard Cleevy!"

"Good old Howard Cleevy," said Molly, and the two of them laughed over that memory for another half a block.

"OK, back to belladonna," said Frances. "So you're telling me this is yet another item from the list of Women Poisoning Themselves for Beauty?" said Frances. "I wonder how many of them dropped dead. Beautiful corpses though, eh?"

"You have a dark mind."

"Says the murderer-chaser."

"Make it murderer-*catcher*," said Molly. "Nicer ring to it."

Frances stopped and stared down at her feet. "Why is it that my shoelaces are chronically untied these days? I never anticipated tying my shoes to be this Herculean task, but it *is*," she said. "Not to mention I can't even see my feet anymore."

"You sure you don't have twins in there?"

"Funny. Hi*lar*ious. Tie my shoe, will ya?"

Molly knelt down, snickering, and took Frances's laces in hand. Something—a quick movement, or maybe it was just a gut feeling—made her lift her eyes and look back down the street. She saw Angeline LaRue, a block behind them, step behind a hedge. But not hurriedly.

Molly finished tying the shoe and stood up. "Lord have mercy," she murmured. "You'll never guess who's following us."

Frances whirled around—as quickly as a pregnant woman can whirl—and saw nothing but empty street and sidewalk. "A ghost that only you can see?"

"Angeline. She's behind that hedge in the Chenault's yard."

"Think she has a poison dart gun or something?"

"You never know," said Molly. "At this point, I'll stake my reputation—heck, I'll even stake La Baraque—on Angeline's guilt. Her stalking me right now just adds to the list of suspicious events. It's *proof* she is up to no good."

They walked on for a block before Frances spoke. "You do know, beloved friend, that the fact that someone who lives in the village is walking on a village street is not actually proof of anything?"

"I'm telling you, she killed her husband."

Frances rubbed her belly as they walked. "I'm not trying to tell you your business. You're the murderer-catcher, not me. But so far? You're not selling it."

Molly shrugged and did not bother trying to convince Frances. Frances, no matter how annoying she might be in the moment, was not the person it was crucial to convince.

"FOR ONCE IN my life I'm not even hungry," said Molly, pulling up her chair at Chez Papa for a late lunch and smiling at Lawrence.

"How curious," he said. "Does this mean, overall, that you are satisfied with your life? Not hungering for...anything?"

"Oh, don't get all metaphorical on me. It's just that I ate an unconscionable number of prunes stuffed with foie gras this morning, and I'm still full."

She gazed at her friend, unsure what tack to take. Should she just come right out and ask about Matthias? Or let him keep his secret?

"Well, I could eat a horse. Which does not appear to be on the menu. I suppose I can make do with a croque monsieur. And while I contemplate that, please tell me: how are things going in your investigation?"

"Honestly," said Molly, glowering at him. "Can I not have a single thought without the entire village knowing about it?"

"Oh, dear one," said Lawrence. "The answer to that, as you well know, is: no. At least, you can't keep anything from *me*. I can read your mind, as I'm sure you realize. You have...patterns, my friend."

"Don't we all," Molly muttered. "Some of us are open-hearted and transparent with our very good friends, and some of us...are not."

They smirked at each other, not really mad but rather enjoying pretending to be mad.

"But seriously, Molls, how are things going? Any headway at all?"

"Not as such," said Molly. "I think I'll have a croque monsieur as well. I believe I can wedge it in if I give it the really good ol' college try."

Lawrence put his fingertips together and waited.

"See, this is the thing," she said, in a voice low enough that the other diners could not hear, though some were trying to. "I am on the trail of poisons, and I am feeling pretty good about that side of things. You wouldn't believe what a toxic world we live in, and I'm not even talking about industrial fumes and chemicals, but beloved plants from our own backyards!"

Lawrence nodded, still waiting.

"You know that Angeline is quite the gardener. So it makes sense, wouldn't you agree, that she would be able to grow a whole long list of poisonous plants if she wanted to. We call that *means* in the investigation business. And then, after using it, all she has to do is pull it up and throw it on the compost pile, and any evidence of it will be totally gone in matter of weeks."

"Ingenious, in a murdering sort of way. All right, I'll give you means. And opportunity—sure, obviously. But what about *motive*, Molly? From all reports, Benoît LaRue was one of the kindest, gentlest men alive. Even if she was unhappily married, why kill him?"

"I haven't gotten that far. I believe I may have explained that motive is actually the weakest of the three, because without means and opportunity, you can have six hundred motives and they won't matter."

"Yes, but—"

"—but I'll need to give a motive if anyone is to believe me. I know, Lawrence, I know. I'm just not focused on that quite yet. Besides, if Florian exhumes the body, and poison is found, I don't think motive is going to be much of a problem. People kill for reasons the rest of us can't imagine. Maybe he had bad breath. Maybe he had secrets. Maybe he....anyway, put all that aside for the moment, will you? Let me explain what I could use some help with."

She let him think that over while she jumped up and put in their lunch order with Nico.

Back at the table, she said in a low voice, "I cannot find a way to access Benoît's medical records. I can't make any guesses about which poisons were used unless I know what his symptoms were —I'm talking about stretching way back, years back, from when he first started getting sick."

"Are you saying you think she used a variety of poisons...for years?"

"I do. At least that's my hypothesis anyway. But so far, I'm nowhere close to proving it."

"You don't wonder just a little whether the idea of that kind of murder is so...well, I mean, it's like something right out of a book, isn't it?"

Molly tried to keep the impatience out of her expression and failed. "I don't care if it's from the movie of the week," she said. "I'm telling you, that woman killed her husband and I just need a little help to prove it. Even knowing what his symptoms were leading up to his death, even how he looked after dying—that might be meaningful. Maybe enough to get the exhumation. Know anyone who might have some insight on that?"

She gave him a penetrating look. *I know*, she tried to communicate with her eyes. *I know about Matthias.*

But Lawrence showed no sign of receiving the message. He shrugged and began asking questions about the armoire she had just bought from Lapin, then about a recipe for chocolate chip cookies made with coconut flour of all things, and finally about where she would travel if money were no object.

But Molly was no slouch when it came to understanding why people do the things they do, and this included her good friend babbling a lot of nonsense because he wanted to keep a secret even when he must suspect that the secret was not a secret anymore.

❧ 39 ❧

"Get over here," growled Florian, tugging on the hem of
Selma's bright red shorts.

She laughed a throaty, pleased-with-life sort of laugh, but did
not budge from the window. "You're the one so paranoid about
Molly Sutton," she said. "I'm just peeking to see if she's around.
She and Ben wander through the meadow all the time, playing
with that dog."

"Any sign of her?"

"Not right now." She sat down on the bed and then flopped
back with a moan. "Know something funny, though? I was
watching yesterday—"

"—quite the little snoop you are," he said affectionately.

"Indeed. Just watching out for your interests, Monsieur Coroner. So anyway, guess who was sitting on the terrace with Molly
yesterday morning?"

"Santa Claus."

"It's June, it couldn't be Santa Claus."

"Julia Child."

"You are a silly, silly man. Angeline LaRue, that's who!"

Florian froze. "What?"

"Yes."

Florian sat up, brow furrowed. He patted his chest though he was not wearing a shirt and had no cigarettes in the pocket anyway. "You just said Angeline LaRue was sitting on the terrace —*here?* At La Baraque? With *Molly?*"

"That is what I just said. You think it's strange too, then?"

"Of course I do. And it's more than strange, it's dangerous."

"You mean dangerous for you?"

Florian lay down beside Selma and trailed his fingertips along her hip. "Yes. For me. At least, that was my instant response, a stab of...well, I don't like to admit it, but...fear. But on reflection, it's not as though Molly's going to be asking Angeline to exhume Benoît's body, right? That's not a conversation that's ever going to happen. So...what in God's name were they talking about?"

"I'm afraid we're a little far away for lip-reading."

"Angeline...surely she must have heard by now...some well-meaning blabbermouth must have told her..."

"Maybe she came over to tell Molly to keep her nose out of her business."

"Hm," said Florian, moving his fingertips up to Selma's neck and along her earlobe.

"You're tickling," she breathed, moving closer.

"People in the village...they don't like Angeline," said Florian, kissing her collarbone. "She's rather a cold fish. She took care of Benoît all these years, so people don't say anything against her. But even all that selfless work was not enough to make anyone actually like her."

"Do you think...is it possible that Molly is right? That Angeline seems selfless on the surface but is a stone-cold killer in reality?"

"I think you watch too much TV."

"I'm just saying—maybe there's a reason no one can stand her. Like even if they're not looking at her and thinking *murderer,* people sense that something about her is off. Wrong. Even...

dangerous. So they keep their distance. Or maybe people have heard things, and that news hasn't reached us yet."

"Certainly possible," said Florian, rubbing her shoulder and kissing her forehead.

"I don't want to talk about Angeline anymore," said Selma. Her face was flushed and she wiggled closer to Florian, who smiled such a wide and loving smile that his friends in the village would not have recognized him.

❧ 40 ❧

"I very much appreciate your seeing me," said Molly, as Matthias let her inside his little house with the green door, only minutes after getting home from work.

"You're quite welcome," said Matthias, rather nervously. "Lawrence made it sound important."

Molly grinned at him. Since Lawrence had asked Matthias to talk to her, her friend was acknowledging that the secret was out (in his roundabout way) and she was glad to have no more secrets —and the fact that Lawrence's boyfriend worked at the coroner's office was icing on the cake, and chocolate buttercream at that.

Matthias was not looking so glad. He sat on the edge of the sofa, looking like he might feel a need to spring up and run at any moment. The furniture in his house was quirky and beautiful; in fact, the entire interior of the little house with the green door was not only lovely but so representative of Matthias and what an interesting person he was that Molly felt she had gotten to know him better simply by sitting in his living room for a few minutes.

"So, I just have one or two questions," she began. She could see she needed to go slowly so as not to startle him. "You picked up Benoît's body the day he died, I understand?"

"I did, yes."

"Had he been dead long?" Her voice gentle.

Matthias's eyes got wide. "I...can't say. For awhile, anyway. His body...wasn't warm. But it wasn't cold either."

"And Florian was there, to determine the time of death?"

"He wasn't, no."

"Was that unusual?"

"It was. Well, not precisely, no. I mean...I personally had not been involved in that part of the coroner's duties before, so strictly speaking, I can't answer any questions about what was usual or not." Matthias stood up and began to pace. "Molly, listen, I want to be helpful to you. Lawrence was telling me some of your accomplishments here in Castillac, and of course I knew your reputation already...you've done such good work, even as far away as Aix-en-Provence."

Molly heard the impending *but*, inwardly cursed, tried not to show it.

"But you've already asked me quite a lot of questions and I'm afraid that the sum of where those questions are headed is going to end with me losing my job. I don't want to make this all about me, but I've worked in the coroner's office for so many years, I wouldn't even know where to begin to find something else. So— regretfully—and respectfully—"

"Oh no," said Molly, her tone still calm but also forceful. "You will *not* be losing your job. Don't have a single worry about that, Matthias. You say you've been working in the coroner's office for so long—it's funny we haven't run into each other, isn't it? What exactly do you do there, if I may ask?"

Matthias looked terribly stressed. He took out a handkerchief and wiped his forehead; Molly thought she saw his hand trembling, ever so slightly. "For years I was doing tech support. IT stuff. You know—computers. But then, budget cut, the old story —so now I continue to do the tech side but also am sort of Florian's right hand. I go out with him when someone dies. Or at least, that is my current job description—as you know, there haven't been many deaths lately."

"None except for Benoît."

"Except for Benoît."

Molly thought for a moment. "Listen," she said, again making an effort to be gentle. "I think I see the situation: Florian, for some reason, wasn't where he was supposed to be on the day Benoît died. You filled in. And so the paperwork that got submitted—with time of death, cause of death, all of those banal details that we will all have describing us someday—was not written out by a seasoned coroner, but...by you? I say that simply to understand, not to get you in any hot water.

"And to be honest, on the face of it, it's Florian who could be in hot water, not you. *He* was the one missing in action, not you. But please understand—I have no interest at all in getting him *or* you into hot water. I'm not in favor of any hot water at all, either way! All I want—my only goal—is justice for Benoît LaRue. That is it, beginning and end."

"I want that too," said Matthias, so quietly she could barely hear him. "He was not my friend, he was a little older. But he was a kind-hearted soul, anyone could see that. Not that anyone is deserving of...well...if you're right about this...but he especially was not."

A long silence.

"Florian told me what to write," said Matthias, again, barely more than a whisper. "And at the time, it seemed...well, maybe not the usual thing, but nothing so terrible. I mean, you know Benoît's health history. It wasn't a suspicious death, not by any of the markers that we usually look to judge that. There was no reason to think—"

"You're right," said Molly. She reached over and patted his arm. "I don't think you missed anything. And I'm not criticizing Florian either. What the two of you did made perfect sense if you're looking at that particular day and that particular body."

"Then why....? Lawrence told me—well, it's common knowledge in the village, even for a hermit like me—that you have... suspicions. Where do the misgivings come from?"

Molly took in a breath and let it out, long and slow, to make sure she stayed calm. Matthias was coming around, she could feel it. As long as she didn't scare him off.

"It started when I heard about his history—which was before he died, actually. I assume you didn't know him? Here's a guy who, to listen to his friends describe him, was a happy fellow, a fun-loving, easy-going *mec*. Especially kind-hearted, as you yourself just said. Yet I overheard Angeline talking about how he'd been sickly for years, went to doctor after doctor, and they told him it's all in his head. We aren't talking about a neurotic person, someone whose nerves got the better of him, someone whose mind is fragile, or goes to dark places, or has any obvious mental or emotional infirmity at all. There's a big mismatch between the supposed diagnosis and who the patient actually was. To me, that's a red flag. An alarm."

Matthias slowly nodded. "Saying it's all in his head—sort of taking an easy way out, isn't it?"

"I believe so. The doctors didn't know why he was sick, so they blamed it on him. It was lazy, at the very least."

Matthias shook his head.

"I know a little about that because I had Lyme disease, and that's a condition that often gets the same sort of diagnosis. It presents with such a wide range of symptoms, and it's become a common illness only fairly recently—anyway, the details of all that don't matter. But it was my own history that made my ears prick up when I heard the same thing happening with Benoît. In my book, when someone says they feel ill, I believe that they feel ill, and aren't pretending. And the next step to take, for any serious medical person, would be to determine the *why*."

Matthias nodded, looking for all the world like a doomed man.

"So that brings us to how you, specifically, could help," said

Molly. "If I knew more about these symptoms, I might be able to link them up with the particular agent that killed him. Since I do not for one second believe it was a collapsing mental state that brought them on. I believe he was poisoned. I would bet anything on it, in fact."

"But I didn't know Benoît, I have no idea what his symptoms were."

"Not for his long illnesses, no. But I wondered, since you were the first and only person to arrive at what I believe was a crime scene, what you could tell me about that morning when you went to the LaRue's. How did he look, did Angeline say anything about the course of his final hours? What were your observations? Any detail, even something that seems insignificant..."

Matthias furrowed his brow. He was lanky and slender and did not look physically strong, and Molly felt an urge to protect him. She wished there were a way to keep him out of the whole mess. Gratefully, she listened as he described that fateful morning, the emotional state of the new widow, and the appearance of Benoît himself.

&.

"Oh, Matthias was helpful, all right. Not that he really wanted to be—or, that's not fair, it's just that in his case, being helpful comes with the possibility of real personal cost. Anyway. I really hope I can get this case resolved and that the irregularities at the coroner's office get swept under the rug in the finest bureaucratic tradition. Best thing for all concerned."

"You sound confident. So tell me, what did he give you?"

Molly was pacing back and forth in the kitchen.

"Ben, it was better than I could have imagined. Matthias is *observant*. He noticed everything. The look of things, the smell, the feel, the psychology—*everything*. He's the best witness you could ever have. First, he thought something was off about Angeline. Said her state of mind seemed to zigzag sort of wildly—one minute she was weeping, and the next, talking about some china she really likes, all animated and smiling, like she was five years old, it was Christmas morning, and she was about to open presents."

"But her husband had just died, only hours before. You wouldn't expect anyone to be acting normally at that moment."

Molly shrugged. "Maybe. But there's more. Matthias described how the bedsheets were soaking wet. How he could smell vomit. How Angeline had obviously made an effort to clean up but there was evidence of...well, let's just say the poor man was expelling from both ends."

Ben waited. Molly kept pacing.

"Now, before you object, I know that these symptoms aren't rare and even all of them together do not definitively lead to one and only one conclusion. It's not as though Matthias reported smelling bitter almonds which would mean cyanide. But...you know how I've been thinking that if Angeline poisoned her husband, the garden would be the logical place to look for those potions? What Matthias described fits oleander poisoning perfectly. The plant is very toxic, Chloe told me, and kills by over-stimulating the heart, producing the exact symptoms he described. The copious sweating and all the rest of it."

"Would an autopsy be able to find traces of oleander?"

"Yes. I believe it would. So there's more work to be done in the direction of Florian. Unfortunately, Florian has his own reasons for not wanting to do an exhumation that have nothing to do with the merits of the case. More on that later. Right now, I have to get over to Angeline's and see whether she has oleander growing in her garden. If she doesn't, this trail gets cooler. And if she does, I want to check to see if the shrub shows signs of recent cutting."

"I want to come with you."

Molly considered. "I don't know, Ben. I think Frances might

be better for this particular job. It's not like little Angeline is going to overpower me if she feels threatened. I don't think I'm in any danger from her, even though I have an idea she would love for me to think so."

"Frances?" Ben looked skeptical.

"Frances can chat the bark off a tree," said Molly. "So if Angeline is there and needs to be distracted while I have a look around, Frances is my girl. She might be able to literally put Angeline to sleep talking endlessly about her pregnancy," Molly added with a laugh.

Ben did not feel so sure.

41

"All I can say is, it's about time I got enlisted by Dufort/Sutton Investigations. All this time I've been sitting on the bench, wondering why the coach hasn't put me in," said Frances, putting on some roomy linen shorts with an elastic waist while Molly waited for her to finish dressing.

"Well, this is your moment then," said Molly. "Your special skills are exactly what is required."

"Tell me again? Give me the whole setup and what you're trying to accomplish. Spare no detail!"

"It's really not complicated," said Molly. "And listen—don't tell anyone about any of this, even Nico. The less information gets back to Angeline, the better."

"Lips are sealed!" said Frances, bubbling over with enthusiasm. "I'm suited up and ready!"

Frances looked effortlessly glamorous, as usual; somehow even her belly looked glamorous. Her skin was pale (as it always was) and glowing, her Cleopatra hair glossy and shining.

"Okay. All we're doing is strolling by Angeline's so I can get a good look at her garden. I need to see if she has any oleander bushes. It would be especially good if I could get up close to it to see if she's been taking cuttings. Your job is to distract Angeline, if she's there, or be a lookout, if she's not. Ideally I'll get to poke around in her garden and see if I can identify any of the other plants Chloe told me about. Did you know you can put cuttings of oleander in water, and make the water poisonous?"

"The things you know," said Frances, shaking her head.

"I just learned it. But I'll tell you, I'm not going to be looking at gardens the same way, with all the information I have now. Did you know even *azaleas* are poisonous?"

"Everybody knows that."

"You are a big fat liar."

"Indeed I am. But I am also a lieutenant at Dufort/Sutton Investigations, and ready for action!" Frances hopped from foot to foot, amazingly agile given her condition.

Molly laughed, wondering if including Frances was going to turn out to be a huge mistake.

Out on the street, Molly had to struggle to keep up with her, as Frances's enthusiasm propelled her down the street at a more rapid pace than Molly's short legs could match. In less than fifteen minutes, Angeline's cottage came into view.

"She's got some gorgeous roses, gotta give her that," said Frances.

It was true; a profusion of light and deep pinks, apricots, whites, a little touch of red here and there, not too much, spilled over the stone wall and some well-designed trellises—with a heady aroma that wafted to Molly and Frances before they reached the garden gate.

"Margot!" called Angeline, appearing suddenly just as Molly and Frances approached.

"Bonjour, Angeline," said Molly, caught a bit off guard.

"Margot?" said Frances, giving Molly the side-eye.

Molly shook her head slightly, trying to communicate to Frances to ignore this.

"Bonjour, Angeline," said Frances, nodding to Molly, her voice loud enough that the next block could hear. "Do you speak English? I speak French, my husband French. But I am a baby French talker, you understand? Anyway—" she pressed on, in French—"I admire this flowers very much. They pretty."

Angeline's eyes were wide but she did not budge from the gate, blocking their way.

Molly looked everywhere she could for an oleander bush but her view was compromised by the wall, by the roses, and by Angeline herself.

She figured flattery might work.

"Your roses are absolutely stunning," Molly started, and she could see right away that Angeline's expression softened and a small smile appeared. "Would you consider—we don't want to impose—but do you have time to give us a little tour of your garden? It looks like it's at the June peak and I'd love to admire it up close."

Angeline stood immobile, frozen with indecision.

"Your mother—she teach you the plants?" said Frances.

"My mother is dead," said Angeline, her smile vanishing.

"Me too!" blurted Frances.

"I'm sorry to hear that," said Molly. "Was it recent?"

"No," said Angeline. She crossed her arms.

Molly wanted to push through the gate and past Angeline but it was not yet the moment for that kind of force. Not yet. She waited, hoping Angeline would relent, but Angeline did not back down, and her small body was big enough to block them from coming through the gate unless they were willing to knock into her.

"Oh well, I'm sure you've got all kinds of things to attend to," said Molly. "Nice to see you." She moved along, reaching for Frances's hand. They walked slowly, looking over the wall at what they could see, complimenting the garden loud enough for Angeline to hear.

Angeline leaned out to watch them. She felt an itchy heat

rising up from her belly, to her chest and then up her neck. As though her blood were about to boil.

She knows, Angeline thought, in agony.

She knows, she knows, she knows.

⁂

AFTER THEY TURNED a corner and were out of view, Frances went back to hopping from one foot to the other, excited as a child. "Well? How'd I do? My maiden voyage as an investigator! I think I was magnificent. Did you think I was magnificent? I know, the language thing gets in the way a bit. But I don't think she even noticed! And listen, I have no idea what an oleander bush looks like, did you see one?"

Molly, as she so often did when around Frances, laughed. "What did you think of her?"

Frances shrugged. "Hard to say. Not very welcoming, that's for sure. I'd say...she looked anxious. Worried."

"Not grieving?"

"No."

"Me neither."

They walked a ways, Frances patting her belly, Molly thinking about Benoît drinking a glass of oleander water. Did Angeline put a sprig of mint in it to disguise any taste?

"And so?" said Frances.

"What?"

"Oleander, Molly! The whole reason for that mission. Did you see it? What does it even look like?"

"Didn't see any. It's not hard to recognize, though I don't think it would be blooming yet. The leaves are a nice spear shape, a smoky light green, not glossy."

"We didn't really get a good look. The garden goes back a ways, there was a lot we couldn't see at all."

"Yes. And...this doesn't make me happy, but I guess there's no reason the oleander absolutely has to be in Angeline's yard anyway. All that's required is that she have access to it somewhere, which would mean if it's here in Castillac, she could sneak over to make some cuttings..."

"Now *that* is a dispiriting thought."

"It really is." Molly rubbed her brow as though to ease a headache. "Just a few hours ago, I was feeling on the brink of figuring this out..."

"Look, Castillac is not that big. I can go home, look up oleander on the net, make sure I know what it looks like, and check out the whole village. I'm so horribly antsy lately, walking around will be the perfect thing for me."

"Would you really? That seems like a big job."

"Well, I'll want a badge. I can't be running all over town when I haven't been properly deputized."

"I'll see what I can do. I think if you see any oleanders, they're likely to be against a wall, or in a protected spot. They don't like a lot of cold."

"Ok, I'm on it! I'll scamper home this minute and get googling. Even if I go into labor, neither snow, nor rain, nor darkness shall keep me from my appointed task!"

"That's some dedication," said Molly, feeling a twinge of regret at involving her friend. "You're not on the verge of labor, are you? Don't you have a few months left?"

"Yes, but you never know. She might be bored in there."

Molly laughed. "OK, thanks, pal."

In a flash, Frances was around a corner and out of sight, and Molly was left alone with her disappointment. It felt as though she had seen the oleander in Angeline's yard so clearly —her imagination had made it absolutely real so that all she had to do was stroll up and see where Angeline had snipped cuttings, take a few photos, and the whole case would be done and dusted. She and Frances saw almost all of the garden from the sidewalk, looking over the wall. It felt perhaps over-optimistic to think an oleander was tucked someplace just out of view.

It wasn't back to the drawing board, not yet. The vision of that bush was still too real—but maybe it was in someone else's yard.

And in the meantime, why not pay a visit on her old friend Florian Nagrand before heading home.

❧

"But what's your objection to letting me see the full report?" she said to Florian, whose face was sweating more than usual.

"My objection, Madame Sutton, is that you are a resident of Castillac and that is all. You are not attached to the coroner's office in any way, no matter how much you wish it were so. You are not part of the family, the gendarmerie, or a lawyer involved with the case, or have any other connection that you might attempt to dream up. You have nothing to do with it, full stop, and you will not be pawing through the paperwork of things that do not concern you. No. You will not. Just let it go."

Molly sat down in the chair in front of Florian's desk, causing him to close his eyes and rub his hand over his face. She glanced over at Matthias but he had been studiously avoiding any eye contact and adjusted his computer screen to hide his face entirely.

"Well, I was just wondering whether there might be some… ah…irregularities with the paperwork," she said amiably.

"What sort of irregularities? What are you implying?"

Molly shrugged. "Nothing. Just wondering. Tell me, does it happen very often that a cause of death has to be adjusted?"

"That is the kind of question I am in no mood to indulge." Florian stood up. "Good day, Madame Sutton. Lovely to see you, as it always, always is."

Molly enjoyed teasing Florian but she felt a little worn out from Frances and not finding the oleander, so she stood up to leave. "Good to see you, Matthias," she said. "And Florian, just to be one hundred percent clear: I am telling you right now that Angeline LaRue poisoned her husband, and all you have to do to set things right is dig him up and run a few tests. I can see several reasons why you wouldn't want to do that. But I suggest you think about whether your situation will be improved if yet more time goes by and you end up being forced into doing so.

"No matter how much people want to sweep this under the rug, I don't think anyone wants a killer to get away with murder. Do they? Do you? I don't think so," she said lightly, and let the door bang on her way out.

42

"So what's the day look like," Ben asked on Saturday morning, Changeover Day.

"Well, Selma Throckmorton has pretty much moved in. I don't think she's ever going to leave, and she's left a note saying she doesn't want any cleaning. So that's the pigeonnier taken care of. Two students will be staying in the annex, but only for two nights, and a family of five in the cottage. The, uh, what are their names again? The Wallaces, from somewhere in the midwest. Iowa, I think. They'll all get here when they get here, we don't need to pick anyone up. Constance is going to do all the cleaning, I checked with her about that already. I have to go into the village—"

Ben smiled, rather a tight smile. "Mm?"

"When I last saw Edmond, he was...behaving oddly. Even for him."

"How so?"

"At first I thought he was mad at me for some reason. Then finally—and I had to press him—he told me he wants me to stay far away from Angeline. But he wouldn't say why. 'He's heard some things' was about all I could get out of him."

"And you think you might give it another go, see what he meant?"

"Well, yeah. What things, is the obvious question. Angeline's past is murky—which doesn't have to be suspicious, she didn't grow up here. But also it means she doesn't have the history that you and the villagers have with each other, where you know, more or less, what people are made of, what their character is. Angeline is a question mark."

Ben nodded. "And the danger—as you well know—is that people will just fill in the gaps with their imaginations. They'll take some little thing and make it into something it's not. I don't mean intentionally, it's just how humans are."

""I'm aware."

"Molly! Don't be insulted. I was just talking, not instructing. I know you know."

"Oh, don't mind me. I've been a little on edge lately, a little overly emotional."

"Well, I hope you can get something out of him. He's so besotted with you, I'm sure you can work some magic."

She grinned at him. "Hope so. I thought about doing a simple apèro tonight, to welcome all the new people. You up for it?"

Ben shrugged. He would always rather be reading a naval history in bed than making small talk with people he'd just met. But he was, thankfully, adaptable. "Whatever you want," he said, pulling his wife into his arms and giving her a smooch on the lips.

❧

MOLLY PASSED CONSTANCE riding her bike on rue de Chêne and gave her a wave, her mind already filled with visions of almond croissants, and who could imagine what seasonal delights Edmond might have on that beautiful June morning?

It was a good thing she had pastry to occupy her mind, since the case of Benoît LaRue seemed, even to her unusually optimistic self, once again on the verge of stalling out completely. This idea of intuition, so derided by most of the world—and possibly especially by the French, who revered Descartes and "I think, therefore I am," which was assuredly not "I have this feeling, and so I'm going to trust it"—was something Molly had secretly come to appreciate deeply. It was not a perfect indicator, but she had begun to wonder whether its imperfections had more to do with her imperfect attention to it than the intuition itself.

These were the kind of thoughts Molly tended to have while speeding the scooter over hill and dale, and she was so focused on them that she missed a turn and had to go back to get to Patisserie Bujold.

What's troubling, she thought, is how clear that intuitive vision of the oleander was. It didn't feel like I made a reasonable hypothesis and that hypothesis turned out to be incorrect. It was that I *saw* the bush in Angeline's yard, saw it as clearly as if I were standing right in front of it, could see the green spear-shaped leaves, clear as day. Could almost but not quite see the vase filled with water that held the cuttings. She supposed the bush could be tucked away in a corner not visible from the street. All was not lost, not quite.

With a sigh she hopped off the scooter and locked it outside the pastry shop. Once inside she realized she had misjudged—it was market day, of course the shop would be crowded and there would be no chance for her to grill Edmond about the gossip about Angeline. She took her place in the long line; she was well back from the display case and couldn't see what was inside, so she employed her usual hobby of eavesdropping, just for something to do while she waited.

Molly closed her eyes.

"...when will the strawberries come in? They are *so* late this year—"

"—realized that chocolate gives me a headache every time I eat it. But honestly, give up chocolate? I am not Superman."

Molly snickered at that.

"—Angeline—"

Molly leaned closer but did not get any of the rest. Dammit, she said to herself, stepping a little too close to the woman in front of her, and getting an elbow in return.

"Molly," said Edmond, when it was finally her turn.

"Nice to see you, Edmond," said Molly. "Six almond croissants, please. Two of those tarts with blueberries and kiwi. A Napoleon." She paused, wondering what would please Ben. "And a coffee eclair." Edmond used tongs to put the croissants in a bag, and the rest into a white cardboard box which he tied with white string.

"I want to talk," she said, in a low enough voice that other customers would not hear. "We're having an apèro tonight, can you come?"

Edmond's face was a demonstration of how awkward it can be when a person feels pleasure and agony at the same time. He adored Molly and would not miss an apèro at La Baraque for the world. And at the same time, the very last thing he wanted to do was have any sort of conversation about Angeline LaRue, which he guessed was on the menu for the evening.

❧ 43 ❧

"For someone who's only lived in Castillac for what, less than five years—and can that really be so? You sure know a lot of people," said Lawrence, looking out at the throng assembling for Molly's Saturday night apèro.

"I sort of kept inviting people I saw this morning at the market," Molly answered, talking with her hand in front of her mouth so no one could lip-read. "And I told them to bring friends if they wanted. Look, isn't that Dr. Boulet over there?"

"Molly!"

"No worries, no worries, I promise not to grill him. At least not where anyone can see. Heh heh."

Lawrence rolled his eyes but Molly gave his arm a squeeze and went over to Ben, who was inundated at the drinks table with a lot of apparently very thirsty guests.

"Can you grab some bottles from the back closet?" he said, juggling bottles and cups.

Molly saluted and went inside, where a gaggle of strangers were looking into her refrigerator.

"Can I help you?" Molly said, more amused than annoyed.

"Oh!" said a woman with an American accent. "Do you live here? We heard—"

"Yes, this is my place. Welcome. You're visiting Castillac?"

"Actually no, we came up from Bergerac because we heard there was going to be this epic party—"

Molly laughed. Really, the ability of Castillacois to transmit information was a constant amazement.

"Okay, welcome! Would one of you come with me a moment?" A young man raised his hand and followed Molly down the hall to the back closet, where Molly filled his arms with bottles of Malbec and told him where to take them.

She went into her bedroom for a moment and closed the door, wanting a moment to think. It pleased her to have the garden at La Baraque filled with guests, but for just a moment she was a little overwhelmed—that feeling she'd been having lately of too many emotions coming on at once. So she stood just inside the bedroom and let the noise of the party flow over her, for once not thinking about murder, or Angeline LaRue, or really anything at all.

&a.

"WHAT IN THE world are you doing in here?" said Frances, her belly coming through the bedroom door before the rest of her. "I've been looking all over for you. Quite a bash, Molls, quite a bash. You make me feel twenty-two again."

"Ha. Happy to oblige. You know, I have to tell you—yet again —you're looking really good. Your face is so bright! I think you're going to want another baby right after having this one." Molly had a sly look as she teased her friend, but to her surprise the teasing did not land.

"I just might, who knows?" said Frances.

Molly's eyes got very wide.

"Listen, you never got me that badge and I was dead serious

about that, but I'll give you my report anyway, since we're alone for a sec," said Frances. "I schooled myself on what an oleander looks like. I would say at this point I know the oleander intimately. Whatever did we do before the internet?"

"Wander around in ignorance," said Molly. "Ok, don't keep up the suspense, did you find any?"

"I didn't go into Angeline's garden because she was home, so that's still your number one with a bullet. But I did cover the entire rest of the village, and I mean every single nook and cranny, and even in a village as small as this, that is a *lot* of nooks and crannies."

Molly nodded encouragingly.

"So there I was, going up and down and over and across, covering every last street and alley. I did a fair amount of trespassing, too. Most of the gardens you can see pretty well from the street, but there were a few with, as I said, nooks and crannies that looked big enough to hide an oleander, so I sneaked right in and got a good look. Good thing I'm pretty quick on my feet because these days visually I am not exactly easy to miss." Frances grinned.

"And?"

"I can say with certainty that the only oleander in all of Castillac—apart from Angeline's, which as I mentioned is still a question mark—resides at 86 rue Montfort. And lest you think I am not a worthy member of the Dufort/Sutton Investigation team, I did not simply note the address but went home and used that crazy internet again to find out whose house it was."

Molly loved Frances, loved her like a sister. But she could be exhausting.

"And?"

"It belongs to one Delphus McDougal. I venture a guess that he is not French," Frances added with a snort.

"Curious," said Molly. "I met them both at Lapin's—Angeline and Delphus—just in the last few weeks. That has to be coincidence though, right? And I guess…I assumed that strolling by Angeline's would be good enough to spot an oleander, if she had one. But like you say, maybe it's in a nook or cranny of her garden, and I'm losing heart over nothing?"

"That's the spirit! You want to sneak over there right this minute and have a look-see?"

"I've got a few guests."

"Eh, there are so many, nobody will notice you're gone! Or maybe Angeline has been snipping from Delphus's bush, so we can make a closer inspection of that." Frances started hopping from one foot to another again.

"So this is your new thing? Frantic hopping?"

"Hahahaha—I know, what's gotten into me? Remember those Mexican jumping beans we used to get as kids? That's what I feel like. If I can't be on the move, I don't know, I get uncomfortable."

"This is from the pregnancy?"

"Who knows? At least it's better than heartburn."

"Okay, well—thanks for all that work, Frances, you've really raised my spirits. I'm going to go join the party and give Ben a hand."

"Got any other jobs for me? I mean, I'd be working without a badge (*hint hint*) but surely there's someone here I can chat up for Dufort/Sutton Investigations. Who do you need information from? Who can I squeeze like an old sponge?"

Molly laughed. "Just enjoy yourself. Hop around and talk to whomever you like. I'm not going to be working either."

They both knew that was not true, but they simply put their arms around each other and went outside, into the fray.

THE YARD between the main house and the cottage was jammed with people, only some of whom Molly recognized. She managed to spot the Wallaces and checked in with them; their five children were tearing through the crowd, enjoying themselves immensely, so the parents were happy too. She craned her neck looking for the students staying in the annex but didn't see them.

And then she recognized the back of someone familiar. It was a wide back, the hair too long and not exactly lush, wearing a linen sport coat which struck Molly as unusual. She moved quickly to catch up with him. But just as she opened her mouth to speak, the man grasped the shoulders of none other than Selma Throckmorton, and kissed her heartily on both cheeks.

Not just heartily, thought Molly, completely and utterly surprised. *Lustfully*.

Florian and Selma were *an item?*

Molly backed up, stepping on the foot of a young man she did not know. She made apologies and turned to find Ben.

"Good heavens!" she said, when she got to him. "You look like you've been in combat."

Ben wiped his brow with his sleeve. "A few people showed up," he said. "But we'll be out of alcohol within the half hour, so I expect we'll see some thinning of the multitudes."

"I'm surprised we lasted this long."

"The gougères were gone in the blink of an eye."

"You're not going to believe—oh look, there's Dr. Boulet! Back in a minute," she said, gone before Ben could try to talk her out of...whatever it was she was up to.

Thankfully, Dr. Boulet had moved to the edge of the crowd so there was space for Molly to approach without squeezing in too close to other people . "Bonsoir, Dr. Boulet," she said, sticking out a hand. "I'm Molly Sutton, *propriétaire* of this bedlam!"

"*Enchanté*," said the doctor, though Molly could see he was considerably less than enchanted, and wished he were talking to someone—anyone—else.

"Your reputation precedes you," he said, with what Molly thought might be an ironic bow.

"I came to see you last week actually," she said. "No, no, I'm feeling just fine. But I wanted to talk to you about—"

"—Benoît LaRue. I know. If ever a secret has been kept in this village, I've never known it to be so. I wish you had come, Molly, so that I could give you the facts of the situation and put your mind at ease. I do understand your wish for justice—we are not in the same line of work, but I think we share something of an impulse to do good, am I correct? So I do not want you to think I am criticizing you for asking questions. The way some might."

Molly nodded, rather enjoying watching the doctor spin a line of bull-merde.

"I was Benoît's doctor for many years. I consulted with the various specialists he went to see—Angeline was diligent in taking him around to anyone who might help, even as far as Bordeaux—and no one knows his case more intimately than I. And so I am pleased to be able to tell you that Benoît LaRue died because the instabilities in his mind led to instabilities in his body, and eventually the damage was too much—systemically, affecting multiple organs—and he sadly expired. I want to assure you that everything that could be done was done, and there was nothing further anyone could do. I will add that Angeline went above and beyond for years trying to help him, to cheer him up, to shift that very stubborn belief he had that he was sick and weak."

Molly smiled at him. She nodded.

"Angeline was the very picture of devotion throughout," he added, giving Molly a stern look.

Molly could well imagine Angeline in the role, and how she must have enjoyed playing it.

"She shouldered the burden of her husband's illness without a single complaint. And, as I said, took him to see anyone who might possibly be able to help. So it is, you understand, something of a...how to put it...clash with reality?...for anyone to cast aspersions on Angeline LaRue, of all people." The doctor raised his chin in order to literally look down his nose at Molly.

But Molly, as usual, was undeterred. She had the learned the French for "aspersions" and was amused by how many in the village kept using the word.

"Thank you for that, Dr. Boulet. I appreciate your sharing it with me. Do you need a refresher?" she asked, pointing to his glass.

"Oh, no. Only one glass for me and then it's off to bed. Thank you for inviting me, it was lovely to meet the famous Molly Sutton at last."

You're such a bad liar, Molly thought, still smiling. He showed up merely to make that speech which he believed covered his behind in case Benoît died of something other than the good doctor diagnosed. Not that it hasn't been a pleasure, she thought, shaking her head and rolling her eyes both at once, as the good doctor moved away into the crowd.

❦

MOLLY ADMITTED to herself that she *would* like to slip away and give Angeline's garden a once-over that second. She regretted not inviting her—it would have been perfect: between Frances and Constance, they could have kept Angeline busy while Molly darted over to the garden on her scooter and did an inspection. It was still light out at 9:30; if there was an oleander there, she would have been able to spot it, and return to the party quickly.

She wondered what oleander smelled like. The internet said it smelled good but smell is something words do almost nothing to express.

She wondered if Benoît knew the smell, whether it was a smell he regularly smelled. Did Angeline start with a very low dose and work her way up to the fatal one? How had the mechanics of the years-long poisonings taken place? A little here, a little there, or did she have a more thought-out plan?

The conversation with Dr. Boulet had only made her more

certain of her hypothesis. He wanted Molly to look silly. He wanted to embarrass her. She had no doubt he was talking to anyone who would listen about these silly embarrassments, all so that his own long neglect of Benoît and incuriosity about the causes of his symptoms would not come to light.

So many people, so many hidden motivations.

Molly stood apart from the crowd, feeling none of her usual urge to jump in and socialize. She felt tired and ready for bed. And even though Ben had been correct and the dearth of wine had caused the crowd to begin to diminish—she had the feeling that this party still had some legs.

MOLLY REMEMBERED A CASE OF RED—CHEAP, but in France, of course even the cheap wine is good—that was stashed in the annex, and went to ask Ben if she should get it. She passed Edmond on the way but he saw her coming and hid behind a shrub, pretending he was interested in its flowerbuds.

"Maybe we should just let this thing die a natural death," said Ben. "I think I've seen more new faces tonight than I have in the last year altogether." He stood up and stretched from side to side. "I sound like an old man, but I am ready for bed."

"Same," said Molly. "It—oh my God, it's *Angeline!*" She clapped her hand over her mouth, having said that last bit too loud. She pointed with an elbow and sure enough, Ben could see Angeline LaRue talking to several people, smiling and waving her hands animatedly, looking as though she didn't have a care in the world.

Molly went straight over and thanked her for coming.

Angeline made excuses to the people she'd been talking to (Molly didn't recognize them) and took Molly's arm, leading her away for some privacy.

"It certainly appears to be a great success," she said, her face flushed.

"What?"

"Your party! I heard about it from Paul-Henri Monsour, your special friend at the gendarmerie, I believe? And really I can't thank you enough for doing it."

Molly was baffled. What did Paul-Henri have to do with anything? What is she talking about, special friend? And those questions were only the beginning.

"I..." Molly tried to formulate a sentence, any sentence, but so many questions and feelings were running around in her head that all she managed was standing there with her mouth open. "I welcome you," she said finally, inwardly cringing.

"I don't let a little thing like being suspected of murder get in the way of friendship," said Angeline, smiling sweetly.

She spoke with such smoothness, her words totally absent of malice or vindictiveness or anything but powdered sugar with perhaps a taste of caramel.

Molly blinked. She returned to herself, not wholly, but enough. If this was how Angeline wanted to play it, all right: she was in. All the way.

"Something we have in common is a love of gardening," Molly said. "Oh I know—to look around the garden here at La Baraque you wouldn't know it!" She made a convincingly self-deprecating chuckle. "I'm a little stuck in the planning stage, if you understand what I mean? I look at gardening catalogs endlessly and admire so many different plants and styles of garden that I haven't been able to commit."

"I understand, though I myself have no problem with commitment. I suppose it's just my nature—when I decide to do a thing, I go all out until that thing is accomplished."

Molly looked at her carefully.

"No matter what anyone else might think," Angeline added. "And no matter what the risk."

"What about microclimate?" asked Molly. "Is your garden—

because of building placement, trees, whatever—a bit warmer than the usual around here?"

Angeline shrugged.

"It allows for so much more variety, don't you think, when you have that extra bit of warmth?"

Again Angeline shrugged. She started looking over Molly's shoulder at the crowd.

"I wonder, Angeline, if your beautiful garden contains any oleander—semi-tropical, as I'm sure you know. You see them so often farther south."

Molly thought she saw Angeline's face turn a shade paler. She wasn't sure.

Angeline tapped her pink manicured forefinger on her chin. "Let's see, oleander, oleander. Pretty pink flowers, I believe?"

Molly nodded. She wished this exchange was on video, because no one was going to believe it.

"I think I do have one," she said, pointing that finger at Molly. "You will have to pay me a visit, and come to see it." And with that, she said it was past her bedtime and she regretfully needed to get home. She thanked Molly again—just short of profusely—and her small figure was swallowed up by the crowd, who must have been hoping more bottles and gougères would appear but who were going to be sorely disappointed.

The sun was just beginning to peek in the window that Sunday morning, but Molly and Ben were awake—in bed, but awake—discussing the party and Angeline's appearance while having their first cup of coffee.

"All right, it's bold, but here goes," said Molly, after Ben had again expressed some doubt about Angeline's guilt. "I say this: if we ever get far enough down this road to be able to say that Angeline has been proven to be one hundred percent innocent, I will resign from Dufort/Sutton Investigations and hang up my detective hat completely and forevermore. *That* is how certain I am."

"Wow. I do give your certainty some weight, you know that."

"I do. I'm not really pushing back against you. It's the people who have various reasons for taking the position I am wrong that have zero to do with actual guilt or innocence. Dr. Boulet, for starters. Obviously he has an interest in protecting his reputation. And I imagine he's not the best at accepting he's made a mistake, either. Arrogant, patronizing—I'm not a fan. His opinion is hardly objective."

"Just between you and me, I never liked him either. Who else?"

"None other than Florian Nagrand himself! If Benoît had died under the usual circumstances—by which I mean, the coroner doing his job the way he was supposed to—Florian might well have discovered the poisoning himself. Or at the very least, he would have been open to hearing my thoughts about it—he doesn't altogether loathe me, though he likes to pretend he does. Yet he was mysteriously out of the office on the day Benoît died. Which just so happened to be after Selma Throckmorton came to La Baraque. The same Selma Throckmorton who keeps extending her stay, who doesn't want anyone coming into the pigeonnier, who has been swanning around in apparently glorious spirits all the time...in short, *who is in love.*"

"With *Florian?*" Ben's skepticism made Molly hoot with laughter.

"Yes indeed, with Florian. There's someone for everyone, that's what somebody smart used to say. I saw him greet her last night. Hilarious because he was trying so hard to play it cool, like they were only acquaintances, when it was a thousand percent obvious they are besotted with each other. *Besotted!*"

Ben laughed and pulled Molly closer. They lay in contented quiet for some time, sipping coffee as the sun rose higher.

"One thing's been nagging at me," said Ben. "You know I grew up with Benoît. He was genuinely a kind-hearted, decent man. Not rich, or anywhere close to it. So what are your thoughts about motive? Why would his wife want to kill him? If it was simply a matter of falling out of love, or growing apart, or something like that—why not just divorce him and move on?"

"You say that as though murderers are as reasonable as non-murderers."

Ben shrugged. "I don't think you can say they're all insane, though. I can't say what psychological issues Angeline may or may not have, but to kill a person because you're just evil through and through and enjoy doing it—I don't believe there are so many of those types among us. Much, much more common for a husband to be murdered because he was cheating, or rich, or abusive. Most often, wives murder their husbands for *reasons*, Molly. So what, in this case, could those reasons be? That is what I've been asking myself."

Molly sat up, the coffee in her belly feeling like it had curdled somehow.

"Lawrence asked this same thing—why kill the nicest man alive, according to all who knew him? And all I say can to that is... I don't know. I've been wondering the same. And I agree that it's less likely she killed for the pure joy of it than for reasons. I've just been trying to prove the act itself, hoping that the reason will come to light somehow along the way."

"But so far..."

"...it hasn't."

BEN SKIPPED breakfast and went off to his surveillance job, and Molly, after thinking about the chutzpah Angeline showed by coming to the apèro the night before, decided to be just as brave herself. She would go over to Angeline's, let herself in through the gate, and have a look around that garden whether Angeline was there or not. If Angeline wanted to come outside and challenge her, all right then, let her try.

It was not enough to know whether an oleander was growing in Angeline's yard. Molly needed to see evidence that the shrub had been pruned, or leaves plucked. Even dirt disturbed around the base opened the possibility of some roots removed.

All of the *Nerium oleander* was poisonous: leaf, stem, branch, root, flower.

It wasn't as though she had to be afraid of tiny Angeline, despite her murdering ways, thought Molly. Though the pink manicure somehow figured into Molly's threat assessment, which perhaps it should not have.

NELL GODDIN

Poor Bobo looked mournful at not getting a walk through the woods, and Molly felt a pang of guilt as she gave her a quick scratch behind the ears and hopped on the scooter. Rue de Chêne was quiet, the village peaceful. The bells at the church rang, setting off a flock of birds. No one on the streets.

A block away from Angeline's, Molly parked and locked up the scooter. She walked down the sidewalk with more confidence than she actually felt, not used to trespassing with quite so much advance intent, and not really wanting any kind of confrontation. But when she reached the gate, she opened it without hesitation, and walked quickly to the back of the garden in case Angeline was looking out of a window.

The roses were indeed superb. Molly felt almost drunk with their perfume as she walked down a narrow pathway of grass, roses on either side in full bloom. Then a long bed of perennials, also in full June regalia—peonies, irises—but so far, no shrubs of any kind.

Molly swallowed hard. She remembered that Delphus McDougal had an oleander so even if nothing was here, her theory was not quite dead yet.

And then she rounded the corner at the bottom of the garden, and saw, against the brick wall on the far side where it would benefit from reflected warmth: an oleander. And it was innocently in bloom, a cloud of pink blossoms.

I knew it!

Glancing toward the cottage, Molly ran to the bush. If Angeline had been taking cuttings, there would be signs of those cuts. Molly started at the top of the shrub—it was about three and a half feet tall and across—and worked her way down, inspecting every branch, every twig, every everything.

She reached the bottom. She found no evidence of cutting at all. Not so much as a leaf missing. She looked again, starting at the bottom and working her way up, achingly slowly, moving from one side to another and even moving partway into the bed to look at the backside of the plant.

Nothing.

A handful of flowers were no longer on their peduncles but Molly saw them sitting innocently on the dirt underneath where they had fallen naturally. She counted them; all there. She knelt on the grass and inspected every single twig to see if there were any missing blossoms...but there were none.

She got a sharp pang of anxiety then, as though—what exactly?—she had stepped into a trap? That Angeline had wanted her to come see this oleander, to see that she had done nothing, was innocent after all?

No, Molly thought, simply. *No.*

She hurried out of the garden and back to the scooter, hoping her visit had gone undetected.

Glum does not come close to describing her mood as she drove to Delphus McDougal's, not speeding, feeling sick to her stomach, exhausted, and at a complete loss for what to do next if his oleander was also completely unmolested.

❧ IV ❦

❧ 45 ❧

1972

It was—in Angeline's memory, the childhood days were all this way, no matter the season—cold and gray, with only dimmed light filtering through the small windows. She was huddled next to the fire. She was a little too old for toys, and so she sat looking into the flames and listening to the stories her parents told.

Her mother was a good storyteller. And on that particular cold, gray morning, she had a real head of steam going, and put a great deal of energy and feeling into the story she was telling Angeline's father, even though it was far from the first time she had told it. Angeline sensed the emotion and it felt as though it poured from her mother straight into her, as though the story itself became part of her in some way.

Anne had been working as an aide to a midwife; she did this job for many years though it paid little. Martine, the midwife she was attached to, for the most part attended women without a lot of money, and sometimes payment was in milk or eggs, once in eggplants. One night, they were seeing to a woman who had been living far from their village. Anne was not certain of where—not

237

then—but the woman's family was local, and when she discovered she was going to have a baby, with no father stepping forward to marry or otherwise take care of her—the woman had come home, where her mother would be able to look after her.

If it survived, the baby was going to be given up for adoption, that was never in question.

None of the story, up to that point, was at all out of the ordinary. Babies come into the world without married parents; it was perhaps not optimal but it was commonplace. Anne remembered thinking how lucky it was for the young woman, that she had parents who welcomed her home and were anxious to do what they could for their daughter, instead of casting her out or shaming her or anything of that sort, even though keeping the baby themselves was not an option because their health was in decline.

The labor had not been an easy one. The baby was large, its heartbeat rather hesitant, and the mother had a slight build and narrow hips. Martine told Anne to be ready for a long night, and as usual, the midwife was correct.

Anne was not naturally a caretaker; that is, she was not a person with gifts of empathy, or an ability to put people at ease and comfort them. Her best qualification for midwifery was that she did not quail at the sight of blood or at any other bodily excrescence, and she did not feel faint or lose heart when things went very wrong, which they sometimes did despite the talent and best efforts of this particular midwife. Anne did her best to comfort the woman, but her best was, to be strictly honest, not so good. The woman was in agony and there was little the two women attending her could do that seemed to ease her pain.

At one point, in the middle of the long night, Martine left the room in order to get some herbs that were boiling in the kitchen downstairs. Anne was alone with the struggling mother, patting her arm and wiping her forehead, and frankly long past the moment when the whole affair had become tiresome for her, and she was looking forward to the end (whatever that turned out to be) and going home at last.

But the door had barely closed behind Martine when the mother's eyes grew wide and she took Anne's hands in hers and clutched them tightly.

"I have to tell you," she murmured. Her voice was not strong but Anne could understand her clearly.

And—a story within a story—this is what the woman related, in between contractions, with tears pouring from her eyes, to the first annoyed and then astonished Anne:

She took care of the children. She loved the little girl and the two little boys like they were her own.

The family was rich. Beyond rich. In politics, with powerful friends. The château was beautiful, not a cold fortress but a warm and grand place to live. There were parties, important meetings, celebrations, backroom deals affecting the entire country, dinners for thirty or forty or sixty people with gold-rimmed Limoges china and so much wine it would make a river. It was a house of much abundance, liveliness, excitement...and power. And she was there, on the fringe of it, playing her own small part.

It seemed like the best job in the whole world.

Except.

The noble family included a grown son. He was off in Paris much of the time and visited rarely. One weekend, he came home. She noticed he was looking at her in a way she did not like—well, truthfully, for a brief moment she deluded herself into believing that maybe he was falling in love with her and she would end up being in the center of this influential family; she got far enough along in this fantasy that she decided she would not hire anyone to look after their children but happily raise them herself.

That was a daydream, a short-lived daydream.

The son came into the nursery just after the children had been put to bed. He smelled of drink and had not bathed in quite some time. She noticed that his fingernails were long and sharp, as were his eyeteeth. He said...unkind things, things you have (hopefully) never heard a person say to another person.

She tried to get away. She tried distracting him, diverting him, tried to feint one way and then dart for the door.

But despite his drunkenness, he was quick. He got her by the arm and then grasped both of her arms so tightly that she had purple marks for weeks in the shape of his fingers.

He forced himself upon her.

This child is his, the woman told Anne. This child is a de la Chabelle. The family didn't even bother denying it. They treated me like a...like an annoying impertinence. Banished me—swatted me away like a fly, a worthless nothing. But my baby does not deserve that. You hear me?

My baby does not deserve that.

✣ 46 ✣

When Ben got back from surveillance he found Molly pacing in the kitchen, as usual waiting for water to boil for more coffee.

"Did something happen?" he asked, looking wary.

"Oh, Ben, I'm just—I don't know what to think. Part of my brain is so insistent that Angeline did this, but the other part is saying well, if that were really true, you'd have found some evidence. And...there is no evidence that I can find. And I have run out of places to look."

Her voice broke and Ben hurried over to wrap his arms around her.

"I went over there," she told him. "There *is* an oleander in Angeline's yard, I wasn't wrong about that. But I looked that thing over with a fine tooth comb, multiple times, and I would be forced to swear that nobody has taken anything—not a leaf, a shred of bark, a flower, much less a cutting—from that bush, maybe ever. It's not a mature plant but it has been happily growing undisturbed next to that brick wall, and nobody has paid it any attention at all."

Ben tried and failed to smooth Molly's hair. "I'm sorry."

"I'm struggling to let it go even though I saw with my own eyes that she cannot have used that bush to make any poisonous concoction. I checked the only other oleander in the village as well, over at Delphus McDougal's."

"People will think you've developed a mad passion for gardening."

"Well, I *am* passionate about gardening," she said. "I just somehow don't get around to it as much as I want to. The thing is —there could be other agents she used. I settled on oleander because the symptoms of that poisoning matched up with what Matthias reported about Benoît's last hours. I suppose I could look through my notes from Chloe and see if there is something else I could track down.

"But the thing is—oleander was my first and most logical choice for several reasons: it's a perennial, and big enough that if she wanted to get rid of it, it would be more difficult than something like Star of Bethlehem which you could pull up and throw on the compost heap and it would disappear completely in a week or two. Getting rid of the oleander would leave a gap in the garden *and* it would take time to decompose in the compost heap. Though I suppose she could have simply driven out into the country and tossed it in a ditch. It's so easy to get attached to a scenario without realizing it's far from the only possibility. It's a wonder we ever solve any murders at all.

"Plus—the symptoms matched *so* perfectly. I really thought I had it nailed. It was my best bet," she finished, mournfully. "And now what? People keep warning me off this case, and I thought they were trying to scare me because they were frightened by Angeline—when the truth is, they realized I was talking nonsense. Maybe I did just cook this up out of nothing."

Ben said nothing. He put a hand on her shoulder.

"But I don't think so," Molly said, very softly.

❦ 47 ❦

Leon Garnier had been getting to the office later and later in the mornings, hoping to avoid Angeline, whose visits thus far had been right at the moment the office was supposed to open. So on that Monday—after spending the weekend continually thinking about Angeline and becoming increasingly anxious—he came into work at nearly eleven o'clock, grateful at least that he worked alone and there was no one to see how late he was.

His working life, spanning over decades, had been easy-going and for the most part satisfying. Leon liked having paperwork organized, liked writing checks to people when they had undergone some loss of person or property, liked walking to work and settling in at his desk, liked the routine of breaking for lunch and making a few calls and maintaining the files and the office in good order.

He had not encountered a situation such as this before, where he felt an almost physical abhorrence at doing his duty, which was clearly spelled out in the signed contract. Benoît LaRue had paid his insurance premiums on time. As far as he knew, there was nothing to suggest—despite some vague rumors that had reached Leon's ear, along with everyone else's in Castillac—that there were irregularities associated with his death. By far the easiest path would simply be for him to write the widow LaRue a check and be done with the whole business. He had done so nearly countless times for others without giving it a thought.

But in this case, even though it was causing him profound disquiet, Leon just could not bring himself to write the check. And he did not have the slightest understanding why.

Leon was relieved to see, as he got closer to the office, that Angeline was not hanging around waiting outside the office door. He did not dare to hope that she had forgotten or given up. She would be back, there was no doubt of this; as he settled in at his desk and opened his computer, shuffling some papers from one stack to another, he had one eye on the street, and felt a sense of doom.

❧ 48 ❧

Lapin slipped into Patisserie Bujold just as Edmond was closing for the day and flipping the door sign to *Fermé*.

"Is this the usual closing time? What about people who want to dash in for some bread for dinner?"

"Oh, hello, Lapin. It *is* early. But I have been feeling...well...the stress we're all under...and I thought all right, it's my shop and I can close it when I want to. And my plan, before your big self loomed in the doorway, was to scurry home, have a quick meal, and get into bed. Watch some TV. Try to forget—"

"I know. I get it. But there's no forgetting."

"I keep going over it in my mind, thinking Hortense must have gotten off course somehow, started talking about a book she was reading or a show or..."

"...anything except the actual Angeline LaRue."

"Yes. *Exactement*."

"We must tell Molly."

"You said that before. I don't disagree. But...you haven't done it."

"*You* haven't done it."

"You realize what this means?"

"That we're two grown men, afraid of a little blonde with pink fingernails?"

"We'd be idiots not to be afraid, is one way to look at it."

"Let's have some eclairs and sit down. Make a plan. Like sensible adults."

Edmond arranged eclairs on two plates and poured them some coffee. He locked the door, then gestured to Lapin to come around the counter so they could sit in the back, where customers couldn't see them.

"Did she really almost set someone on fire?" Lapin said, barely audible, as though Angeline was in the next room.

"That is what Hortense said. The story she told was a bit complicated. No, not really. What is complicated was Hortense's reaction to the events, which was not what one would expect."

"Go through the whole thing again. And I promise I will find a way to tell Molly."

Edmond bit into an eclair and then rubbed his face. "I'll give you the highlights, not the whole thing. I can't face it."

Lapin nodded.

"All right, as Hortense related, it was like this: they were schoolmates, maybe around twelve or thirteen? This was in—I can't remember the name of the village. Never heard of it. Anyway, Hortense was being bullied by a rich kid in their class, named Lulu de Benfort. That's a rich girl's name, eh? Lulu was making fun of Hortense's clothes. Day after day, leaving her in tears."

"Kids can be monsters."

"Indeed. At any rate, Angeline stuck up for Hortense—those are Hortense's words, not mine. She said that Angeline somehow lured that rich girl to the edge of the woods, got her tied to a tree, and was just about to douse her with gasoline and set her on fire, but Hortense got there in time and intervened.

"And what I meant about Hortense's reaction—she seemed to think this was evidence of how much Angeline cared for her, the great lengths Angeline was willing to go on her behalf. When it's pretty clear—

"—that Angeline is a psychopath who was using Hortense's troubles as an excuse to torture that girl."

"Not only torture. It sounds like she really might have killed her. And I believe she would have."

Lapin and Edmond felt the truth of this and fear welled up in them both just as it had the first time they heard Hortense's story. They could not look at each other as they each tried to master their feelings.

"We need to protect Molly."

"At all costs. But Lapin, as we discussed, if it gets back to Angeline that we're telling people about this? She's going to come after us too."

"Is it possible that Hortense is simply spinning a yarn, trying to look important, and none of this even happened?"

They looked at each other, wanting to see that the other thought that was even a small possibility. But it was not and they did not lie to themselves or each other about it, but rather sat in their fear and argued about which one of them was going to be the one to tell Molly the details, since their vague warnings had been brushed aside.

"Angeline! I'm so happy to see you," said Paul-Henri, trotting over to her side of the street and pulling down the jacket of his uniform to stop it from riding up.

Angeline was decidedly less happy to see him, but she put on a big smile and came out through the gate, putting her hand on his arm as they kissed cheeks. "And I am happy to see you, too," she said, tucking her chin slightly and looking up at him with wide eyes.

Paul-Henri blushed. "It's about Molly Sutton," he said, lowering his voice though there was no one on the street. "I hate to have to tell you this—if anyone should be allowed some rest, some time to recover, to heal after all you've been through—it's you. I thought the whole business with Sutton had died down and she had finally come to her senses and let it drop. For days I heard nothing and I believe she had stopped pressuring Florian. But that has changed, I'm sorry to say. I'm afraid I've just been notified that she came in to the office of the coroner on Friday, and I can only assume she was there to continue to harass him about the exhumation of poor Benoît."

"Assume?" said Angeline, her voice cracking just slightly.

"I mean only that the report I received noted Sutton going into the coroner's office in the morning but ah, we don't actually know what was said within. I do believe we can make an educated guess, though, don't you? There haven't been any other deaths since Benoît's, after all."

Angeline tried to think. Hearing the name "Molly Sutton" had sent a stab of fear into her lower back and made it hard work to keep up any pretense of flirtation with Paul-Henri. "I don't know what she has against me," Angeline said, squeezing his arm.

"Don't you worry about her," said Paul-Henri, puffing out his chest. "Florian Nagrand—he's no pushover. He's not about to take orders from Sutton, or anyone else for that matter," he added, thinking of a dust-up he had had with Nagrand the year before, when he had learned just how stubborn and unwilling to take direction the coroner was. "But I must tell you, so you can be on your guard: there is something of a complication. Did you hear about Florian and the woman staying at Sutton's gîte?"

"What?" Angeline, having few to zero friends, had the least access to gossip of anyone in Castillac. "No, tell me!"

"Well," said Paul-Henri, "of course the Castillacois love nothing better than a bit of gossip—and the word on the street is that on the very day that Benoît died—please let me express, again, my sincerest condolences—"

Angeline nearly screamed at him to get to the point but managed to contain herself.

"Well, apparently our coroner is absolutely intoxicated by this British woman. Completely lost his mind," he said, chuckling, and enjoying the pictures of this enslaved Florian that his imagination served up. "So on that *exact day*, the day your poor Benoît breathed his last, Florian was, according to sources, shacking up with one of Molly's guests in one of her gîtes. The pigeonnier, to be precise. Instead of doing his job."

Angeline, obviously, knew that Florian had not come to her

house to see about Benoît, but she had not thought about what that might mean.

"Later on they had lunch at Chez Papa together and my source told me they were practically making love right there at the table. Couldn't keep their hands off each other. So of course, as you may be working out—" continued Paul-Henri, "the problem is that Matthias de Clare, who is quite a decent fellow and all that, but not someone properly trained—"

"I see," said Angeline.

For the first time, Paul-Henri felt a chill in Angeline's voice that made him hesitate. But he brushed it off and continued. "It's probably nothing. But it does, perhaps—just a smidgen—open the door to Sutton's importuning. Just a crack. Because Nagrand did not actually—"

"I understand. I get it. Listen, Paul-Henri, you're such a dear for catching me up and I appreciate you so much. I've got so many things I need to take care of today that I must be off. I'm just going to have to wish Molly Sutton well and hope that this grudge she's developed will wither of its own accord. Maybe I will pay her a visit tomorrow to see if I can smooth things over, what do you think?"

"Excellent plan of action," said Paul-Henri.

They said their goodbyes and Paul-Henri stood watching her walk down the sidewalk back to her garden. She was in a hurry and her shoes clip-clopped, making a sound that pleased him. He didn't understand why so many in the village didn't like her, or even seemed frightened of her. She was a pretty little cupcake and she needs me, he thought, smiling to himself. He turned back to the gendarmerie, imagining how grateful Angeline would be when he turned out to be the most stalwart, the most supportive and understanding fellow in the entire village, someone she could lean on, depend on.

Maybe even—well, such thoughts are unprofessional, he

thought, tugging on his jacket and watching her until she turned a corner.

☙

WITH A SENSE OF SATISFIED COMPLETION, Leon put a sheaf of papers into the file where they belonged and closed the drawer. He looked at his watch and saw that it was nearly time for lunch —if he walked slowly to the Café de la Place, he would be there just in time to beat any rush, not that he had ever had to wait for a table for Monday lunch.

He rolled his chair back, thinking about *cassoulet* even though it was really a cold weather dish, and just as he stood up, he caught a flash of pink outside the office and saw it was Angeline— of course it was—and the dread he had been feeling since last week blossomed through his body, making him nauseated.

I don't believe in ESP, he thought. I don't believe in psychics, or tarot, or fortunetelling, or astrology. I don't even believe in God.

So why is it that I have this strong feeling, a feeling I cannot shake no matter how I try, that Angeline LaRue killed her husband?

It's not because of the rumors swirling around, about Molly Sutton thinking the same, he thought. I don't know Sutton and her opinions are not influencing me. What I know is people, and how to read them. And Angeline LaRue…

He watched her as she came through the door to his office, and it felt—bizarrely—as though his body made a duplicate copy of itself, and one copy stayed to deal with Angeline and the other copy left the room completely, and went to the loft of a nearby barn and settled into a haystack where this woman could not find him.

"Bonjour, Angeline," said the remaining copy, coming out from behind the desk to kiss cheeks with her. "I'm happy to tell you that today is the day you will get your payment. Allow me to apologize profusely for the process being so slow. I know it can feel interminable, when funds that you are counting on are delayed."

He sat down at the desk and pulled out the ledger with checks. The number owed was clear in his mind and he did not need to look that up. With a feeling of numbness, he wrote the check, tore it out of the book, and handed it over, trying for a celebratory expression, and failing miserably.

"So you see," said Angeline, tucked in at a corner table at Chez Papa and leaning in to speak softly to Hortense, "the woman has some axe to grind with me, who can say why? Perhaps I remind her of a cool girl in school who bullied her?" She shook her head and presented a baffled, sorrowful expression. "Impossible to know. You know I have been nothing but warm and welcoming to her, so it's just...it's just a mystery. And it...it makes my heart hurt." At this last, Angeline nearly snickered aloud, but managed to hold it together. She tapped her fingernails on the table because being with Hortense made her feel impatient.

"I've never met her," said Hortense. She had never met Molly, seen Molly, had anything at all to do with Molly or Molly's friends, so she cast about trying to find a way to be an active part of the conversation. "I've never met her, but that doesn't mean I like her," she added with a tone of triumph, thinking she had hit just the right note.

"I've tried to be friendly, I really have."

"I'm sure. I can't imagine what her problem is." Hortense was aware that Angeline was not the most popular woman in Castillac, but she chose not to think about that.

"Well, you know, people who aren't from here..."

"Yes, she's a stranger, isn't she? A *foreigner*. American, isn't it? You hear all kinds of things..."

"Their eating habits!" Angeline rolled her eyes.

"Oh yes! And they're so loud. Does this Molly Sutton go all over town shouting?"

"Probably. It's what they do."

Hortense furrowed her brow at the thought of this unpleasant foreign *they* that Angeline had deftly put into her mind.

"Anyway, I'm afraid Sutton's taken against me and there's not a thing I can do about it. I've gone to visit her, to try to offer an olive branch—even though I haven't the slightest idea why she persecutes me so." Angeline looked down at the table, trying to decide if it was the right moment to turn on the waterworks.

"She should just leave Castillac and go home to America. We don't need her here," said Hortense, feeling the burst of well-being that can come from disparaging someone else.

"Funny you should say that," said Angeline, lowering her voice to a bare whisper. She paused, not one hundred, or eighty, or even *sixty* percent certain that Hortense would go where she wanted her to go. "You might think this is...*really* out there..."

"What?" said Hortense, leaning halfway across the table out of excitement, not wanting to miss a word. "*What* is out there?"

"It's just that I...I don't feel safe, not with Sutton blabbing her lies to everyone in the village."

"Safe? She can't do anything to you. You haven't done anything wrong!"

"That's no protection. Her scheming lies could land me in *prison*, Hortense! You know how the world works."

Hortense had no idea how the world worked, but she was willing, even enthusiastic, to believe whatever Angeline told her. "Well, what can you do?" Hortense said, looking up at the ceiling while she thought. "I know! Maybe you could spread some rumors about *her*, and she would get so sick of it she might leave the village?"

Angeline pretended to consider this. "That's good," she said, giving Hortense a warm, complicit smile. "But I've been thinking

—and I know, it's out there, as I said, but I honestly feel boxed into such a corner. I literally fear for my life, dear friend."

"Oh, Angeline, I'm so sorry it's gotten to such a point. So go on, tell me...what are you thinking of doing?"

"I've been thinking—bear with me now—what if I—if *we*—rid Castillac of her...for good?"

Hortense was leaning so far across the table that the edge was cutting painfully into her stomach, but she did not move back. "What are you...you mean, like...when you say 'rid,' are you...do you mean *get rid,* like...all the way? *Permanently?*"

Angeline knew this was a precarious moment. Either Hortense was in the trap or she was not, in which case she would instantly become a liability. Slowly, almost imperceptibly, Angeline nodded.

Hortense slid back into her chair. Her face was flushed with the deep pleasure from Angeline's confiding in her about a plan so unusual, so dangerous—and even asking for her help. Once upon a time, Angeline had come to her aid in a dramatic fashion, taking quite a risk. It was time to repay her. Hortense tucked her lank hair behind her ears, and looking Angeline right in the eye, not hesitating or appearing conflicted in the least—she nodded.

"You're my ride or die," Hortense whispered. "I won't let you down."

※ 50 ※

1968

"Maybe I have mentioned it before, and so what if I have?" said Anne, raking her hands through her hair. The door was open and some welcome fresh air came into the small room where she sat cutting onions while her husband tried to read the newspaper and little Angeline played in the doorway.

"I'm only saying, it's water under the bridge, Anne. Water under the bridge."

"And I'm saying you can take your idiotic platitudes and shove them. If I want to tell the story more than once, I shall."

Artur tried to sigh quietly and not rattle the pages of his newspaper, as these things could send Anne into even more of a fury. He slumped down in his chair, knowing there was nothing to do but wait out the storm.

"I came home that night with a golden ticket," Anne growled, slicing onions at a rapid clip. "That baby should have been ours. Ours! We could have brought him to the de la Chabelle's chateau and insisted they claim him as their own. Insisted they support him in a way appropriate to his connection."

Artur wanted to interrupt to say that the powerful and aristocratic family would never in a million years have done anything of the kind—what, allow themselves to be squeezed by a nobody with a random baby whose mother was not even alive to point a finger at the father, with no way to prove parentage?* It was fantasy of the highest order, he thought. But he had learned, through repeated tries, such common sense did not get through, especially not when Anne was on a tear, as she was now.

"The mother died that night," said Anne, tears running down her face, not of sorrow but a regret so huge that time did not diminish it. "I should have brought that baby home on the spot. The only reason I did not is that I foolishly, naively believed that going through the proper channels would be safer. Never did I imagine that you would refuse to adopt him altogether!"

Artur lifted the paper up and made a face behind it.

"Maman?" said Angeline, who had been listening intently as she played, as she always did. "Would I have had a brother, if Papa had said yes?"

"Indeed you would," said Anne. "We would have adopted him that very week and you would have come along as you did, in the following year. You would have a brother. A very rich, very connected brother. And we would have had a different life. A *real* life."

Artur did not lower the newspaper or utter a word, though he had plenty to say.

With delicate movement of her fingers, Angeline made the chevalier puppet gallop smoothly across the floor. The silver helmet was dirty and the lance had broken off years ago. In a low voice that her parents could not hear, she murmured to the knight: "You'll protect me, sir? You'll slay all the dragons, won't you?"

Anne continued. "And it is insult to injury that he's not even in our village anymore, adopted by Somebody LaRue, all the way in Castillac. We have no way to maintain the connection at all.

And naming him Benoît?" Anne laughed a mirthless laugh. "If any child were not blessed, it would be him. Cast out from his real family, neglected and unacknowledged. The stupid LaRues have no idea what they have."

Anne put down the knife and pushed the pile of onions away, then leaned her forehead on the table and wept.

* *DNA* TESTING *for paternity only became possible in 1988.*

❧ 51 ❧

Hortense had left Chez Papa feeling invigorated and proud. Yes, what Angeline was asking her to do was considerable, true enough...but at first, as she started for home, she was already working out where to buy the rat poison and what kind of soup she might make to put it in, something to disguise what must be a terrible taste. She felt different on her walk home—important. *Needed.*

But as excited as Hortense had been, once she was home alone in her same old shabby apartment, the excitement began to wear off and the whole affair took on a decidedly different flavor.

First off, why in the world would Molly Sutton, a person she had never met, accept a pot of soup from a stranger? Hortense could think of no pretext that seemed the least bit likely to succeed. And more than that....

What had seemed thrilling, now seemed reckless.

What had seemed like a way to show her devotion to her friend, now seemed like a way to get herself in a heap of trouble.

What had seemed like a moment of real intimacy now felt as though she was on her own and taking a huge risk, also on her own.

In short: Hortense firmly decided against doing what Angeline had told her to do. Instead of going to the hardware store to buy rat poison, she got in bed in the middle of the afternoon, frozen with indecision about what to do next.

She had glimmerings of understanding—she could see that being asked to be accomplice to a murder—wait, not merely accomplice but the primary killer—had, when Angeline suggested it, felt like an immense compliment. Of all the people in Castillac to ask, she, Hortense, had been chosen. Lying in bed with the summer coverlet pulled up to her chin, she could still feel the glow that the compliment had given her.

In the moment, those feelings had been so potent that they had made the actual thing Angeline was asking to recede into the distance, not so visible.

But once Angeline was not there to fan the glowing embers, other feelings crowded in that did not feel nearly as good. Hortense was gullible. She often believed what she wished were true rather than what was true. Yet this one time, miraculously, there was a kind of mental friction when she remembered those moments at Chez Papa with Angeline, as though for the first time in their long friendship, Hortense could feel the gap between what Angeline said and what Angeline meant.

It was true that when they were kids, Angeline had leapt into the breach and taken the dramatic action of stopping that nasty Lulu de Benfort. Hortense had never been bullied again, and that was thanks to Angeline's not being afraid of taking action.

But suddenly—with a chill—Hortense wondered for the first time whether Angeline had intended to kill Lulu de Benfort. Would she have lit the match if Hortense had not appeared just at the last moment?

She wondered whether what Angeline did was not so much for Hortense, but for Angeline's own reasons. For her *pleasure*.

Hortense shivered under the coverlet.

For the first time, Hortense wondered if she was being used.

She wondered if Angeline had just tried to prevail upon her to do some dirty work that she did not want to do herself. Because Angeline did not want to get caught, but perhaps would not mind so much if Hortense got caught.

Once these thoughts crowded into her head, Hortense could not unthink them. She slid farther under the coverlet until only the top of her head was showing.

Molly Sutton might be truly awful. She might be a loud American who ate horrible things and poked her nose where it didn't belong. But, thought Hortense, even if she *is* gossiping about my friend? Even if she *is* making things up and overall being an unpleasant pain in the neck? That did not, to Hortense's mind, come anywhere close to adding up to deserving to be murdered.

Could I kill someone if they really, really deserved it? She wondered.

Possibly.

But this is not that moment. Angeline was on her own for this one.

⚜

INSTEAD OF GOING to the Cafe de la Place, Leon hustled back to his apartment on rue Lalique. He kept—ridiculously—touching his face with his fingers as though to make sure he was still in existence. He had never, in his many years in insurance, had this kind of reaction to a client. Or to anyone else he had ever come into contact with. It was inexplicable. It was bizarre.

He made a short detour to Patisserie Bujold to get a baguette, and then stood in his kitchen in a very un-French manner, eating a quickly assembled *jambon-beurre* without sitting down. He stood over the sink, letting the shattered crumbs of the baguette fall where he would not have to wipe them up, so upset he did not even taste the excellent ham or the wonderfully creamy butter.

Leon had expected that finally writing the check and giving it to Angeline would provide significant relief from his anxieties. It had not. He did not have qualms about keeping his—what would you call it? Feeling? Intuition?—to himself because mostly he did not believe it to be true but a kind of trick his mind was playing, for reasons unknown. But this current state of mind, so deeply anxious he felt on the brink of a panic attack, was untenable. Perhaps he should go out to La Baraque and meet this Molly Sutton, see what she has to say about the matter, and tell her about this unaccountable conviction he had that Angeline LaRue had killed her husband. Would telling someone release him from this torment?

He felt absolutely ridiculous even contemplating doing such a thing. But that was nothing compared to the fear that was settling into his very bones and preventing him, apparently, from resuming his normal life.

And yet: if he did talk to Molly Sutton, and word got back to Angeline? Leon shuddered. The copy of himself (that had not dissipated after writing the check) saw the shudder and tried to laugh it off, but could not.

❧ 52 ❧

Angeline was not a woman who trusted others. Her natural inclination was to think the worst, and she believed experience had proved her correct more often than not.

So even though the conversation with Hortense at Chez Papa had seemed to go very well, with that heartfelt declaration of devotion coming at the end...Angeline did not necessarily believe that Hortense would follow through.

She certainly was not going to leave it at that and hope for the best. She needed to *know*.

The next day she loitered on the sidewalk a block away from Hortense's apartment building, seemingly engrossed in a neighbor's garden but keeping a close eye on the building's door so Hortense could not slip out unnoticed. She had put her hair in a high ponytail, which normally she never did, and was wearing a black T-shirt and black pants, also not her usual.

She was not fond of loitering. Increasingly, as the minutes ticked by, she felt more irritation and then rage at Hortense. She supposed it was possible that Hortense had left Chez Papa the day before and gone straight to the hardware store, picked up the rat poison, and was at this very moment making the soup.

That seemed possible, if not likely. Angeline went to the door and pressed the buzzer to Hortense's apartment, hoping that all she needed to do was cheer her friend on, and give her a little bolstering up before the soup was delivered.

It wouldn't take much soup to make Sutton collapse—but even if it took more, Angeline had a feeling that Sutton's gluttony would be her downfall.

She pressed the buzzer again, then again.

It was eight o'clock in the morning. Angeline could think of no reason for Hortense not to be home. No reason, that is, that favored the outcome she was looking for.

She felt a welling up of anger at Hortense, knowing she had not followed through with Angeline's instructions. If you want a thing done, she thought, you have to do it yourself. It is the way of the world.

Alas.

❧ 53 ❧

It was an ordinary Tuesday and Molly and Ben had enjoyed yet another late morning in bed, both of them treasuring these luxurious moments that they understood would be hard to come by once there was a baby or young child in the house. After coffee and a croissant, Ben left for Périgueux to see some old friends at the gendarmerie in that larger city, putting out some feelers to get more investigative work.

Molly was at loose ends. She sat on the terrace having another cup of coffee, considering what to do with her day. There were always flowerbeds to weed, or maybe she could do something ambitious in the kitchen and surprise Ben for dinner. The week's gîte guests were active and independent, and had long since taken off for the day (except for Selma Throckmorton, thought Molly with a grin). In the back of her mind, way way back, there were lists of poisonous plants and the symptoms they caused...but whenever such thoughts rose to the foreground, she swatted them away as best she could. The oleander had not been touched, and that was the end of it.

She didn't hear the knock. It was only when Angeline out of

frustration banged on the door with both fists that Molly realized someone was there.

"Oh," she said, opening the door. "It's you."

"Bonjour, Molly," said Angeline, sweeping past her with a grandeur that made Molly's eyes widen. Well, Molly thought, if she's come to kill me, at least she's got my name right.

"I've brought a peace offering," said Angeline. "I don't know how we got off on the wrong foot, but we have, and I'd like to smooth things over if I can. I've brought you something I think you'll like. I heard you were fond of pastry—Edmond Nugent is one of my oldest and dearest friends—and, well, not to toot my own horn, but I fancy myself as having something of a talent for it. Before I was married, I thought I might be a *patissière*, go to Escoffier and all that." She smiled, pleased with herself for coming up with the lie on the spot.

"Really?" said Molly. "I've sort of kept that as a second—or third—career for myself, in the back of my mind."

"Pastry is, after all, the epitome of French civilization," said Angeline, demonstrating her preternatural ability to read other people like a book.

"We absolutely agree on that," said Molly, looking at the small package Angeline was holding, her mouth beginning to water in spite of herself. "What is it?" she asked, unable to feign indifference when it came to a mysterious pastry.

"Oh, just a little something I threw together. I think you'll find the pastry layers have that characteristic crispness along with softer, chewy bits. Of course I had to guess what sort of flavoring you like so I just went with chocolate because who doesn't like chocolate?"

"Heathens," said Molly, waiting with impatience for Angeline to unwrap the package so she could see it. She had made eggs and bacon for breakfast but given Ben most of it, not feeling all that hungry, but now her stomach was growling a symphony of anticipation.

Angeline put the package on the kitchen counter and slowly took the wrapping off as though she were revealing the crown jewels. And Molly was the best audience she could hope for. Angeline could see Molly's eyes sparkle, see how she licked her lips. The woman was practically drooling, Angeline thought. This couldn't be going any better.

After a few more minutes of awkward small talk, Angeline said goodbye. And that's a final goodbye, she thought with a chuckle as she set off down rue de Chêne for the village.

The night before, she had plucked some new growth from the yew growing in the Latour's backyard, taken it home, pulled off all the needles, and pulverized them in a mortar. Then she began the arduous labor of making the pastry, mixing the powdered yew into the layers of pastry as well as into the chocolate filling, so there would be no way to take a bite without ingesting yew.

And yew, as any prospective poisoner knows, is very, very toxic.

After putting the pastry in the oven, Angeline carefully washed the mortar and pestle, her hands, all the bowls and cutting boards and any other utensil that had come in contact with the yew. She was grateful to the Latours for installing such a valuable plant. Apart from its legendary toxicity, as a bonus, it had no antidote. Not that anyone was likely to work out what was causing poor Molly's symptoms in time.

If ever.

❧ 54 ❧

S he pulled the straw hat down so that most of her face was in shadow. The hat was not flattering, Hortense knew, but she had no time to try to find a disguise and it was the best she could do.

She waited on the train platform for the train to pull into the Castillac station. It only came once a day and was so slow and took so long to get just to Bergerac, that it was never crowded. Hortense tapped her fingers on her thighs. That morning when her buzzer sounded she had nearly leapt out of her skin, never imagining that Angeline would actually come to her apartment, as she had never done so before. Hortense had gotten back under the covers and waited until Angeline left, finally settling on the solution of getting out of town as soon as possible.

She had no car and limited funds so the train was really the only option, and she had no plan yet for what she would do once she got off the train. Bergerac did not seem far enough away; she had to get somewhere that Angeline would not come looking for her.

Hortense shuddered at that prospect.

Eventually the poky train pulled into the station and Hortense climbed aboard and found a seat, tripping over the stair because the hat partly blocked her vision. She settled into a window seat so she could monitor the platform for Angeline—could almost see her coming through the swinging door, her face red, looking for Hortense, raging—

After an interminable wait, the train slowly eased out of the station and chugged its way towards Bergerac. Hortense took a deep breath for the first time in what felt like a month.

෴

ANGELINE HAD BARELY LEFT the driveway of La Baraque when Molly had the pastry in her hands. She held it aloft, turning it, admiring the darker brown edges and the way the chocolate oozed out from between the layers. The dusting of powdered sugar looked professionally done and Molly had to hand it to Angeline: if in fact she had made this pastry from scratch, she had done an admirable job.

Molly put the pastry on the counter. At least, it was admirable from the perspective of how it looked. How it tasted, Molly couldn't say.

Well, maybe she could have just a nibble.

The oleander was untouched. Angeline was innocent.

Wasn't she?

Molly picked the pastry up. A bit of chocolate managed to find its way to her wrist, and she almost licked it off.

The oleander was untouched, that was true. Molly had tried to face the dead end of the investigation with good grace. But that didn't mean she believed Angeline was innocent.

There was no way in hell Molly was going to eat something Angeline LaRue had made and brought to her house, not wishing to take the compliment "to die for" literally.

Maybe the oleander was not the key, but the key was somewhere, if only Molly could figure out where to look for it.

❧

"No worries, I just talked to her on the phone this morning," said Lawrence to Matthias as they cleared the breakfast dishes.

"You're sure? Because she was in the office on Friday, giving it to Florian. I have to admit, I enjoy watching her work him over."

"Molly is a force to be reckoned with," laughed Lawrence. "But I promise you, when I talked to her yesterday she told me she had let the whole thing go since she couldn't find any actual evidence. She didn't come right out and say it, but it seemed like she might be thinking she had jumped the gun a little bit, out of... what should I call it? Over-identification with the victim? She really feels for Benoît. And she hinted—just barely—that maybe those feelings had led her astray."

"Glad to hear it. Even though work will be far less interesting without her coming over to rake Florian over the coals. Which he deserves for any number of reasons."

"I will say I'm going to miss providing the mysterious insider info, now that she knows about you. It was so entertaining—and I felt so important!—when I could text her about a victim and she didn't know how I knew."

"Alas, all the secrets are coming out," said Matthias, reaching over to take Lawrence's hand, which made Lawrence, grown up as he was, blush.

$\mathbf{\mathscr{L}}$ 55 $\mathbf{\mathscr{R}}$

I n the middle of that peaceful Tuesday afternoon, the weather perfect, Molly was back in bed. She felt vaguely guilty about it, knowing there were always tasks that needed doing, and not wanting Ben to have to do them all. But she felt so tired lately, and on top of that, now her stomach felt upset.

She even skipped the usual early afternoon coffee, though a headache was coming on that she could tell was going to be a blockbuster.

She had dropped off the pastry Angeline made at the gendarmerie, asking that it be analyzed for poison, but while Charlot and Paul-Henri had not laughed in her face, Molly had the clear impression that once the door was closed, they would be rolling their eyes and smirking at her. She didn't care about that. But she was very curious about what was in that pastry and hoped they followed through with the testing, and were quick about it.

She lay in bed, looking at the trees outside the bedroom window, wondering how soon the adoption would take place, while moving her hand over her belly, around and around, trying to make the stomachache go away.

꘠

ANGELINE WAS FEELING STRESSED.

She was still angry at Hortense but at the same time excited by the image of Molly Sutton eating the pastry she had made for her. And what a special pastry it is, she muttered, pacing in the kitchen of the cottage. Angeline went out to the garden but she was blind to its beauty; even the heavenly aroma of the roses did not reach her nose.

Surely the yew had done its job, she told herself. Hortense's failure won't matter at all, because I have already succeeded myself.

She went back inside and carefully chose her outfit. A tight-fitting skirt, flats with a little bow, a blouse that had pink edging at the collar and short sleeves. A hint of makeup, carefully and judiciously applied. It was time to go find out what had happened with Sutton.

As she walked to Chez Papa, thinking she would sit at the bar where any gossip would find its way, especially gossip as juicy as the collapse and untimely demise of Molly Sutton, she felt the same twinge she had experienced after the death of Benoît: a rather depressed feeling, on realizing that her triumph would have to stay private, and she would enjoy no admiration or even notoriety about what she had accomplished.

There's nothing to be done about that, she thought, smoothing her skirt as she approached the bistro. She could see several people sitting at the bar having their lunch, and she walked in resigned to getting her merriment from hearing the news she so wanted to hear.

꘠

AND IN LESS THAN fifteen minutes, Angeline was back on the street. She had joined into the conversation, then steered it this way and that, and it appeared that no one had any idea of anything unfortunate happening to Molly Sutton.

She was not only disappointed but surprised. When she gave her the pastry, she could see Sutton's eyes glittering, the woman had practically drooled—and the pastry did look incredible, with its dark chocolate filling oozing out and a dusting of confectioner's sugar on top. Angeline would have made a hefty bet that Molly had gobbled it up before Angeline had even left the driveway.

She did not like to be wrong. Nor to fail. That was one thing that made things easy with Benoît: she cooked something, he ate it, no questions asked.

Angeline did not think she was wrong about food being the correct vehicle when it came to Sutton. And if a pastry didn't do it, what would?

✦ 56 ✦

B eing a woman of action, the very next day, Angeline got
dressed, no makeup, made the necessary preparations, and
set out for the walk to La Baraque. She was hoping not to meet
anyone along the way, and even though it was nearly ten o'clock
and a beautiful sunny day, the streets were empty, which she took
as a good omen.

Adrenaline was coursing through her and she made it to La
Baraque in record time. The scooter was there, and the car, and
she paused a moment, trying to work out her next steps. She did
not want to see Ben Dufort. Even if he had given up being chief
at the gendarmerie a long time ago, he still had an aura of law
enforcement that she wanted nothing to do with.

Angeline stood for a moment on rue de Chêne, facing the
house. This was do or die. She did not think she had more
chances to fail.

She knocked on the door, giving it some oomph since she
suspected Sutton was half deaf.

No answer.

Slowly Angeline lifted the door handle. The bolt clicked, the
door swung open without a creak.

Angeline stepped inside and looked around. The kitchen and living room were empty. She considered calling out and decided against it.

She walked over to the kitchen, reached into her bag and pulled out a jar of honey and set it on the counter.

She turned and went to the door, looking back to admire the jar sitting there by itself, the honey catching the light.

Bye Sutton, she murmured softly, and headed for home.

❧ 57 ❧

At eleven o'clock Molly finally dragged herself out of bed and staggered into the kitchen to make some coffee.

Ahh, she thought, looking outside at the flowerbed while she waited for the water to boil. I'll weed this morning, think how grateful the peonies will be, and it will clear my mind and set me back to rights.

She turned around and saw the jar of honey sitting on the counter, glowing amber in the midday light.

Oh that Ben! He is the best of the best, she thought. So sweet of him. I think I will put a big spoonful of this lovely honey in my coffee. That deep glowing color! I've been feeling so blah lately, it will be wonderfully soothing.

Molly opened the jar and spooned a big spoonful into a mug, watching it drip down and pool at the bottom. The water was boiling and she poured it into the French press and waited— impatiently, as usual—though privately she considered this the best moment of the day, anticipating the first cup of coffee. And so much better this time, with honey from Ben to sweeten the morning.

She had nothing pressing to do. The day would be spent weeding, messing round with Ben, drinking more coffee, and thinking about the adoption (no matter how far away it might be). Her life really could not be any better.

&.

AS THE COFFEE finished dripping through, Molly took a moment to close her eyes and feel appreciation for her life in Castillac. She loved the village more than she would have thought possible, despite its apparently having more than its share of unfortunate events.

She took her coffee out to the terrace and sat in the sunshine. She lifted the cup to her lips just as she heard a crash from the other side of the house. She put the mug down and raced around to see Constance on the ground, tangled up in her bicycle, with Bobo dancing around her barking.

"What in the world," laughed Molly.

"This blasted dog!" shouted Constance, who was on the loud side for a French-person. "She has a thing against this bike! If I walk, we have no problem, she comes up and wags and says hello like a normal dog. But when she sees the bike? She thinks it's like a guided missile aimed at La Baraque to kill you and she will do anything to stop it!"

Molly helped Constance up, still laughing. "Bobo is the best. 'No one will ever love you like your dog,' is what my mother used to say."

"Not a very optimistic view of humans," grumbled Constance, brushing gravel off her knees.

"True," said Molly. "So what brings you out to La Baraque before Changeover Day?"

"Well, I was wondering...Thomas has some plans for Saturday, they involve a picnic among other top secret things I am not supposed to know about. So I was wondering if I could get some of the cleaning out of the way today, so I could be free then? Thomas can't get off work any other time."

"Well, no," said Molly, never at her best before having any coffee. "The guests are still here and won't be gone until 10:00 Saturday morning. So I don't see how that will work."

Constance looked crestfallen. "But the picnic..."

Molly pulled herself together. "Let me think. Selma is staying yet another week, so the pigeonnier is off the list. The students are leaving the annex but there's no one coming this week to take their place, so that cleaning could wait. I can handle the cottage by myself. So..."

"I can go?"

"All I ask is that you come back at some point during the week to clean the annex. But it doesn't matter what day."

Constance kissed Molly on both cheeks and then did it again for emphasis. "Love you!" she called, hopping on the bike and speeding out of the driveway.

With a sigh, Molly headed back to the terrace, hoping her coffee hadn't gotten too cold.

❧ 58 ❧

The phone was ringing so Molly detoured into the house to answer it.

"Molly!" It was Lapin.

"Bonjour, Lapin. What's up?"

"Just—if you would come into the shop, *tout de suite?* On the double, as your American gangsters like to say."

"They do?"

"It's—look, Anne-Marie is insisting I...I need to talk to you about something. And woe is me if I don't get you in here, she's been browbeating me so hard that I'm in tatters."

Molly laughed. "Um, does it have to be right this second?"

"If you want me to survive Anne-Marie, yes indeed it does."

So with a longing glance at the mug of now-cold coffee sitting on the terrace table, Molly sighed, gave Bobo a quick pet and took off for the village.

She was not all that interested in whatever it was Lapin was going on about. She figured she had gotten dragged into the middle of a fight between him and his wife and it didn't really have anything to do with her. She would swing by Patisserie

Bujold to get a coffee and perhaps an almond croissant before making her way to Lapin's, thereby nicely salvaging the morning.

❦

THUS FORTIFIED, she came into Lapin's shop and he hurried right over to greet her.

"Thank you very *very* much for coming right away. I know it's been...that you've..."

"What is the matter?"

"Ohh," he said, wiping his brow and leading her to the back of the shop. "It's only—Angeline—."

"We really don't need to talk about her. I hit a dead end, Lapin. Am I still suspicious? Absolutely. But I realized that maybe it's not my job to spend every minute trying to uncover every wrongdoing in the world. All I ever wanted was a quiet life, doing a little gardening..."

"Uh huh. Sure." Lapin looked amused though he was wringing his hands and sweat was popping out on his brow. "You should know that some in the village—not the loud ones, you understand—have been on your side from the beginning. I mean—your side vs. Angeline's."

Molly felt a vague interest stirring. But it was faint. She wanted to get home to that peony bed, she really did.

"And by 'some'," he said, "who I mean is: Anne-Marie."

"Always a level-headed woman," said Molly with a smile.

"She said that when she heard you suspected Angeline of killing Benoît, the words YES SHE DID flashed into her mind, bright as a billboard in Times Square."

"Times Square, gangsters—you're quite the American today, Lapin."

"And so it's because of Anne-Marie that I asked you to come. Because there's something else. Something I should have told you a long time ago, but I'm...as I think you know...I'm a terrible coward."

"Oh, Lapin, don't beat yourself up. Like I said, I've moved on. My hypotheses didn't pan out and that's the end of it. You have any interesting estates lately? I could use a bedside table. Mine has a funny leg and I've given up trying to wedge something under it that will make it level."

"I don't want to talk about bedside tables!"

"Lapin? Are you all right?"

"Just let me—first I want to show you this thing so I can tell Anne-Marie the mission was accomplished."

"All right," said Molly. "Let's get it done."

He led the way down one of the narrow aisles to the back, where the chest with the china service was. He undid the straps and opened the top. Molly looked in.

"Um...is this supposed to mean something to me?"

"It's a service for thirty. Can you imagine?"

"No, I cannot. Is that all? Am I released? It's time to start thinking about lunch."

"Here's the thing, Molly. Angeline is obsessed...I don't think that's too strong a word...*obsessed* with this china. She comes in here regularly asking to see it. I'm sure if she had two centimes to rub together, she would have bought it. But I've got another customer interested in it so I'm not willing to let it go for a song. And if you're about to suggest I should give her a whopping discount out of acknowledgment to my friendship with Benoît, you can just forget it. No one ever ran a successful business that way, let me tell you."

"I wasn't going to suggest anything of the kind," said Molly. "I still don't understand what any of this has to do with me. It looks like a lovely service—the gold leaf is impressive, for sure, and look at that little black heart in the crest, I've never seen anything like that before—but I can't imagine having thirty people to dinner.

Oh, but..." she looked at her friend closely. "You aren't trying to sell me the service."

"No." He looked at her pointedly.

"Lapin! Just please for the love of God, spell it out! I don't get it! What's the china supposed to mean?"

"She comes back here—Angeline, I mean—and she likes to take out a few plates and set them out, like she's pretending to be at a fancy dinner. Sort of like a child would, you understand? Pretending? And she murmurs to herself. It's downright creepy, if you want to know the truth. It's very uncomfortable, seeing an adult act that way."

Again Molly felt a glimmer of interest. What did the china service mean to Angeline? Did it mean something...useful?

Lapin lowered his voice, though there were no customers in the shop. "I never worked out what she was doing, I just thought she was a little nutty, but harmless. But now...hear me out. This last time, she finally let a little information slip: Angeline thinks the service belonged to Benoît's family," he said, almost too quiet for Molly to hear.

"It's not LaRue china," said Molly. "The initials are D-L-C."

"I know. But Benoît was not a LaRue by blood. He was *adopted*. And D-L-C—that's one of the most prominent—and loaded—families in all of France. De la Chabelle."

They looked at each other. Molly felt blood rushing all around her head and for a moment she felt faint.

"You're saying—Benoît LaRue was really Benoît *de la Chabelle?*" she asked. "Even I have heard of them."

"Could be. I don't know, I can't say. Might be Angeline just daydreaming. But if he was? If by some bizarre chance Benoît belonged up in Normandy with one of the fanciest families in all of France—and somehow ended up here in Castillac, at the LaRues? I can't imagine he would tell anyone, much less do anything about it. He was the most modest person in the world, Molly."

"The opposite of his wife, then," she said.

And Lapin nodded. Widened his eyes, and nodded some more.

"And that's not all," he said. He had dreaded this moment, the retelling of Hortense's story about Angeline. The dread did not lessen as the moment arrived. But the story was making its way around the village and Molly, above anyone, deserved to hear it. It was long past time he put his fears of retribution to the side.

"It's about who she is and what she's capable of," he began, his voice so soft it did not sound like his at all.

"You're right, it *is* a risk," said Florian, who was lying on his back, naked on the bed, enjoying the warmth of a sunbeam coming in through one of the pigeonnier windows.

"It could cost you your job. I thought that's what you've been so desperate to prevent?"

"I know." He reached up to Selma's face and ran his fingertips along her jaw, as though memorizing every inch. "But the thing is —everyone knows now, about us. That day in Chez Papa, we were a little indiscreet," he said, smiling at the memory. "You drive me to such—anyway, people know I wasn't in the office the day Benoît died. They know that Matthias filled out all the forms and he wasn't qualified to do so. That was nothing but dereliction of duty on my part and there's no way to spin it, now that our secret is out."

He ran his fingertip over her lips, making her smile.

"I can't explain it away, not now. And when I say everyone knows? I'm talking especially about my hateful boss, Peter Bonheur. I cringe to think about it. But cringing, obviously, doesn't solve anything. So...please excuse this endless explanation, chérie...I figured the best thing for me to do was go ahead with the exhumation. Either it will reveal nothing, no toxins, and support our conclusion of a natural death—in which case, what's Bonheur going to complain about, really? Maybe I did cut some corners but the work of the coroner's office was correct anyway. Or...it will show that Molly Sutton has been right all along."

"In which case, you'll be on the side of revealing a murder and back on the right side of things. I mean, even if Bonheur is furious about your office making an error, public opinion should shift to your side, right? And that will count for a lot." Selma did not necessarily think this all to be true, but was trying to be positive.

"That's my thinking. My hope, anyway."

"When is it happening?"

"Already underway. I gave the order early in the week, so the casket has already been dug up and tests are being run as we speak."

"I'm not sure which outcome to hope for."

"Me neither, my love. Me neither."

❧ 59 ❧

The peony bed would have to wait.

When Molly got back from Lapin's, she went straight to her computer for a date with Mr. Google. When she put in "de la Chabelle," the hits went on for pages and pages. She read about the history of the family, how they had slowly amassed power over centuries—centuries!—and how they had managed to avoid being decimated by the French Revolution. A few members of the family had met with the guillotine but they were not the decision makers, and the family had kept possession of their château and lands and come away mostly unscathed. Now *that's* political savvy, thought Molly.

Currently, three members of the de la Chabelle family were in politics—not surprisingly, rather far to the right. "Protect your assets" might be the family motto, thought Molly as she looked at photographs of the chateau which included a magnificent garden of many acres, while the interior of the building was beautiful, certainly, and also livable, not a crusty old museum piece but a place for the refined, the rich, and the influential to gather in comfort and understated luxury.

Molly had never met Benoît. All she had to go on was what his

NELL GODDIN

friends could guess about what this connection—if it was even real—would have meant to him.

The other looming question in Molly's mind was: what did it mean to the de la Chabelles? What circumstance might have led to a member of the family being adopted far from home, apparently in secret?

She did not think it took an enormous leap of imagination to guess what those circumstances might have been. A male child would almost certainly be greeted with much delight in a noble family...unless one of the parents was unfit for some reason. Would bastardy be an instant rejection? If not, maybe the mother was poor, and the de la Chabelles felt it would be an embarrassing match and would not allow their son to marry her. Maybe it was a de la Chabelle daughter who was wild and got herself pregnant by a dashing soldier or even a laborer—again, deemed unfit by the family.

Molly could think of nearly endless permutations by which a child could be conceived by a de la Chabelle, which the de la Chabelles would not want to acknowledge.

Was there some way of proving that this was what happened to Benoît? Or was Angeline deluded and having fantasies of grandeur, and Benoît was simply the son of a local woman who for whatever reason (most likely financial) had decided to give him up? Molly thought the latter was certainly possible, even probable. The fact that Angeline behaved as though she expected people to be throwing rose petals in her path wherever she walked—that was proof of nothing.

Well, I might as well dive right in, thought Molly. With quite a bit of digging she was able to find a phone number, and without hesitation she called it, and was surprised that a person actually answered.

"Yes, may I help you?" the woman's voice said.

Molly imagined the woman in that spacious salon she had

seen in the photographs, with the enormous sofas in a fawn-colored velvet, sun pouring through the windows.

"Oh, I hope so! My name is Molly Sutton. I'm calling on behalf of...well...I'm hoping to talk to someone who could talk to me about the history of the de la Chabelle family, specifically about forty or forty-five years ago?"

"Excuse me," said the voice, and Molly thought she had never heard a more melodious phone voice, as though the richness of the de la Chabelle bank accounts even affected the voices of their assistants. "Could you tell me what is this in reference to?"

Molly decided, in the instant, to go for broke. "I'd like the family's response to a claim from one Benoît LaRue of Castillac, that he has de la Chabelle blood."

The line went dead.

BEN WAS SHAKING HIS HEAD. "You can't have thought that would work, Molly."

She laughed. "No. It was a little impulsive, I admit. Well, downright foolish."

"You can't just go around calling aristocratic families up out of the blue and accusing them of stowing bastard children away in the provinces."

"I guess I did that, didn't I?"

Ben threw his head back and laughed. She joined right in and they laughed until their bellies hurt.

"But you do see...that china changes things," she said.

Ben shrugged. "Maybe. A very distant maybe. It could easily —*easily*—be that Angeline is simply not mentally stable and would be given to imagining herself a countess no matter whom she'd married. What Lapin describes fits with that. She so desperately wants to be more important than she is that she makes up a whole story about it. And actually? I'm not even sure I would call that mentally unstable, people do it all the time—live in a fantasy world, when reality is not to their liking.

"Right, but most people know that their fantasies are fantasies."

Ben shrugged. "Maybe."

"On the other hand, I was thinking, well, Lapin says Delphus McDougal is sort of obsessed with that china service too, and as far as I know, he hasn't murdered anyone or got any illegitimate babies stashed in his attic. I guess Angeline could just be attracted to the china because it looks rich. Well, it *is* rich." Molly paced, wiggling her fingers, trying to think. "But even if she is delusional and is making the whole de la Chabelle connection up, it doesn't really matter, does it? It still provides a motive for killing Benoît. It fills one big hole in my investigation—I never could get the slightest understanding of why someone would kill the nicest man alive instead of simply divorcing him. But this could be the motive—either way—whether it is true or just that she just believes it's true—she would be *furious* at Benoît for not contacting the de la Chabelles and demanding something from them. Even just money, if acknowledgement was out of the question."

Ben considered this. "Angeline wanted to parlay the connection into..."

"Everything! Probably, knowing her grandiosity, she dreamed of being welcomed into the de la Chabelle family and getting to lounge around on those fawn-colored velvet sofas. Any amount of wheedling and threats would be worth it to be called *Comtesse*. But failing that, she'd take a cash payout to keep quiet. Though I doubt that would ever happen, not these days. Once upon a time —maybe it was still the case when Benoît was born—having a child out of wedlock was a big deal. Something to put some effort into hiding. At least that was true for us plebes. But now? Is it even a thing now that so many young people make families without bothering to get married at all?"

"I'm too old to answer that question."

"Pascal would know. I'll email him. Well, my darling husband, you won't be surprised to hear this whole fancy china situation has breathed some life into what I thought was a totally dead investigation. And I haven't even told you the story about Angeline as a teenager, which will make your hair stand on end. But right now I've got plenty more googling to do, and then I want to pay Angeline a visit. This can't wait another second."

"Molly—"

"I know, I'll be careful!" She gave him a good smooch before sitting down at the computer, the kind of smooch that says you mean it.

❧ 60 ❧

That Saturday dawned gray, the first wet day in a long while. Paul-Henri was off duty. He had some information he was sure Angeline would want to know, but he was not at all sure about how to deliver it. Should he text her? Should he wander about her neighborhood hoping to run into her?

Way in the back of his mind, he wondered why he was so anxious about making a misstep when all he wanted to do was tell her something she would want to know. And should have been told through the proper channels, though he had a feeling that had not happened, and he was right.

He dressed carefully, as he always did. His off-duty clothes were neatly pressed, his sneakers a blinding white. He looked at himself in the mirror and thought perhaps it was time to grow a mustache—but it was difficult to decide which style was most suitable. He did not like the idea of getting criticized by Chief Charlot for choosing the wrong one.

The light sprinkle was cool on his face as he set out for Angeline's neighborhood. He walked a few blocks, humming to himself.

Then with sudden decisiveness he pulled out his phone and texted Angeline, asking her to meet him on the corner of rue Simenon and rue Goulue.

There. Now she will come to me, he thought with a hungry anticipation.

In normal circumstances, Angeline would never have rushed out of the house to meet a man who texted her. She would have made him wait whether she wanted to see him or not, perhaps never showing up at all.

But Paul-Henri Monsour, junior officer—that was different.

He saw her leave the house without locking her door, pulling a light sweater around her shoulders, her hair in charming disarray.

"Oh chérie," he said, then hesitating because *chérie* was too familiar. "Listen, I...there's something I thought you would be interested to know."

Angeline felt a pit in her belly like she had never felt before. She had no idea what Paul-Henri was going to say, but her body knew that whatever it was, it was bad.

Very bad.

And her body was not wrong.

"It's business of the gendarmerie and I really shouldn't be saying anything to anyone," he murmured. "Your husband, Benoît..."

"*Yes?*" said Angeline, despairing at his slowness.

"I only just heard. The order came from the office of the coroner to exhume him. Days ago. I have no idea how I didn't hear about this earlier—I expect it's already taken place. You should have been notified, as next of kin?"

The blood ran from Angeline's face and she was very pale. "What did you say?"

"They've exhumed Benoît—"

"Shut up! Stop your babbling!"

And then she slapped him hard across the face.

Molly was impatiently waiting for Constance when she
remembered that Constance wasn't coming that Saturday and
Molly was on her own. She was in quite a hurry, so distracted she
forgot about the honey and threw back a cup of black coffee
while explaining to Ben the questions she planned to ask Angeline, gathered her cleaning supplies and the vacuum, ready to
clean the cottage.

Then she poked her head back inside to call out to Ben,
thanking him for the honey. Ben was puzzled, but went back to
his naval history, happy to have a rainy day for reading.

The Wallaces had left at dawn, so Molly tore through the
chores and was done hours earlier than on a normal Changeover
Day. She left the vacuum and mop in the cottage because she was
in a wild hurry to get to Angeline's and talk to her.

The case was as good as solved, she believed, except for a last
few dangling threads. Molly now had motive, thanks to the de la
Chabelle china. She had opportunity, because what would be
easier than poisoning someone who was bed-bound in your own
house? It was only means that remained. If Angeline hadn't used
oleander, how had she poisoned her husband?

Molly pulled up to the LaRue cottage and parked the scooter.
Castillacois were beginning to stir, on their way to the market
despite the light rain. Molly rapped on Angeline's door.

No answer.

Was she at the market? wondered Molly. She knocked again.
No answer. Then she pressed down the door handle and the door
swung open. Molly stepped inside.

Not technically breaking and entering, she thought. The door
was practically wide open.

"Angeline?" she called. She took a few steps down the hallway
and leaned into the stairwell. "Angeline, are you home?"

No answer.

Molly slowly inhaled. She didn't move at first, but stood by the stairs taking it all in—the herbaceous smell of the house, mixed with wood polish. The sparse furnishings in the living room. The windowsill that could use a fresh coat of paint.

There was a mirror on the wall next to the door. Molly looked at herself—she saw her expression had some fear in it—and she also saw the jagged crack that ran almost from the top of the mirror all the way down, as though something had slammed into it.

She heard something and cocked an ear. "Angeline?" she called again.

No answer.

Molly walked carefully into the kitchen, trying to make as little noise as possible. In a moment of semi-paranoia, she looked around for a video camera, feeling as though she were being watched.

The kitchen was neat and tidy. A little too neat for Molly's taste, as though no one actually cooked there, though she knew Angeline did. She wanted to go upstairs and have a look around but was too nervous about Angeline's coming back and catching her. There would be no explaining it away if she were caught rummaging in the widow's bedroom. She turned around and went into a small sitting room on the other side of the stairs.

There was not much for decoration. A shabby armchair with plaid upholstery. A small woodstove. A set of shelves but no books. Molly walked over to see the objects on the shelves more closely. A rough clay pot, a pair of brass candlesticks. And a worn marionette, its strings dangling down in a tangle. Molly bent her head to look at it. The chevalier had red hair coming out from under his helmet and a broken lance.

Molly picked up the marionette, its wooden legs clattering, and inspected the shield, which was made of wood and was drawn on, possibly by a child.

A crest with a small black heart, in circle of gold. (In this case, yellow crayon.)

Just like the D-L-C china, thought Molly. She did not believe for a moment that this marionette had belonged to the de la Chabelles. It looked like something from Angeline's own childhood—played with until it was nearly worn to nothing. Not a rich child's toy.

It appeared that this obsession with the de la Chabelles started long ago, if indeed the marionette had belonged to Angeline when she was little. How had she found out about the de la Chabelle connection, if it was even true? There are always mysteries within mysteries, Molly thought, some of which never get solved.

Molly went out the kitchen door to the garden and stood on the small deck, just as the sun came out. A light fog was close to the ground and the sun glinted on the wet roses and shrubs as she thought about small black hearts, about social class and money and what it was like not to have either of those things but want them desperately. A stream of bees glowed in the sun as they came out from the hive to feed.

Molly stood rooted, watching them.

Oh. *Oh.*

She dug her phone out of her pocket and texted Ben:

Don't eat the honey!!!!!

And before she could decide on the next right step, she heard Angeline walking into the house. Through the front door that Molly had left open. In seconds she was through the kitchen and out to the deck.

"You!" said Angeline, pointing a finger at her. "What are you doing in my house? Haven't you caused enough trouble? Get *out*, you wretched, horrible woman! You *ghoul!*"

For the first time in Angeline's presence, Molly was scared. Angeline was so petite, so...*pink*...that Molly had never felt the slightest concern for her safety around her; after all, a poisoner was not likely to be someone who would crack your skull open when you weren't looking.

Though it occurred to her now that "not likely" was not the same as "won't happen."

As Angeline got closer, Molly was afraid. She could sense a cold recklessness in Angeline, and slowly she backed away from her. But she needed some answers, and wasn't willing—not yet—to give up on getting them.

"Angeline," she said calmly (though her heart was racing). "I think I understand, finally."

Angeline shook her head, then stopped. "Why did you have to get involved in my business? Why are you persecuting me so? You didn't even know Benoît! "

"No, I didn't. Though many of my friends—" Molly stopped, decided to change course. "It must have been so frustrating, being married to someone who..."

"Nicest man alive," sneered Angeline in a sing-song voice, and Molly felt a flash of fear go down her back. She kept her knees slightly bent, her weight on the balls of her feet, in case she needed to bolt. For the second time she felt as though Angeline was capable of...anything.

"Well, maybe he was the nicest man to everyone else," said Molly soothingly. "But to you? He was depriving you of so much, and for what? That's the part I still don't quite get. Benoît had this important connection—the de la Chabelles, for heaven's sake, so famous and so powerful—why wouldn't he let you be part of that world, even if it didn't matter to him?"

Angeline stared at her. Her expression went through shock to fury, her mouth twisted into a sneer. She started to speak but instead in a flash she grabbed a hoe that was leaning against the house and came after Molly, quick as a snake.

Molly turned and ran, glancing back because she didn't dare have Angeline out of her sight.

At the scooter, Molly stopped. A moment in slow motion, as

she saw Angeline running towards her with the hoe raised over her head, her angelic blonde hair bedraggled in the rain, her face so full of rage that it jolted Molly into action, and she turned the key in the ignition, blessing that good new mechanic as the scooter revved beautifully and she skidded away just before Angeline got to her.

✦ 61 ✦

When she was about five blocks away, Molly pulled over so she could call Chief Charlot.

"Bonjour, Chief. I know this is sudden, but Angeline did kill Benoît, and I think I know how," said Molly, too loud, heart still racing, looking back to make sure Angeline wasn't coming after her. "I was just at her house. And she just came after me with a hoe, so if you want, you could just start with attempted assault and then take it from there. I'd guess she's a flight risk."

Charlot was no fool. She certainly didn't love taking instructions from Molly Sutton, but neither did she love making gross errors and allowing murderers to go free because she was too proud to listen.

"I'll send Paul-Henri," said Charlot. "It's his day off but no matter. And Molly—please come to the gendarmerie right away for a chat."

Molly paused, wondering how to refuse. Finally she said, "Okay, I'll wait for Paul-Henri, be his backup, and then come straight to the gendarmerie once he has her in custody." And then she hung up, cringing because she knew Charlot was probably fuming. But she couldn't just ride away from Angeline now, giving her all the time she needed to get away.

Again Molly looked back towards Angeline's but the streets were quiet. She was hesitant to start the scooter up again, thinking Angeline might be lurking and listening for it.

So, awkwardly, Molly hopped off and pushed the scooter along the road, circling around towards the gendarmerie, hoping to catch Paul-Henri. She had an idea that Paul-Henri might need some convincing that Angeline was dangerous, and of course she was right.

ૐ

As MOLLY CIRCLED AROUND, she caught up with Paul-Henri. Quietly she pushed the heavy scooter as hard as she could to catch up to him. When she was closing in, she called his name softly and he turned.

"Well, now," said Paul-Henri, unprepared for a confrontation with Molly. "What's this, anyway? The Chief has asked me to bring in Angeline—not that you have any right to that information," he added, mad at himself for giving Molly anything.

"I have to warn you," said Molly, catching up to him and putting her hand on his arm. "She is acting unhinged. She chased me with a hoe! And not for fun, Paul-Henri. If she had caught me, I think she'd have split my skull with it."

Paul-Henri recoiled. "Now really, Madame Sutton, this time your imagination—"

They heard a small engine start up.

"Hurry!" said Molly, hopping on the scooter and starting it up. "Don't let her get away!" She sped off around the corner to Angeline's house, which was only a half block away.

Paul-Henri ran as fast as he could, which was not very fast.

A battered car, lipstick red and barely bigger than a toy, was chugging down the street away from them. Molly could see blonde hair through the rear view and chastised herself for not having scoped out Angeline's car situation in advance...but she was positive that Angeline was driving.

Molly accelerated as Angeline rounded another corner, pushing the scooter faster than she ever had before.

Paul-Henri kept running but was hopelessly behind.

Molly was gaining on Angeline. Just as the red car slowed to make another turn, Molly gunned the scooter and shot ahead, skidding on the wet pavement in front of the car and falling to the ground in one rather loud and graceful swoop.

Molly's leg was scraped up but she was okay, and she jumped up to see Angeline wrench open the door to the little red car and take off running down the street, back towards her house.

Molly called to Paul-Henri, "On foot! She's coming your way!" and then she felt a little woozy, sat down on the curb, and fainted.

A week later.

Molly was looking forward to the celebration at Chez Papa—who wouldn't be relishing the idea of getting clapped on the back and told she had been right all along? The fainting had been a little embarrassing but the swerve in front of Angeline's car had done the job, to the great admiration of the villagers. Paul-Henri got credit for intercepting Angeline on the street and following orders to bring her to the gendarmerie, no matter how confused his feelings had been in the moment. Chief Charlot had been gracious and appreciative, which made Molly beam with pleasure.

When Paul-Henri had searched Angeline's car after putting her in jail, he had found a packed bag and a Swiss passport, which did help to convince him that Angeline hadn't been going to the market in the red car, which was the lame story she had tried to tell him.

Molly and Ben could see people spilling into the street as they approached the bistro. "Ben," said Molly suddenly, "what if I can't stop myself from saying 'I told you so'? What if I'm insufferably smug?"

Ben laughed. "The words 'I told you so' are waving in the air wherever you go right now, six feet tall, and I expect it will take some time before they fade. And as for being smug—don't you think you deserve to feel that way, just for a moment? I'll let you know if you get carried away."

Molly grinned, liking the idea of being followed around by a waving banner *and* being allowed five minutes of smugness. As they approached the crowd, applause broke out and Molly tightened her grip on Ben's hand, feeling suddenly shy.

"Here, here!" crowed Lapin, who considered himself a crucial part of the investigation's success, as indeed he was. He pushed his way over and slung an arm around Molly.

"Hip hip hooray for Molly!" cried Leon Garnier, his face bright red as he had begun celebrating some hours earlier.

"Now Madame Sutton," said a red-headed woman Molly did not recognize, "Please, please, come in, have a drink, and tell us *all* the details. You've been holed up at La Baraque all week and we have questions!"

"So many questions!" shouted another person Molly had never met, and the crowd laughed.

Molly came through the door of *Chez Papa* once again feeling a bit like a victorious soldier home from a long war.

"Did she really come after you with a hoe?"

"I want to go back in time and tell Benoît it's time for a road trip to Normandy!"

"Big things come in small packages, that's what I always say. Maybe in this case not 'big' but 'dangerous'."

"Nico," said Molly, "I'm suddenly dying of thirst, Make me a big glass of Perrier, willya?"

"No kir?"

"Later..."

Edmond Nugent approached, the very picture of sheepishness. He kissed cheeks with Molly and said simply, "I am so sorry I did not speak up sooner. I was trying, in my imbecile way, to protect you. Please forgive me."

Molly laughed and said all was good. She was beaming and her face was rosy and bright.

"So little old Benoît LaRue turns out to be part of one of the fanciest families in France!" said a gray-haired woman perched on the stool next to Molly. "That rascal!"

"Well, to be strictly sure, we'd need a DNA test," said Molly. "And curious as we might be, no one has legal standing to order that except Angeline, ironically enough. Certainly the de la Chabelles have no interest in such a thing. And someone in that family would need to take the test as well."

"I would think Angeline would be the first one to want proof!"

Molly laughed. "I know. She is probably desperate to know for sure. But...it would hurt her case rather badly, since that de la Chabelle connection is central to her motive for killing Benoît. So I doubt she's going to."

"Maybe she's just crazy enough to want to be right, even if it means spending most of the rest of her life in prison."

Molly nodded. "Would not surprise me, to be honest. I mean, she tried to kill me twice. Or maybe it was three times?" Molly shook her head. Then she saw, out of the corner of her eye, Hortense sitting at a table in the corner. By herself, shoulders slumped. But with a glitter in her eyes, as though contemplating with great relief how her life was going to unfold without Angeline.

Ben was telling a group of enraptured listeners about how the honey that sat on the kitchen counter at La Baraque for three days had indeed tested positive for the toxin found in oleander.

"That was how she did it," he said. "She had a beehive right there in her garden, the bees pollinated the oleander and brought all that poisonous pollen back to the hive. The toxicology report came back from our poor Benoît, and confirmed that he did in fact die of oleander poisoning. Just as Molly said all along," he couldn't resist adding.

"Poisoned honey. So brilliant…and so evil," said a young man who in that moment decided on a career as a detective.

Florian came over, his arm tightly around Selma's ample waist. "Madame Sutton," he said, and made a courtly bow, in which a world of apology was expressed.

"Florian, Selma," said Molly, grinning so hard it hurt. She had never felt how wonderful it can be to find yourself in a moment where words are not necessary.

Selma said, "I just cannot wait to tell everyone at home that the propriétaire of my gîte turned out to be a real-life Sherlock Holmes!"

Florian startled. "You're not thinking of going home?"

Frances came over and rubbed Molly's shoulders and Molly felt so touched by this that tears sprang to her eyes. She'd been feeling so emotional lately.

Molly had felt tired a lot too. Even though she was happy to be at Chez Papa celebrating with her friends—and making new ones—already she was longing for sleep. She felt vaguely sick to her stomach, especially in the mornings, and even almond croissants didn't seem appealing. This had been going on for a few weeks, with no one—not Ben, not Frances, not Molly herself—wondering about the cause of this latest mystery.

Sometimes all you can do is get from one minute to the next. It's so easy to miss the forest for the trees.

Lawrence, to give credit where credit is due, had his suspicions. On a recent trip to Paris, he bought some exquisite, tiny clothing, with ribbons of silk and lace but not too much, just in case he was right.

THE END

GLOSSARY

Chapter 1
    gîtes...................rentals, usually by the week
    rebonjour.........hello again
    magnifique........magnificent

Chapter 2
    chérie.............dear

Chapter 7
    au contraire......on the contrary
    la bombe...........the bomb (i.e. sexy)

Chapter 8
    SAMU..............Service d'aide médicale urgente (ambulance)

Chapter 9
    pichet.............small pitcher

Chapter 10
    recré..............short for recréation, or recess

Priez pour vos morts........pray for your dead

Chapter 11
épicerie...............small grocery

Chapter 12
frites.........French fries
croque monsieur..........grilled ham and cheese

Chapter 14
exactement.............exactly
poubelle............... garbage can

Chapter 15
chatelaine.............woman of the manor
oranais aux abricots....apricot pastry with pastry cream

Chapter 16
sobranade...............stew with beans, pork belly, turnip

Chapter 17
de rigeur...............a must

Chapter 18
salade Périgourdine.....salad of lettuce, duck giblets, and walnuts
foie gras................goose liver
ma petite chou...........my little cabbage (term of affection)

Chapter 19
chevalier..................knight
maternelle...............nursery school

Chapter 24

à tout à l'heure.....see you later

Chapter 25
ébenistes..................very high quality cabinetmaker, 17th century
au revoir..................goodbye

Chapter 28
Comedie française.........French National Theater

Chapter 30
froideur.....................frostiness

Chapter 32
apèro...........................cocktail party

Chapter 33
merde........................poop (vulgar)

Chapter 35
Liberté, Egalité, Fraternité.....liberty, equality, fraternity (motto of the French Revolution)

Chapter 40
mec..................................good guy

Chapter 43
proprietaire...........................proprietor
enchanteé.............................enchanted

Chapter 48
fermé........................closed

Chapter 49

cassoulet......................stew of beans, duck, and pork

Chapter 52
jambon-beurre...................typical French sandwich of ham and butter on a baguette

Chapter 53
patissière........................female pastry chef

Chapter 59
comtesse..........................countess

ACKNOWLEDGMENTS

So much gratitude to Tommy Glass, Nancy Kelley, Paul Ardoin, Nellie Baumer, Barbara Mosley, and as ever, the best readers in the world.

Merci bien.

ALSO BY NELL GODDIN

The Third Girl (Molly Sutton Mysteries 1)

The Luckiest Woman Ever (Molly Sutton Mysteries 2)

The Prisoner of Castillac (Molly Sutton Mysteries 3)

Murder for Love (Molly Sutton Mysteries 4)

The Château Murder (Molly Sutton Mysteries 5)

Murder on Vacation (Molly Sutton Mysteries 6)

An Official Killing (Molly Sutton Mysteries 7)

Death in Darkness (Molly Sutton Mysteries 8)

No Honor Among Thieves (Molly Sutton Mysteries 9)

Bittersweet Oblivion (Molly Sutton Mysteries 11)

You can get Nell's ebooks or audiobooks (or give them as gifts) at her Shopify store: goddinbooks.com

For paperbacks, go to Amazon or Barnes & Noble online, or order them at your local bookstore.

ABOUT THE AUTHOR

Nell Goddin has worked as a radio reporter, SAT tutor, short-order omelet chef, and baker. She tried waitressing but was fired twice.

Nell grew up in Richmond, Virginia and has lived in New England, New York City, and France. She has degrees from Dartmouth College and Columbia University.

www.goddinbooks.com
nell@goddinbooks.com

20240102070617